The Ultimate Price

Battalion 1 Series: Book 4

Theo Mann

The Invisible Publishing Company

Battalion 1 Series

Contents

Chapter 1

C aptain Corban Rhodes adjusted the grid lines surrounding his Striker's cockpit. The Grid gave him a full 360° view of the battlefield below him.

Aemon Legion Platoons fought street to street through the devastated landscape. Mechanized Masks ground troops assaulted the platoons, forced them to fall back, and the platoons diverted to other streets and neighborhoods trying to gain ground against the Masks.

Masks invasion ships and Legion Ravagers fought tooth and nail in the atmosphere over what was left of the city.

Rhodes had to dodge one barrage of fusion charges after another pelting back and forth across his Striker's bow.

Two faces hovered in The Grid in front of him. "I'm scanning The Grid for any sign of implants, but nothing's coming up," Fisher told him. "There are too many destroyed Masks down there. They must be disguising the implants."

"We don't even know if Coulter, Dietz, and Lauer are still on the planet," Rhodes replied. "The Masks could have recaptured them, taken them on board an invasion ship, and removed them from the field."

"Then they'll be impossible to find," Rio pointed out. "We wouldn't be able to track which ship they're on. We would just have to wait until the Masks deploy the men in battle. Then we would be able to find them and hopefully retrieve them the same way we found you."

"That isn't good enough," Rhodes replied. "The three of them have already been stranded for three days. If the Masks had them, we would know by now."

"Then how are we going to find them?" Fisher asked.

Rhodes made one last sweep of The Grid, but he didn't see anything Fisher and Rio didn't already tell him about.

The Grid offered a detailed layout of the city, the battle, and everyone involved in it. The Grid returned biometric information on the Legion soldiers fighting in the platoons.

The Grid also read the electronic components of the Masks' machine bodies, their energy readings, and even some of their neural patterns.

Rhodes had seen all those readings before. They were identical to the readings he should have been seeing from Battalion 1's implants.

He plummeted past another air battle between Ravagers and invasion ships. Both sides fired at him, but Rio flew too fast.

Rhodes sailed clear, dropped low over the city, and wove between a few ruined buildings. Their charred frames stuck up over mountains of rubble, dead bodies, and Masks blown to pieces.

Rhodes searched The Grid again and again. He never found any trace of Corporal Eddie Coulter, Sergeant Jairo Dietz, or Lieutenant Heath Lauer.

Rhodes didn't see any sign of their Strikers, Elio, Enoch, and Baron, either.

"Lauer won't be with the others," Fisher pointed out. "He was miles away when we went down."

"We don't know *when* he went down," Rio countered.

"You didn't see what happened to Coulter and Dietz?" Rhodes asked. "They were with you when you picked me up."

"Rio took too much damage when he got hit," Fisher replied. "He wouldn't have recorded anything that happened to Coulter and Dietz."

Rhodes interfaced with the rest of the battalion. Lieutenant Dane Rhinehart, Lieutenant Ted Oakes, Corporal Rudy Fuentes, and Alyssa Thackery flew in formation around and behind Rhodes.

The other Strikers had to veer away from gunfire and around buildings. Their interface spread The Grid all the way to the edge of town, but they still didn't find anything.

"How did you get separated from Lauer?" Rhodes asked Oakes.

"We drove the Masks as far as the edge of town," Oakes replied. "We waited until they started loading onto their invasion ships and retreating out into the countryside. Then we pulled away to rendezvous with the *Ero* like you told us to. That's when the invasion ships turned on us and hit Lauer."

"Did you see where he went down?"

"It was every man for himself," Rhinehart replied. "We had to scatter. I think he got hit over there."

Rhinehart indicated a spot at the far northwest corner of the Grid. It was nowhere near where the three men had been bombarding the Masks ground troops.

"There's nothing there now," Thackery pointed out. "The Masks must be hiding their signal. We would be able to see them otherwise."

"Not necessarily," Fisher countered. "I can think of a few other explanations for why we wouldn't detect any sign of the three missing men."

"What other explanations are there?" she asked.

"For a start, all three of them might have lost power," Fisher told her. "They could be blending in with the debris of destroyed Mask parts. The Masks would be able to conceal all three of them in completely different parts of the city."

"They did it to me," she pointed out.

"They did it to you in one spot. They did it to you and an invasion ship that happened to be directly above you. Then the captain flew into range and the same thing happened to him. The field continued to suppress The Grid for both of you as long as you stayed together and close enough for the Masks to maintain it. The field collapsed once you both got far enough away."

"That's an interesting theory, but it doesn't help us find Coulter, Dietz, and Lauer," Rhinehart interrupted. "How can we find them if they're blending in with a bunch of destroyed Masks parts? The longer they stay on this planet, the more likely they are to get recaptured."

"I have an idea," Rhodes chimed in. "Roll back the sequence of events from when you first picked me up."

Rhodes and the rest of the battalion had to fly around in the skies over the battlefield to keep out of the Ravagers' way.

The Masks definitely noticed the battalion in the area. The invasion ships kept breaking away from the battle to come after the Striker group.

Rhodes and his subordinates understood by now not to engage with the invasion ships or even get close to them.

The invasion ships could hit targets a long way off. One hit would bring down a Striker. Then the battalion would be looking for another stranded person in this wasteland.

Fisher brought up the sequence of events on The Grid. Rhodes watched Dietz and Coulter descend in their Strikers, Aries and Baron. The two ships stood guard while Rio picked up Rhodes.

The three ships started to lift off the ground. Aries and Baron flanked Rio to give him cover.

Then three more invasion ships swooped in and attacked the Strikers. The invasion ships' gunfire flattened Rio to the ground and the Striker took heavy damage.

He barely managed to get away, but not before Rhodes got severely injured. The readings got scrambled. Rhodes couldn't see much about how it all happened.

By the time Rio soared clear into the atmosphere to rendezvous with the Ravager *Ero,* Dietz and Coulter were gone.

The same playback showed Oakes and Rhinehart on approach to the Ravager, too. Lauer was nowhere in sight.

"This isn't going to work," Rhodes muttered. "Interface with the *Ero,* Fisher."

"What will that tell you?" Rio asked.

"The Ravagers would have recorded everything that happened during the battle. The *Ero* must have seen where the three Strikers went down."

"I sure hope you're right," Oakes murmured. "I hate to think of them injured and stranded—especially if they don't have power."

"They could be dead already," Thackery pointed out. "We could be looking for three dead bodies."

Rhodes didn't dignify that with an answer. Even if Coulter, Dietz, and Lauer were dead, Rhodes had to find out one way or the other. He couldn't just leave them behind.

Fisher brought up another replay sequence from the *Ero.* He was right. The Ravager had been stationed in orbit through the whole battle.

The ship recorded Dietz and Coulter flying in opposite directions to get away from the invasion ship's gunfire.

Rio's crash drew the invasion ships' attention away from Dietz and Coulter long enough for the two Strikers to get clear.

They circled the city in opposite directions. The air battle between the invasion ships and the Ravagers prevented Dietz and Coulter from gaining altitude to return to the *Ero*.

They met back up on the other side of town—the northern side. Oakes and Rhinehart were already gone. So was Lauer.

Dietz and Coulter wouldn't have seen Lauer after he went down. They wouldn't realize they were anywhere near him.

Then another four invasion ships attacked Dietz and Coulter from the north. These must have been the same invasion ships that lifted off the Masks ground troops—the troops Oakes, Lauer, and Rhinehart worked so hard to drive out of town.

The invasion ships knocked Dietz and Coulter out of the sky, too. They and their Strikers lost power and they vanished off the *Ero's* scans.

Rhodes pinpointed the exact spot where the two Strikers went down. Then he rolled back more footage of the attack against Oakes, Lauer, and Rhinehart.

"No way!" Thackery breathed. "Dietz and Coulter are less than half a mile away from Lauer!"

"I'm going down there to get them," Rhodes announced. "The rest of you stay airborne."

"We'll stand guard, Captain," Oakes told him. "We won't let the invasion ships come after you."

"Don't stand guard," Rhodes ordered. "Draw them away. They're more interested in capturing all of you. If you stay here, you'll only wind up getting into another fight trying to defend me. Protect yourselves. That's more important. You can lead the invasion ships away from me while you're at it. Open the cockpit, Rio."

Rio sighed. "I'm getting really tired of those words."

The cockpit popped and Rhodes launched out into the smoky atmosphere over the city. It wasn't even a city anymore. The ongoing battle had reduced it to another wasteland of destroyed buildings, twisted ship parts, and mangled bodies.

He activated The Grid and plotted a course to the spot where Dietz and Coulter went down. Rhodes would have to find them first. Then, if he got lucky, he would be able to go after Lauer.

Chapter 2

R hodes ignited his boosters, dove deep into the heart of the city, and dodged between buildings getting closer to the coordinates on The Grid. He still didn't pick up any sign of Dietz or Coulter.

The ongoing battle had pulverized this part of town to rubble, but the battle wasn't here anymore.

Rhodes kept a close watch on The Grid to make sure no Masks ground troops came near him. He didn't want any Legion platoons coming near him, either.

The invasion ships held off, too. The Strikers obeyed his orders by cycling around and around the city. They flew anywhere but over Rhodes's position.

The invasion ships kept trying to intercept the Strikers, but the rest of the battalion flew far enough apart from each other. The Masks couldn't pinpoint more than one of them at a time.

This left the invasion ships vulnerable to Ravager attack. Rhodes had this part of the city to himself.

He slowed on approach to the place where Dietz and Coulter went down. Trying to find them in the rubble would be nearly impossible without some electronic signal coming from their implants.

Rhodes didn't know how losing power would affect anyone from Battalion 1. No one knew how anything would affect Battalion 1. The project was so experimental. No one could predict anything.

He landed on a mountain of debris ten feet from where Dietz and Coulter should have fallen. Rhodes looked around at a whole lot of nothing.

He stepped on broken pieces of Masks tangled up with the twisted human remains. The Grid adjusted to Rhodes's every move and read the mounds underfoot. None of the bodies belonged to Dietz or Coulter.

Rhodes stumbled over the uneven surface. What did he really hope to find down here?

He adjusted The Grid to check for any shape that might match a Striker, but he didn't pick up anything like that, either.

"How long do you want to keep looking?" Fisher asked. "We should probably go look for Lauer before the Masks get wind that we're down here."

Rhodes nodded. He didn't want to admit just how hopeless this search was.

Now he saw it firsthand. Dietz and Coulter couldn't be alive down here. No one could be.

He started to turn away when The Grid in front of him changed. A dog face appeared on the interface right next to Fisher.

The dog didn't have a body. The grid lines that made up the face kept shifting, stretching, and adjusting. "Captain Rhodes!" the dog exclaimed. "Thank heaven you're here! You have to help us!"

"Murphy! Where the hell are you?" Rhodes looked around again. "I've been looking everywhere."

"Zen and I have been masking our location to hide from the Masks. We're under the debris."

"Are Baron and Aries with you?" Rhodes asked.

"Dietz and Coulter are hiding inside Aries. Baron is next to us. We all took damage and we couldn't get into the atmosphere. We used The Grid to burrow under the debris so the Masks wouldn't find us."

"Never mind about that. Just show me where you are. We're going to get you out of here."

Murphy did something to The Grid and he, Dietz, Coulter, Zen, Aries, and Baron all materialized on The Grid out of nowhere. They were almost directly underneath where Rhodes was standing.

Rhodes gulped when he saw how bad the situation was. Dietz's life signs fluctuated dangerously. Zen was malfunctioning and kept jittering in The Grid.

He tried to talk to Rhodes, but only a scratchy sound came out. Part of Coulter's chest implant had gotten crushed.

He was barely hanging on, but Murphy was still fully operational and functioning normally.

Neither of the Striker SAMs appeared on the interface. Neither Striker had any power at all.

Neither of them had a Striker shape anymore, either. They must have used the last of their power to alter their grid lines to get into this hiding place before they both shut down.

Rhodes scrambled over to them and used his laser to carve his way through the rubble. He signaled the location to the rest of the battalion, but he ordered everyone to stay clear.

He melted a bunch of twisted metal fragments away and exposed Baron's roof. Multiple fusion blasts had caved in the fuselage.

Murphy kept showing Rhodes everything under the mounds of trash covering the two Strikers and the two men.

Rhodes went to work clearing the crap away from Aries next. Rhodes dreaded what he would find when he got the cockpit open. It was a miracle the two men survived for three days down here.

Rhodes checked their life sign readings a few more times, but he didn't see anything that gave him any hope.

"Just hold on a little longer," he panted. "We'll get you out and back on board the *Ero*. You did great staying hidden this long."

"It wasn't hard," Murphy told him. "Coulter has been delirious from the drug withdrawals and Dietz has been unconscious almost the entire time."

Rhodes didn't answer. He got off easy spending his withdrawal period in a conversion cycle on board the *Ero*.

Dietz and Coulter must have been living a nightmare all this time—and that was saying nothing about what Murphy must have been going through.

Rhodes concentrated all his effort on clearing the debris away from Aries's cockpit. Rhodes passed his hand across the glass and saw Dietz and Coulter for the first time.

They looked as bad in real life as they did in The Grid. Rhodes didn't like the idea of taking them out of here. He didn't want to move them at all, but he had to.

He modified his hand into a prying tool and wrenched open the cockpit. "Thank you so much for coming for us, Captain," Murphy exclaimed. "I feared the worst."

"We have to get you back to the *Ero* right away." Rhodes interfaced with the rest of the battalion. "Come down here, Rio. I need you to lift off Dietz and Coulter. The rest of you stay airborne and keep the invasion ships away."

"What about you?" Fisher asked.

"I'm going after Lauer. He could be hiding somewhere, too."

"What do you want to do about the Aries and Baron?" Oakes asked. "You said we wouldn't leave anyone behind. They could fall into the Masks' hands if we leave without them."

"That will be for the Legion brass to decide. Ravagers would have to lift the Strikers out of here. At least we know now where they are."

Coulter uncurled himself from his hiding place. He could support his weight, but he didn't look up to make eye contact with Rhodes. Coulter kept his head down and turned aside.

"Is he malfunctioning?" Rhodes asked Murphy.

"He's still in withdrawals. He won't talk to me or look at me. He's semi-catatonic, but his brainwaves are all reading as normal. I've been trying to help him, but it seems like the best way to help him is to just leave him alone."

Rhodes made the most cursory assessment of Coulter's injuries. Rhodes wouldn't be able to do anything to fix the damage to Coulter's implants. Only Drs. Osborne and Trudeau could do that.

Rio's engines howled across the landscape. The Striker looped around a few buildings in the distance before he made sure the coast was clear.

Rhodes had to support Coulter. He stumbled a few times and leaned on Rhodes. Rhodes walked Coulter a few yards away from Aries and then lowered Coulter against one of the rubble piles.

"You're gonna be okay, Eddie," Rhodes murmured. "We found you. We're gonna take you back to the *Ero.* You're safe now. You're free from the Masks. Everything is going to be all right. You'll see."

"Thank you, Captain," Murphy replied.

"Keep an eye on him while I get Dietz out. Come on in and pick up Coulter, Rio."

Rhodes didn't watch Rio descend between the mountains of debris. The Striker extended its landing gear to set down in front of Coulter.

Rhodes bent over Aries's cockpit. Rhodes didn't see any external damage to Dietz's implants or his organic tissue.

That didn't mean anything, though. The organic side of his face looked like he was already dead. The skin had gone ashen grey and waxy around his lips.

His one organic eye hovered a third of the way open. The eyelid no longer looked like real human skin and a milky white film covered the eye. Dietz was barely breathing.

Rhodes instinctively turned to Zen for answers, but the SAM couldn't communicate with Rhodes, either.

Dietz's life sign readings told Rhodes only too plainly how precarious the situation was. Dietz had to get off the planet right now. He might not even survive even if he did get off the planet.

Rhodes bent all the way over to pick up Dietz, but Rhodes couldn't reach him from up here. Rhodes changed his grid lines, stretched his arms into two long, jointed tentacles, and scooped up Dietz as gently as he could.

Dietz's body flopped and his limbs all drooped down when Rhodes picked him up. Dietz's head lolled back and his mouth fell open. Damn, he looked bad!

"I'm trying to interface with Zen," Fisher announced. "I don't think Zen is malfunctioning. Dietz's condition is causing Zen to act like this. If we can stabilize Dietz, Zen should come back online."

Rhodes stood up and carried Dietz over to where Coulter lay. Rio was just touching down when a boom startled Rhodes into looking up.

He had a split second to see an invasion ship zooming straight for him. Blasts of fusion fire pounded the city below as the ship soared overhead.

Rhodes ducked and barely kept his grip on Dietz. Rhodes might have thought the invasion ship was coming after him and his friends, but it wasn't.

A second later, a Ravager followed the invasion ship and drove it farther away. The Ravager bombarded the invasion ship with dozens of volleys. The Ravager's gunfire pelted off the invasion ship's hull and deflected to the ground.

Rhodes tried to cover Dietz with his body, but a second later, another invasion ship thundered into view from the western horizon.

This one definitely slowed and circled over Rhodes's position. The battalion's implants attracted the Masks with an irresistible pull.

The second invasion ship fired on the mound next to Coulter. He curled into a fetal ball, turned his head away, and huddled against the rubble for protection, but it couldn't protect him.

Rhodes sprang up. "Take Dietz and Coulter, Rio! Get them out of here!"

Rio popped his cockpit cover again. Rhodes transformed his arms again to pick up Dietz to put him into the seat.

At that moment, an almighty blast of fusion fire hit Rio from the side, smacked the Striker away, and slammed him into a different mound.

Rhodes lost sight of Rio in the confusion. Rhodes lost sight of everything in the confusion—everything except Dietz.

Rhodes wrapped his snake arms around Dietz and held on for dear life. Rhodes couldn't lose this one man—not after everything Rhodes went through to find Dietz.

Rhodes lunged out of the way to avoid another shot of fusion fire, but it struck Rio again.

The third blast knocked the Striker even farther away from Rhodes. He couldn't get anywhere near Rio.

Rhodes reacted without thinking, morphed his grid lines into eight flexible arms, and dropped on four of them to support himself.

He snatched Dietz and Coulter with his other four arms and took off into the city at high speed. He didn't care about anything other than getting away from the invasion ship's gunfire.

He did care about Rio, but Rhodes couldn't help his Striker now.

Rhodes interfaced with him, but Rio was already gunning his engines and launching into the atmosphere to flee from the invasion ship, too. Good. Rhodes didn't want Rio anywhere in danger right now.

Murphy's voice broke through Rhodes's fog. "Find a place to hide, Captain! I can conceal us so the Masks won't be able to detect us."

Rhodes floundered back to his senses and adjusted his course to head west. "Lauer is out here somewhere. We have to find him."

"I know where he is. I'll show you, but it will be harder for you to rescue three injured men than two."

"Don't confuse me with details, pal," Rhodes muttered. "Just make sure the Masks don't recapture us."

"There." Murphy showed Rhodes a destroyed building a few blocks away. "Hide in there."

Rhodes darted under the torn structure. The giant metal dome roof had partially collapsed. It formed a hollow protected on all sides by metal.

Rhodes scuttled inside and lowered Dietz and Coulter onto the floor. Dietz's body sank onto the ground. He was barely alive at all.

Coulter retreated against the wall, pulled his knees to his chest, and turned his face away so he wouldn't make eye contact with Rhodes.

"It's okay, Eddie," Rhodes murmured. "You're free now. You never have to go back to the Masks. The battalion will come and get us. You're going to be okay."

Of course Coulter didn't answer. Rhodes didn't expect him to.

Rhodes didn't blame Coulter for going all fetal and catatonic. God only knew what he and Dietz had been going through these last three days.

Murphy watched Coulter with that deep understanding gaze Rhodes had come to expect from Fisher. Murphy must have been pulling out all the stops to help Coulter, but without effect.

"Are you sure we're concealed here?" Rhodes asked.

"Interface with the other Strikers. They can scan the surface. They'll tell you if they can detect you. If they can't, the Masks can't detect us, either."

It only took Rhodes a few seconds to interface with the rest of the battalion. Their Grids didn't pick up any sign of Rhodes's location.

"Stay in touch with us, Sir," Rhinehart told him. "We can't help you if we can't see you."

"Don't help me. Keep out of the way. The best way you can help me is by keeping yourselves safe."

"We'll have to come down eventually to pick you up," Thackery pointed out.

"We won't do that until it's safe." Rhodes checked The Grid. "Show me where Lauer is, Murphy."

Murphy brought up what he said was Lauer's location on The Grid. Of course Rhodes didn't see a damn thing over there.

"This is not the way to run an operation," he muttered to himself.

"I wish I could be more help, Captain, but I assure you he is there."

"You mean he *was* there. He might have gone down there, but if he's concealing himself somehow, he could be anywhere. He could have moved."

"You're right, of course, Captain. I wish I could go with you to help you find him."

"Stay here." Rhodes checked himself. Murphy couldn't go anywhere. "Keep an eye on Dietz and Coulter for me. If anything goes wrong, call in the Strikers to lift you off—but don't do it unless it's an absolute emergency."

"Isn't Dietz's condition emergency enough?" Fisher asked.

"His condition will be a hell of a lot worse if the Strikers get shot down." Rhodes stood up. "I'm going to get Lauer. Stay here."

Rhodes cast one last fleeting glance at his subordinates and the surroundings. Nothing had changed in the last five minutes.

He ducked out of their hiding place and set off at a fast walk across the devastated landscape. He had to get as far away from Dietz and Coulter as possible before someone spotted him.

Chapter 3

Rhodes closed in on the place where Murphy said Lauer went down. Rhodes revolved The Grid back and forth in front of his own eyes. Lauer wasn't on The Grid at all. How the hell was he concealing himself?

He might be dead, but Rhodes didn't think so. Heath Lauer was just too damn tough. He was by far the toughest man in all of Battalion 1. If Dietz and Coulter stayed alive out here, Lauer must have done the same thing.

Rhodes found himself sweeping his gaze across the piles of wreckage and mutilated bodies. He wouldn't have been able to recognize Lauer among them even if he'd been there.

Rhodes got to the spot Murphy indicated. It turned out to be a relatively flat spot with a bare stretch of pavement fifteen feet wide between a demolished building on one side and another mountain of dead Masks on the other.

Rhodes paced down the pile of Mask parts. It would have been the perfect place for someone in Battalion 1 to hide. The Masks' components would hide Lauer's implants.

The pile contained plenty of dead Legion soldiers, too. Their organic limbs would work just as well to hide Lauer's organic skin. Was he here?

Rhodes got to the end of the pile. He almost turned away when he spotted Elio half-buried under the mounds of stuff.

Rhodes went over to the ship and touched its sides. Nothing happened. The Striker was completely without power.

"Can you interface with Elio?" Rhodes asked Fisher.

"I'm trying. He isn't responding."

"There must be a way. We can't just abandon him here. Maybe he shut himself down to hide from the Masks."

Rhodes stepped onto the wing and modified his hand again to pry the cockpit cover open.

He wedged it under the rim and wrenched. At that moment, a powerful electric burst erupted from the ship's fuselage.

The charge hit Rhodes hard and smacked him off. He went flying and crashed into the building.

Rhodes shook the stars out of his head and started to pick himself up when Elio appeared on the interface. He had a shaggy, almost spider-like appearance with multiple eyes, jointed, fanged mandibles, and spiky bristles surrounding his cheeks.

"Captain Rhodes! I am so sorry!" Elio husked. "I had no idea it was you."

"Are you....are you okay, Elio?" Rhodes stammered. "We were trying to find Lauer."

"He told me to shut down all power so the Masks wouldn't find me. I am so sorry, Captain! Are you hurt? I feel terrible. I thought the Masks were trying to capture me."

"Don't worry about it, man. You did the right thing. Where is Lauer now? He isn't showing up on The Grid."

"I'm sorry, Captain. I can't tell you that. He told me to land here and shut down power. Then he took off running into the battle. That was the last time I saw him. I've been shut down ever since."

Rhodes inched toward the Striker. "Are you damaged in any way, Elio? Are you perfectly functional? Oakes and Rhinehart said you got hit by an invasion ship."

"I did, but I landed on my own. Lauer told me to pretend to be more damaged than I was."

"Good idea," Rhodes murmured.

"I'm only worried that the Masks will be able to find me, now that I'm powered up."

"You're right. I want you to launch and rejoin the rest of the battalion. They're in the atmosphere. Rio and the others will look out for you. I'll stay here and find Lauer."

"How will you find him if he doesn't show up on The Grid?"

"Who the hell knows?" Rhodes growled. "He could be anywhere. I just don't want you in any more danger. Your signal will bring the Masks running. Launch now, Elio. I'm really glad I found you."

"Of course, Captain. Thank you for coming back for me. I wish I could do something to help you find Lauer."

"You can. Keep yourself safe and stand ready to come and pick him up as soon as I find him. Once I do that, the other Strikers will lift off Dietz and Coulter. Then we can all go home."

"What's wrong with Dietz and Coulter?" Elio asked.

"I don't have time to explain it right now. Get out of here. That's an order."

"Of course, Captain."

Elio fired up his engines. Rhodes stepped out of the way and watched the Striker shake off the rubble. Then Elio lifted off and launched into the atmosphere.

Rhodes watched him out of sight. The other Strikers swooped over to surround Elio and then they all vanished into the distance. That was one person rescued, at least. Now Rhodes had to deal with the other three.

He turned around to check the surroundings again even though he knew he wouldn't find anything. Whatever Lauer used to conceal himself worked too well.

That was the moment Rhodes noticed Masks ground troops moving through the city. They'd always been there fighting the Legion platoons in other parts of the battlefield.

Now they headed this way, but they didn't come toward Rhodes.

"They're on course to intercept Dietz and Coulter," Fisher pointed out.

"Like hell they will," Rhodes muttered and took off for Dietz's and Coulter's hiding place. "Murphy! The Masks are coming your way!"

"What am I supposed to do about it?" Murphy asked. "The interface is still showing that we're concealed. The Masks could be going after something else, though I can't detect any……"

He broke off when a single human life sign blipped onto The Grid. It appeared five blocks north of Dietz's and Coulter's hiding place. Then the signal vanished as quickly as it appeared.

"Lauer!" Rhodes whispered. "What the hell is he doing?"

"It looks like he's trying to lure the Masks away from Dietz and Coulter," Fisher pointed out.

"It isn't working. They're still heading straight for them." Rhodes fired his boosters and launched into the air. He just barely made it back to the hiding place before the Masks showed up.

They definitely must have detected the two men hiding there. The Masks raised their rifles to aim at the caved-in dome. They didn't pay any attention to Rhodes until he flew right into their path.

He unloaded his lasers on them and released a dozen Viper missiles from the ports on his back to take out as many Masks as he could.

Vipers and lasers seemed to do the most damage to their outer metal housing.

He hacked his way into their ranks, blocked them from getting near the hiding place, and battled the Masks away.

He would have liked to find some way to make them forget that they ever knew any members of Battalion 1 were hiding here, but that was no longer possible.

Dozens of Masks assembled from all over. They crowded in behind the forwardmost ground troops. More Masks pushed forward no matter how many Rhodes killed.

He took down fifty of them. His Vipers kept exploding in the back ranks, but he couldn't stem the tide.

The Grid showed him more ground troops coming this way. It also showed him Legion platoons heading in the same direction to assault the Masks in this little bottleneck.

He tried to drive the Masks a little farther away, but they were the ones who forced him to retreat closer to the dome. He bumped into it. He couldn't retreat any further than this.

Without warning, a punch of fusion rifle fire struck him in the chest and thumped him against the dome even harder.

The Masks took advantage of that moment when he stopped firing. They surged forward to finish him off.

They would finish off Dietz and Coulter, too—if the Masks didn't throw all three of them back into captivity. Rhodes couldn't stand that.

He was just making up his mind to finish off himself, Dietz, and Coulter rather than become the Masks' prisoners again.

He brought his weapon around to aim at the Masks one last time, but at that moment, another spray of laser shots belched into the Masks' horde from the side.

Rhodes caught one glimpse of Lauer storming into view. At the same instant, four Strikers dropped out of the sky, peppered the ground troops with more laser fire, and drew the Masks away from Rhodes.

He couldn't wait any longer. He dove into the hiding place, used the grid lines to change himself into a Striker, and sprouted multiple arms to pick up Dietz and Coulter.

He put the two men in his cockpit, blasted his engines, and skimmed out from under the dome on the other side—away from the battle.

Lauer bombarded the Masks with laser fire, but he fought them alone now. Rhodes couldn't live with himself if he left anyone behind, especially not the man who just saved Rhodes, Dietz, and Coulter.

Rhodes hurtled out of the dome and started climbing, but he doubled back right away and tilted his nose toward the ground. He fired his engines again—except that these weren't Striker engines.

They were his normal boosters. They weren't designed to carry the weight of three men—much less four.

Rhodes pushed that thought away. He didn't let himself think about the problems. He had to save Lauer as much as Rhodes had to save Dietz and Coulter.

Rhodes let gravity pull him toward the ground, picked up speed, and streaked past the battle, but Rhodes didn't fly low enough to get anywhere the Masks.

He extended another long, snaking arm, grabbed Lauer off the ground, and flew off with him before the Masks knew what was happening.

Their gunfire followed Lauer away, but it was too late. Rhodes took off flying for the rear of the battle—back toward the Legion position.

He couldn't gain altitude until he cleared away from the Ravagers and invasion ships.

He raced past the platoons moving in to engage with the Masks. Without warning, one of the soldiers raised his Jackhammer and fired directly into Rhodes's underside.

That one shot gave permission for all the other soldiers to fire at Rhodes, too. A dozen fusion blasts smashed through his housing and he lost his grip on Lauer.

"CAPTAIN!!" Lauer bellowed, but he was already wheeling off into the clear blue sky miles over the city.

Rhodes lost awareness of where he was. He concentrated all his mental power on keeping his shape as a Striker. He had to protect Dietz and Coulter at all costs, but Rhodes couldn't even right himself.

He started to fall only to get caught by Lauer. Lauer extended two long, whip arms from his sides to catch Rhodes.

Lauer had to change his plans when more invasion ships broke away from the battle to intercept him.

He swiveled his lasers toward the invasion ships, opened fire, and modified his legs to catch Rhodes instead.

Rhodes stayed in the form of a Striker. His brain finally cleared enough for him to straighten himself out, but he couldn't fly away with Dietz and Coulter—not with the invasion ships moving in.

Lauer lowered Rhodes back down to the ground—to a different part of the city. Lauer set the Striker on the pavement.

"This is no good, Captain," he muttered. "Everyone knows where we are now."

"I don't dare put Dietz and Coulter down again," Rhodes panted. "I might have to take off with them again.

Lauer interfaced with him and they surveyed The Grid for any way out of here. The rest of the battalion joined them in the interface.

"To hell with this," Rhinehart snarled. "Just launch and beat it back to the *Ero*. We'll defend you. It beats the hell out of farting around on this rotten planet."

"The invasion ships are keeping us grounded," Rhodes replied. "They know we're here. They're doing everything to stop us from leaving."

"That last hit didn't come from any invasion ship," Lauer muttered. "The Legion platoons fired on you—the ungrateful bastards."

"Allow me to make a suggestion, Captain," Wild interjected.

"Please," Rhodes replied. "Help me out."

"You're using the shape of a Striker now. You could use Aries's and Baron's strategy, use your grid lines to dig under these mountains or scrap metal, and conceal your whereabouts. Then, when you get to a part of the city where the Masks aren't looking for you, you can launch and make it into orbit before the invasion ships catch up with you."

"What an excellent idea," Murphy exclaimed.

"I'm no slouch," Wild mumbled back.

"All right. We'll do it," Rhodes replied. "Lauer, I want you to head off in a different direction from me. Get clear and take off into the atmosphere. Get above the battle and rendezvous with the *Ero.*"

"Are you stupid?" Lauer countered. "You think I'd run off and save myself while you're down here with two of our injured comrades? To hell with that. If you want me to go off in a different direction, at least let me take one of the men with me. Then we'll be equally loaded."

"Fine. Be that way. Use your grid lines to make yourself into a Striker. You can take Dietz."

Chapter 4

L auer transformed himself into a Striker and Rhodes transferred Dietz to the cockpit. They accomplished the operation just in time before the Masks started to converge on their location again.

"Go!" Rhodes ordered. "Get out of here! As soon as we make it past the air battle, the rest of you get out of the atmosphere and rendezvous with the *Ero,* too. Don't stick around."

He didn't wait for anyone to reply. He used his grid lines to flatten himself into a burrowing line moving under the mountains of bodies and rubble.

Murphy took control of Coulter's grid lines and morphed Coulter to match Rhodes's shape. Lauer and Wild manipulated Dietz's grid lines and squashed him to fit inside Lauer's cockpit.

Rhodes lost sight of them snaking through the landscape. The piles of Masks parts concealed them.

The Grid didn't work as well from in here, but Rhodes didn't care so much about that. He dug into the mounds and found a concealed spot where he could still read the battle outside.

The Masks ground troops and Legion platoons kept shifting from one part of town to another. They never stayed in one place for long.

Rhodes checked the air battle. It was moving off, too. It left a clear area of sky between the city and the Legion fleet in orbit around the planet. The *Ero* was up there.

Rhodes was just about to make his move when Fisher broke in on his thoughts. "We have a problem, Captain."

"Another one? What is it now?"

"Listen."

Fisher did something else to The Grid. Rhodes had never seen anyone do anything like this. He didn't know it was possible until Fisher did it.

He widened The Grid so Rhodes could see the whole battlefield landscape. Then Fisher zeroed The Grid to one city block. It was on the other side of the firefight Rhodes and his men just left behind.

The Masks ground troops and Legion platoons kept trading gunfire—but not all the Legion soldiers fought with the platoons.

A squad of twenty soldiers had broken away from the rest to follow Rhodes and Lauer.

This one squad tracked Rhodes and Lauer to the place Lauer set Rhodes down—the place where Rhodes and Lauer just separated.

The Grid added audio to the visual reading of the soldiers' movements. "I swear they just came this way," a lieutenant told his men.

"You're dreaming, Scofield," another returned. "You'll never find them. They can hide anywhere."

"They betrayed the Legion," Scofield fired back. "They attacked the platoons and killed hundreds of soldiers on Rono and again on Keonus. We have to find them and eliminate them."

"You better be careful what you wish for," a third man added. "The brass wants these guys back alive. They never said anything about hunting them down and killing them."

"The brass doesn't know what they're doing—and you're a damn coward, Malloy," Scofield spat. "We lost a lot of good men in those battles. Do you want to be the one responsible for it happening again?"

"We wouldn't be," Malloy pointed out. "The brass is making that decision."

"Why don't you go back home and suck your thumb, then." Scofield turned to the first man. "Did you find anything over there, Hollister?"

Hollister passed a device back and forth across the ground. "I'm picking up disturbances in the underlayer over here. It's leading in this direction."

The soldiers followed Rhodes's trail. Whatever device Hollister was using definitely showed the soldiers which direction Rhodes went.

"Great," Rhodes muttered under his breath. "So they want revenge for what we did."

"There's more, Captain. Look."

Fisher adjusted The Grid again. The soldiers were so busy tracking Rhodes that they didn't see another group of Masks ground troops moving on the squad. The soldiers' device didn't show them that.

"It seems a simple enough solution to let the Masks kill those men," Murphy pointed out. "They won't cause us any more problems."

"Letting the Masks kill those men will confirm to any survivors that we're working for the Masks." Rhodes checked on Coulter again. "I guess I can't put him down here."

"What are you going to do?" Fisher asked.

"I'm going to save those soldiers. I don't have a choice. I can't let the Masks wipe them out—not without doing something about it."

"I might be able to modify The Grid to create a protected place for Coulter down here," Murphy suggested.

Rio, Zion, and Enoch broke in on the interface. "Let us come down and pick up Coulter, Captain," Rio suggested. "Don't put him in any more danger than he already is."

"It's too risky," Rhodes replied. "Stay out of danger."

"All of this is too risky," Fisher pointed out. "You can't save everyone—especially not people who are trying to kill you."

Rhodes didn't listen. He waited until the soldiers got closer to his position. The Masks circled the squad. The squad remained oblivious to the danger until the soldiers located Rhodes hiding right there under the rubble mounds.

"He's here!" Hollister called to his friends. "He's right here!"

"Stand by to open fire as soon as he tries to escape," Scofield ordered. "You saw the way our Jackhammers brought him down earlier. We can bring him down again if we all hit him at once."

The soldiers gathered around Rhodes's hiding place. They trained their Jackhammers on the debris over Rhodes's head. "This is a terrible idea," Fisher muttered.

Rhodes made another instant decision. He could burst out of here, transform himself back into a Striker, blast into the sky, and get into orbit before the soldiers had a chance to land a single shot on him.

The soldiers would fall to the Masks if he did that. The Masks might even attack the soldiers first. That would give Rhodes a perfect cover to take Coulter off the planet.

Lauer and Dietz were already out in orbit heading for the *Ero.* Rhodes didn't have to worry about them anymore.

Rhodes just could not bring himself to be directly responsible for any more Legion deaths. These soldiers had a right to hate him. He did kill Legion soldiers—a lot of them.

He always knew those men had friends and families somewhere. He didn't blame any of them for hating him.

Throwing himself in front of a gun wouldn't bring those soldiers back, but he couldn't run away and leave even more Legion soldiers to die. That was asking too much.

He gathered his grid lines to make his move, but he waited until the very last minute. He had to make this count.

"He isn't coming out," Malloy remarked.

"I can see he isn't coming out, genius!" Scofield snapped. "Fire on my order. We'll blast the son of a bitch out. We won't wait for him to launch."

"Are you sure about this?" Hollister asked. "These guys have more weaponry than a whole platoon put together."

"Just do what I tell you," Scofield ordered. "He's one guy. He can't defeat all of us shooting at the same time."

The other soldiers exchanged glances behind Scofield's back. At least the rest of the squad wasn't as hysterically vengeful as Scofield.

Plenty of other Legion soldiers were bound to be, though. They wouldn't forget what the battalion did in Masks custody. The battalion was bound to come to a reckoning.

Scofield opened his mouth and inhaled. "Fire!" he ordered.

The moment he said that word, the Masks ground troops pivoted out of a side street and opened fire on the soldiers.

Rhodes shot out of the pile with all his might—right into the path of the Masks' fire. Their rifles smashed into his housing just as hard here as they did outside Dietz's and Coulter's hiding place.

Rhodes spread his grid lines as wide as he could to take the assault. He blocked the Masks' gunfire from hitting the soldiers, but the impact knocked him off his feet.

He felt himself losing control of The Grid. He couldn't hold onto Coulter anymore.

The soldiers spun around to defend themselves, but Rhodes protected them from the Masks. The soldiers aimed their Jackhammers at his back, but they didn't fire.

They stared in shock as he lurched and staggered under the barrage. The Masks fired dozens of times before they realized they were hitting a member of the battalion instead of Legion soldiers.

The force of the Masks' rifle fire knocked Coulter away. Rhodes's grid lines reverted back to their default state and he turned back into a man, but at least he could use his weapons now.

He raised both arms and opened fire with everything he had. He still wouldn't have been able to defend himself against so many Masks, but miraculously, Coulter snapped out of his stupor right at that moment.

He stumbled away from Rhodes, caught his balance, and then he spun around and opened fire with his lasers, too.

He fired five Vipers into the Masks. Those explosions startled Rhodes back to his senses.

He fired his Vipers, too, held out one arm to his side, and yelled to the soldiers behind him. "Get back! Fall back to the platoon! Fall back!"

Scofield stared at him in stupid shock. Hollister and Malloy recovered first.

They grabbed Scofield by his arms and towed him into another street heading south.

Rhodes swung his lasers forward. Coulter sidestepped closer to Rhodes and they both herded the soldiers out of danger until the Masks retreated in a different direction.

Chapter 5

Rhodes crouched next to a wall and moved his face right in front of Coulter's eyes. "Eddie! Are you okay?"

Coulter twisted his head aside and refused to look at him.

Rhodes gripped Coulter's shoulder. "You did great. We're going to get you out of here." Rhodes checked the interface.

"Can we come down and get you now?" Rio asked. "Please?"

"Yeah," Rhodes gasped. "You can come."

"Coulter's brainwave patterns are normalizing," Murphy reported. "I don't know why he's still acting like this."

"Leave him alone. He's still going through withdrawals." Rhodes couldn't stop squeezing Coulter's shoulder. "You're a champion. You're gonna be just fine, Eddie. I know it."

Coulter still didn't respond. "Rio, Zion, and Enoch are on approach," Fisher told Rhodes.

Rhodes stood up....and came face to face with the soldiers he'd just saved—the soldiers who had been hunting him to kill him.

Rhodes locked his gaze on Scofield. This guy didn't stand a chance against Rhodes, but Rhodes didn't want any animosity between himself and the platoons.

"Do you have something you want to say to me, Lieutenant?" Rhodes asked in a dangerous undertone.

Scofield opened his mouth to speak. None of the other soldiers would face Rhodes.

Scofield didn't seem to be able to make a sound, and right then, another burst of gunfire erupted three blocks away. A different mob of soldiers backed into the same street.

They traded gunfire with the enemy on the other side. Rhodes spun around and raised his weapons to help defend the soldiers.

Coulter started to get to his feet, but a second later, a third wave of Legion platoons attacked and drove the Masks farther north.

That left three more platoons stranded with Rhodes, Coulter, and Scofield's squad.

The platoons rotated northward to keep their weapons trained on the Masks.

That was the moment when the platoons noticed Rhodes and Scofield's squad squaring off right there in the middle of the battle zone.

One man forced his way out of the crowd and stormed up to Rhodes and Scofield. It was Captain Tate Vernick from the 249th.

Rhodes didn't recognize any of the men with him. They didn't belong to any platoon Rhodes ever fought with before. Vernick must have gotten transferred.

Vernick glanced back and forth between Rhodes and Scofield. Rhodes knew Vernick too well not to recognize that look. "Is there a problem here, Captain?"

"That's what I was just trying to figure out," Rhodes replied.

Vernick turned to Scofield. "What's your problem, Lieutenant? Do you know who this is? This is Captain Corban Rhodes from Battalion 1. The Legion brass has been trying to find him for months."

"Months!" Rhodes exclaimed. "Has it been that long?"

"You didn't know? The whole Legion is on alert looking for you and your people."

"He killed hundreds of Legion soldiers!" Scofield blurted out. "He might even have killed thousands! You weren't there on Rono! You didn't see!" He turned on Rhodes and spat through gritted teeth. "I was there! We all were! Do you think we could ever forget that?"

Rhodes did his best to shrug it away. "I don't blame you for hating me. I hate what I did on Rono, too. Would it mean anything to you if you knew we worked our asses off to try to stop it? Would it mean anything to you if you knew we didn't do it of our own free will? The Masks took control of us. We fought them all the way."

"I don't believe you!" Scofield fired back. "You're a traitor to the Legion—all of you!" He shot a deadly glance at Coulter, too.

That look threatened to snap what was left of Rhodes's patience. He didn't begrudge anyone hating him.

No one better threaten Coulter—not in his fragile state. He had enough to worry about without dealing with these accusations.

"All of that is for the brass to figure out," Vernick interjected. "Fall back with the platoon, Lieutenant. Lieutenant! I'm talking to you!"

Vernick got right in Scofield's face and then shoved between him and Rhodes. Vernick pushed Scofield away and made the whole squad back off.

Rhodes stayed where he was. Vernick kept his back to Rhodes until Scofield shot them all a glare over his shoulder and stormed off heading south.

Vernick finally turned around and narrowed his eyes at Rhodes. "We haven't heard the last of this."

"I know," Rhodes mumbled.

"Was that true? Did the Masks really control you to make you attack the Legion?"

"You don't think I attacked Legion platoons on my own, do you?" Rhodes compressed his lips to get himself under control. "Sorry. I don't blame anyone for doubting us."

"No, of course I don't think you attacked Legion platoons on your own. It's just...." Vernick's eyes darted to the platoon behind him. "People are saying all kinds of shit about you."

"Don't tell me," Rhodes muttered. "I don't want to know."

"We're supposed to fall back south, too. The 765th is still out there occupying the Masks. We're supposed to retreat under the 765th's cover. You should come with us."

Rhodes glanced at Coulter. "Maybe that isn't such a good idea. I have a guy who needs medical attention. I'm going to call in my Strikers to lift him off. Will you and your men be all....."

Rhodes trailed off when something else happened to The Grid. He'd never experienced anything like it before.

He'd been trying to interface with the Strikers to find out where they were and how easily he could get one or two of them down here to evacuate himself and Coulter.

The Grid flashed a different set of readings in front of his eyes. He didn't understand them—not at a conscious level.

Some distant part of him already knew what the Masks were going to do. It was the kind of inner knowing he experienced when he was the Masks' prisoner.

They used these signals to communicate their orders to him and the battalion. The orders didn't come through The Grid the way they normally would—not unless he was in the Fort Bastion landscape or somewhere else the Masks wanted to simulate the Legion.

He read the whole battlefield—but not through The Grid. This was the strangest sensation in the world.

He understood exactly what the Masks were thinking, what they were planning, and where they would move their troops next. He still had a residual connection to them.

Vernick read Rhodes's mind. "What's wrong?"

"The Masks are moving in behind the 765th. The Masks are using one flank to occupy the 765th. Another flank is cutting behind them. The Masks are on their way south to ambush you once you start to retreat."

"What can we do about it?"

Rhodes shook himself awake. "Keep falling back. The Masks know where you are and too many platoons are already falling back in that direction. They would know what was up if they saw you change your plans at the last minute."

Vernick raised his eyebrows. "What *is* up?"

Rhodes waved that away. "Just keep going. Get everyone back behind the line....and take this guy with you." He pulled Coulter forward.

"NO!!" Coulter burst to life, yanked his arm out of Rhodes's grip, and fought to free himself. He still wouldn't look at anyone.

"You have to fall back, Eddie," Rhodes told him. "It's too dangerous for you out here. We're only going through all this to get you back to the battalion."

"NO!" Coulter snapped again, but he kept his head turned to avoid all eye contact. "I'm going with you."

"I can't let you do that."

"Try to stop me," Coulter snarled under his breath.

Rhodes glanced at Murphy through the interface. Murphy only shrugged. "He can be very determined when he wants to be, Captain."

Rhodes gave it up and turned back to Vernick. "Get your platoons out of the city."

"What are you going to do?"

"I'll cover you and create a distraction."

"What if they ambush you?"

"They won't." Rhodes didn't explain how he knew this. The Masks would never be able to ambush him again. He knew everything they knew.

He pushed Vernick away. "Go, Tate. Get out of here."

Rhodes didn't wait for Vernick to leave. Rhodes took off heading north. Coulter followed him.

Rhodes didn't try to talk to Coulter. Taking Coulter back into a warzone might just be the dumbest thing Rhodes had ever done in his career.

He somehow understood why Coulter had to do this. No soldier in his right mind would want to get carried off the field when he could still fight. Coulter wasn't wounded enough for that—not physically.

Rhodes didn't have it in him to deny Coulter if he was still mentally with it enough to want to fight the Masks. Everyone in the battalion deserved to fight the enemy. No one in this war had suffered more than Battalion 1.

Rhodes had to cut a wide circuit north to get around the 765th Platoon. They still engaged with the Masks to the north, but they wouldn't stay that way.

The 765th would only stick around long enough to give the other platoons a chance to withdraw. Then the 765th would do the same thing.

As soon as the 765th left the city, the Masks would overrun all that territory. Rhodes didn't see how the Legion would ever get this city back, but that was someone else's decision.

The Legion had no reason to get this city back. There was nothing left of it to get back. The Legion might as well cut its losses and make its stand somewhere else the Masks were trying to destroy.

Rhodes found a building on the city's eastern flank. From here, he could see the Masks ground troops that were planning to pull a surprise attack on the retreating platoons.

Rhodes's connection gave him an innate understanding of the Masks' plans. Whatever they did to try to integrate the battalion must have stuck even after Rhodes and his people escaped.

Rhodes didn't grasp all the intricacies of that connection. He didn't need to. He just had to exploit it.

That unspoken link made him glance at Coulter at the same moment Coulter glanced up at him. Coulter's vision cleared and he made direct eye contact.

Gratitude gripped Rhodes's heart that he had Coulter with him. Rhodes didn't have to do this alone—not that he was worried about it.

He inched another quarter of a mile farther south. The Masks angled into position to rush across the platoons' path.

The Masks planned to block the platoons from rejoining the Legion. The platoons would have to fight their way through the Masks to get to safety.

If anything, the Masks might even be able to force the platoons back into the city where they would have to fight all over again.

"How do you want to do this, Captain?" Murphy asked.

It didn't sound like Murphy at all except that those words used Murphy's voice. It sounded more like something Coulter would say.

Rhodes pretended not to notice. Their connection was doing something strange. Maybe the Masks were interfacing with the battalion without realizing it.

Rhodes waved Coulter farther south—farther south even than the Masks' position. Rhodes positioned himself and Coulter where they would be able to cut off the Masks from getting anywhere near the platoons.

The Masks would have no choice but to confront Rhodes and Coulter while the platoons escaped behind the Legion line.

That was Rhodes's plan, at least. The other alternative was to leave these platoons to die just like the others.

Coulter glanced over at Rhodes one more time and nodded. That was good enough for Rhodes.

He fired his boosters just as the Masks made their move. Rhodes and Coulter streaked north, zoomed between the Masks and the platoons, and both men opened fire.

The Masks already held their weapons raised ready to gun down the platoons, but they hadn't opened fire yet.

Rhodes and Coulter caught them off guard exactly the way Rhodes hoped. He and Coulter flattened dozens of Masks before the Masks recovered enough to get off one shot.

Both Rhodes and Coulter used lasers, but they also unleashed plenty of Vipers, too. The explosions startled the platoons.

A bunch of men raised their weapons to open fire on the Masks. The soldiers would have hit Rhodes and Coulter instead, but Vernick yelled at them to keep moving south.

The platoons streamed away faster. Rhodes couldn't watch to see where they went or whether they got away in time.

The Masks realized the maneuver and opened fire on Rhodes and Coulter. Rifle fire hammered both men. Coulter jerked under the Masks' assault and collapsed on one knee.

Rhodes tried to fight his way toward him, but more Masks gunfire slapped Rhodes off his feet. He staggered closer to the fleeing platoons.

He braced himself to stand his ground, passed his lasers back and forth across the enemy ranks, and dug deep to get back over to Coulter.

Rhodes made it a few feet from Coulter's position before another brutal volley of enemy gunfire hit Rhodes in the face.

His head swam, but he kept shooting. He tasted blood and then his best efforts to stay upright failed.

He toppled, crashed down on his chest, and barely stayed conscious enough to pivot his weapons forward to hold the enemy at bay.

The Masks advanced. Rhodes couldn't concentrate well enough to see on The Grid if the platoons were getting away. Rhodes and Coulter couldn't stop the Masks from pulling their flanking maneuver now.

Rhodes kept shooting. He probably would have died still shooting as many Masks as possible. Coulter didn't stop, either.

They both lay crumpled on the pavement unloading lasers and Vipers on the enemy until, after what seemed like an eternity, another surge of Legion platoons flooded the area coming from the north.

Soldiers from the 765th raced past Rhodes and Coulter without stopping. The platoons traded gunfire with the Masks and then five Strikers pelted out of the west bombarding the Masks with fusion blasts.

A shockwave hit Rhodes in the face. He didn't think he passed out, but when his vision cleared, he lay on his stomach on the pavement staring at an empty street. He and Coulter were alone.

The Grid still worked, but the interface didn't. He heard Fisher and Murphy talking to him, but Rhodes couldn't make out what they were saying.

He checked The Grid to find out where the enemy was. It took him a second to realize that he wasn't as alone as he thought.

The platoons filed past him in the southbound street where he'd just been protecting them. None of them stopped to help him and Coulter.

Rhodes forced himself onto his hands and knees and crawled over to Coulter. Rhodes's vision kept slipping in and out of focus.

Coulter slouched on his knees staring straight ahead—toward where the Masks just had been. They weren't here now.

"Eddie..." Rhodes choked.

Coulter glanced at him. Coulter didn't hold eye contact as well as he did before the battalion escaped from the Masks, but he kept getting better by the minute.

He barely looked at Rhodes before Coulter struggled to his feet. Rhodes couldn't tell how injured Coulter was or if he was injured at all.

He jammed his shoulder under Rhodes's armpit and Coulter forced Rhodes to his feet. Rhodes stumbled. He couldn't balance.

Coulter held him up, turned him around, and both men set off staggering south with the platoons.

Chapter 6

C oulter followed the retreating 765th Platoon toward a giant Legion staging area south of the city. Rhodes didn't even know which city it was or which planet he was on.

It didn't matter because they were all the same. Soldiers streamed in all directions. Dusters, Predators, and freighters came and went all over a massive field dotted with temporary buildings.

A dozen Ravagers came down to take the platoons on board. It sure looked like the Legion was withdrawing from this planet.

Coulter stumbled through the throng going....somewhere. Rhodes couldn't think clearly enough to ask.

"The command dome is over there," Murphy pointed out. "We should go there if the brass is so keen to get us back. They'll be able to send us back to the *Ero*."

"Forget the command dome," Fisher countered. "The Strikers can come and get us here. Captain Rhodes needs medical attention. He can only get that on the *Ero*. The brass would only delay us."

"We can't call the Strikers if we can't interface with them," Murphy returned. "You think you're so smart, but you don't think of a little detail like that. We need the brass to contact the *Ero* and the *Ero* would have to contact the Strikers. The Strikers probably don't even know where we are."

"Which officers are at the command dome?" Fisher asked.

"How should I know if I can't interface with the Legion?" Murphy repeated.

Coulter responded to their conversation by turning toward the command dome. He only made it a few dozen yards before a completely different group of officers came toward him and Rhodes. These officers didn't come from the command dome.

Rhodes didn't recognize any of them—except Scofield. He was the only lieutenant in the group. Everyone else was a captain or above.

Two colonels squared their shoulders in front of Rhodes and Coulter. "Captain Rhodes?" one of them snapped. "Captain Rhodes of Battalion 1?"

Rhodes tried to answer, but his brain didn't connect to his mouth. He sagged off Coulter's shoulder. Just keeping his eyes open was as much as Rhodes could manage right now.

The colonel waited for Rhodes to say something. When he didn't, the colonel went through another convulsion of squaring his shoulders.

"Captain Corban Rhodes, you're under arrest for treason against the Treaty of Aemon Cluster." The colonel glanced at Coulter. "You both are." He waved to the men behind him. "Take them."

Scofield stood there staring while a bunch of armed Legion guards came forward and surrounded Rhodes and Coulter. They took Rhodes off Coulter's hands.

Rhodes wanted to tell Coulter not to resist, but he didn't. He cooperated with everything and walked off with the soldiers guarding him.

Rhodes stumbled when he lost Coulter's support. The soldiers moved in to prop Rhodes up, but they didn't get there in time. He collapsed on the ground and passed out.

He woke up lying on a metal bench in a bare cell. Bars separated him from the next cell where Coulter sat on an identical bench.

Coulter leaned against the wall and stared at Rhodes through the bars. Rhodes hauled himself upright. "Eddie...." Rhodes frowned. "Are you okay?"

"I'm fine," Coulter replied in his old nonchalant tone. "I went through the rest of my withdrawals. I'm okay now. Thank you for getting me out of there."

"Are we.....?" Rhodes furrowed his brow some more when he looked around.

He didn't see Fisher in the corner of The Grid, but Rhodes sensed that Fisher was there. He was making himself silent and invisible the way he often did when Rhodes first woke up from a conversion cycle.

It took him a minute before he recognized where he was. He and Coulter were in the brig of a Legion Ravager.

"We're on the *Ero,*" Coulter told him. "The brass didn't know how to treat your injuries, so they sent us back here. Dr. Osborne has been in here a few dozen times taking care of you since we got arrested."

"Why are *you* under arrest? You were under my command ever since we got captured. If someone is holding me responsible for what we did, you should be clear."

Coulter shrugged. "I have no idea what's going on out there. I can't interface with anyone—but I can only assume you and I are the only ones under arrest. None of the rest of the battalion has gotten locked up in here."

Rhodes sank back against the wall. He still felt weak—as if he'd been in a long conversion cycle.

He couldn't have been in a conversion cycle, though, because he wasn't in a capsule or one of the Masks' standing conversion stations. He'd been lying on this bench until just now.

"I'm sorry I got you into this," he murmured. "I'm sorry about all of this."

"You have nothing to be sorry about," Coulter countered. "You're the one who's been doing the most for all of us. We're on the *Ero* now because of you."

"I just hate what I see happening to all of you. I hate what I see the Legion doing to all of us."

Coulter only shrugged again, but he didn't look away. His eyes sparkled as clearly as ever. "None of that is your fault. I wish I could have been clearer while we were in The Grid. I wish I could have seen more clearly what was going on so I could be more help to you. It kills me that Dietz was the one who got to be that for you." Coulter finally lowered his eyes. "I guess we all misjudged him."

"I don't suppose you know what happened to him, do you? Did Dr. Osborne say anything?"

"He said everyone in the battalion is fine. He says they all got out."

Rhodes wilted again. "Thank God! I don't care if the brass locks me up as long as the rest of you are okay."

"Okay isn't the word I would use to describe how we're doing."

Rhodes didn't open his eyes. He really, really needed to go through a conversion cycle—a real one.

Everything that happened since the Masks captured him was starting to catch up with him—as if it already wasn't catching up with him.

He wished he could be stronger for Coulter right now, but Rhodes couldn't summon the energy to be anything to anyone right now.

If the Legion kept him locked up in the brig, then no one expected Rhodes to do anything or be anything. He just had to sit here—which was somehow so much worse than sitting around in the barracks at Coleridge Station.

He was still sitting there with his eyes closed when Dr. Osborne returned. He brought four armed Legion soldiers with him.

They were the ones who unlocked Rhodes's cell so Dr. Osborne could come in and examine Rhodes. Then the soldiers locked Dr. Osborne into the cell while the soldiers stood guard outside.

Dr. Osborne checked his device while he took readings on all of Rhodes's systems. "You're exhibiting a stress response from not having gone through a proper conversion cycle."

"I know," Rhodes muttered. "I feel it."

"We're working around the clock to get the brass to release you to the lab for medical treatment, but they don't want to cooperate. They say you're dangerous even when you're inactive in a conversion cycle."

"Can't you at least get Eddie released? Tell them I ordered him to do everything. I don't care what you have to tell them. Just get him released."

"Colonel Kraft, Colonel Neff, and General Hyde are already doing all of that."

Rhodes's head shot up. "They are? They're here?"

"They've been in non-stop negotiations with the Legion brass to get you sent back to Coleridge Station, but the brass is insisting that you at least face an inquiry into what happened."

"Don't you have Grid readings from everything that happened to us? You should be able to download all of that from The Grid. You would be able to see everything from the minute we got captured."

"Yes, we have all that. That's the evidence Kraft, Neff, and Hyde are using to explain your actions, but the brass doesn't want to accept it. They think the Masks might have doctored it."

"Why would they doctor it to implicate themselves?"

Osborne shrugged and bent over to stare closely at something on Rhodes's facial implant. "You can't make this shit up." He touched

Rhodes's implant on his cheek. "Do you feel like you have normal sensation in your face? You took damage to your facial implants when you got shot."

"I feel fine now."

"Everything is reading as normal as it possibly can until you go through a conversion cycle. Just try to be patient. The brass is all hot to bring you to an inquiry, so I don't think you'll be stuck in here for much longer."

The soldiers let him out and then locked the cell with Rhodes inside. He shut his eyes, stretched out on the bench, and did his best to relax.

It didn't work out too well, though. He couldn't sleep like a normal human being. The strain sapped his nerves and made him jittery.

He lay there for ten minutes before Fisher expanded. "I won't ask how you're feeling this morning, Captain."

"I'm afraid I'm not going to be very good company for a while, pal. You might want to back into your cave until they fix me."

"I don't have a cave, Captain."

"You know what I mean."

Fisher didn't go away. He stayed there staring at Rhodes exactly the way Coulter did.

Rhodes kept his eyes shut, but he still saw Fisher even then. Fisher didn't go away.

Rhodes couldn't decide whether to be happy about that or not. Fisher's company had always been a blessing and a curse.

On the one hand, Fisher saw Rhodes at his lowest point. On the other hand, Fisher occupied that low point along with Rhodes.

Now Coulter was seeing Rhodes like that, too.

Coulter held up better than Rhodes did. Rhodes didn't understand why because Coulter couldn't have gone through a conversion cycle in the brig, either.

Coulter didn't explain it and Rhodes didn't ask. Coulter just sat there watching Rhodes with that mysterious intensity. What was Coulter thinking right now?

Chapter 7

Rhodes must have fallen into some partial stupor. He woke up hours later when Dr. Osborne came back with the same soldiers.

"You're being called to a meeting with the brass," Osborne informed him. "They want to question you to see if you should go before an inquiry or not."

"Why wouldn't I when I did what they say I did?"

"You should know better than to admit to something like that. Anyway, they aren't trying to determine guilt or innocence. They just want to talk to you before they decide whether to hold a formal inquiry. Then they'll release you to the lab and you can go through a conversion cycle. Nothing is more important than that right now."

"What about me, Doc?" Coulter asked.

"You're coming, too. They want to hold an inquiry on you, too."

"Why on Earth would they do that?" Rhodes demanded. "He didn't do anything."

"Neither did you, but the brass wants its pound of flesh. Come on."

Dr. Osborne tapped on his device for a minute before the soldiers unlocked the two cells. The soldiers stood guard while Rhodes and Coulter followed Dr. Osborne outside.

The soldiers didn't try to restrain the two prisoners, which was strange considering how dangerous Rhodes and Coulter were supposed to be.

The party headed off down the corridor. Everything else about the *Ero* looked the way Rhodes remembered it.

"Eddie says you said the rest of the battalion is all right," Rhodes began. "Did Dietz make a full recovery?"

"He's fine. I don't know why the brass are treating you and Coulter differently from everyone who came back earlier."

"Maybe it had something to do with soldiers and officers on the battlefield who wanted revenge and got me and Eddie arrested in the first place."

"I don't know about that," Dr. Osborne replied. "I don't understand any of this if you really want to know the truth. Nothing anyone is doing makes much sense. The only people in this whole thing who are thinking clearly are Colonel Kraft, Colonel Neff, and General Hyde."

"Remind me to thank General Brewster for coming out and showing his support," Rhodes muttered under his breath.

"He wanted to, but General Hyde told him to put a sock in it and make himself invisible." Dr. Osborne bit back a sudden burst of irrepressible laughter. "She said his reputation as a raving lunatic would only make this harder for you."

Rhodes looked away. "She must be thinking clearly if she said all that."

"The three of them are your best friends in all this. If you get out of this, it will be thanks to their efforts."

They had to cut their conversation short when they got to the *Ero's* bridge. Captain Ackerman stopped what he was doing and led

Rhodes, Coulter, and Dr. Osborne into a conference room adjacent to the bridge.

Colonel Paxton Kraft, Colonel Neff, and General Hyde were already there with half a dozen other officers Rhodes didn't know. Dr. Trudeau stood at the table, too.

"Welcome back, Captain," General Hyde began. "You did an excellent job of bringing all your subordinates back to the Legion. You have our undying gratitude."

Rhodes glanced at the other officers. None of them looked even marginally grateful to get Rhodes back.

He mumbled, "Yes, Ma'am," and he and Coulter took their places at the only places left at the table—at the very far end closest to the door.

Everyone remained standing, so Rhodes and Coulter remained standing, too.

General Hyde waved at the other officers at the table. She introduced them one after the other even though Rhodes could read their nametags just as fast.

"This is Admiral Wilson Stabler, Colonel Harlan Volk, General Dennis Wolcott, Captain Otis Lake, Admiral Donald Hassel, and General Albert Guzman. These are the officers who've been called in to decide if you should face disciplinary action for your role in the deaths of so many Legion soldiers at the Battle of Rono and the Battle of Keonus."

Rhodes only nodded. "I understand all that. What I don't understand is why Corporal Coulter is facing disciplinary action for the same thing. He shouldn't be. He's lower-ranked than anyone else in the battalion. He should have been cleared a long time ago."

Admiral Stabler spoke up across the table. He was an aging man with white hair and sagging cheeks, but the rest of him still looked as strong as a man a fraction his age.

"I can assure you, Captain," he told Rhodes. "The outcome of this investigation will apply to the whole battalion. Whatever we decide for you will affect the entire battalion."

"Is that supposed to be a threat?" Rhodes heard himself stepping out of line, but he didn't care about anything except getting Coulter out of the brig. "If I'm facing disciplinary action on behalf of the whole battalion, then Coulter should be back with the rest of them where he can get the medical treatment he deserves."

"We haven't decided whether you'll face disciplinary action or not," Colonel Volk replied.

"All the more reason Coulter should be released," Rhodes returned. "You have two choices. Hold me in the brig and charge me on behalf of the whole battalion or charge the whole battalion and throw everyone in the brig. You have no reason to hold one man."

Admiral Stabler sighed and looked away. "You make a good point, Captain. Corporal Coulter will be released."

"Yes!" Fisher blurted out and immediately shut his mouth. He retreated into the corner of Rhodes's vision.

Rhodes pretended not to notice. "Was there anything else you wanted to talk to me about?"

"We were hoping you could give us some insight into the Masks' movements," General Hyde replied. "Captain Vernick seems to be under the impression that you had advanced knowledge of an ambush the Masks planned to pull on the platoons. Is that true?"

"I knew about the ambush, but I can't tell you anything about the Masks' movements. The connection only lasted a split second. It hasn't happened before or since. I've been the brig the whole time, so I haven't been near them."

"We were actually more concerned with your actions while you were in the Masks' custody," Captain Lake interjected. "Multiple officers witnessed you and your battalion attack Legion platoons on Rono and again on Keonus. You killed dozens or even hundreds of Legion soldiers."

Rhodes did his best to keep his head straight and hold eye contact with everyone at once. "Yes, that's true. We did."

"What explanation can you offer for this?" Captain Lake demanded. "You've been charged with treason and multiple counts of murder."

"We've already gone over this a dozen times, Otis," General Hyde interrupted. "We have all the evidence that suggests the Masks controlled the battalion and forced them to kill those soldiers."

"I want to hear it from Rhodes," Lake returned and faced Rhodes across the table. "Is that your defense—that the Masks controlled you and forced you to kill those soldiers? I would remind you that you're speaking on behalf of the whole battalion."

"The Grid evidence already proves the battalion was interfacing with each other during the assault," Colonel Neff added. "Captain Rhodes would have known which of his subordinates attacked the platoons under the Masks' control and which didn't."

"That's exactly what I'm saying," Captain Lake countered. "Captain Rhodes can tell us which if any of his subordinates was under the Masks' control and which weren't." He turned and leveled Rhodes with a drilling stare. "Were *all* of your subordinates under the Masks' control at the time? Did any of them act of their own volition?"

Rhodes hesitated. Was he really about to rat out Fuentes—and maybe Lauer and Thackery, too?

Admitting that any of them acted of their own volition would be a death sentence. Was Rhodes really prepared to go that far?

"If you were under the Masks' control, you would be exonerated," General Hyde reminded him. "The people who were actually responsible for this atrocity would get what they deserve. You and the other innocent members of the battalion would be released and returned to duty where you belong."

Rhodes still didn't answer. Returned to duty—so they could do it all again?

When Rhodes still didn't answer, Colonel Volk turned to Coulter. "What about you, Corporal? Do you know if any of your comrades acted of their own volition when it came to killing those soldiers?"

"I....." Coulter cast a sidelong glance at Rhodes. Rhodes couldn't meet his gaze. "I think you better take this to an inquiry, Sir. I don't think I'm in any position to answer that question."

"Is that because you don't know or because you want to protect your friends?" Captain Lake asked.

Coulter shrugged. "Does it matter?"

"I'm disappointed in you, son," Admiral Stabler blustered. "You're dismissed to the battalion's capsule hold. You stay here, Captain."

Coulter saluted the table, said, "Yes, Sir," and let himself out of the room as quickly and quietly as he could.

That left Rhodes to face the firing squad.

"I just want to assure you, Captain, that we have all the evidence on The Grid feed," General Hyde told him.

"Then why are you even questioning me about it? You should already know."

"We're questioning you and considering conducting an inquiry into this matter because the families and loved ones of the slain soldiers want answers."

"Don't you already have that?"

"Why do you think the Masks protected you on the battlefield?" Captain Lake asked. "They attacked Lieutenant Scofield's squad when they were about to shoot you."

"I don't know. Maybe the Masks wanted to recapture me. How should I know why they did it?"

"What do you think of the SAMs' assessment that the Masks and the SAMs are the same?" Admiral Stabler asked.

Rhodes spun around. He shouldn't have been surprised by this. These people had access to every nuance of The Grid the battalion had been going through from day one.

Rhodes pulled himself together with an effort. "It makes sense, doesn't it? Almost all the Masks' technology is the same as the Legion's......"

"The Masks aren't SAMs no matter what the SAMs say," Colonel Volk growled.

It was the first time he'd spoken. He was a young man of thirty with jet-black hair and black eyes, but he gave the impression of sagging old age even more than Admiral Stabler did.

"The Masks say they're the same as the SAMs, too," Rhodes pointed out. "That's what the Masks say—that they captured us to fill in the gaps in their programming that the SAMs have and the Masks don't."

"What do you think that means?" General Hyde asked. "What gaps do you think they need to fill? The cityscape they showed you seemed complete."

Rhodes didn't tell her about the heavy air of despair and hopelessness infecting that cityscape. He might have made a mistake about that. Maybe the cityscape was as perfect as B said it was.

"If you can't give us the answers we need, we'll have no choice but to hold an inquiry into your loyalty to the Treaty of Aemon Cluster," Captain Lake told Rhodes.

"If I can't give you the answer you need here, I won't be able to give them at the inquiry, either," Rhodes pointed out.

"You and the battalion are the only people who can help us understand the Masks," Colonel Neff replied.

"I don't understand the Masks," Rhodes told him. "I would tell you if I did."

"So you actually think the Masks and the SAMs are the same technology?" Colonel Volk asked. "You actually think the Masks came from failed and discarded SAMs from the Battalion 1 project?"

"Where else could the Masks have come from?" Rhodes asked. "The Masks used The Grid the same way we do. It doesn't seem reasonable to assume they developed The Grid independently from us, does it?"

Some of the officers exchanged glances.

Others didn't. "I'm afraid we have no choice but to hold an inquiry into this matter," Colonel Volk went on. "We can't risk the battalion causing another bloodbath like the last one."

Rhodes only nodded again. "I'm only surprised you haven't held an inquiry before now. I thought you would have held one right away."

"You'll go back to the brig until...."

"This is outrageous!" Dr. Trudeau interrupted. "You've denied him critical medical care for days! This is as much a violation of the Treaty of Aemon as anything he's done. You have to send him to the lab immediately! This is cruel and inhumane punishment when he hasn't even been charged with a crime!"

Colonel Kraft spoke up for the first time. He hardly ever spoke at these meetings. When he did, his words carried the weight of worlds.

"Captain Rhodes will be released to Dr. Osborne's custody and returned to the lab for medical treatment," Colonel Kraft murmured under his breath. "He's already agreed to face the inquiry. We don't have to consider him a flight risk or a threat to any Legion personnel." He nodded to Rhodes. "You're dismissed, Captain."

Rhodes muttered, "Thank you, Sir," and left the conference room. The officers remained standing in tense silence until Rhodes, Osborne, and Trudeau shut the door behind them.

"Those bastards!" Trudeau hissed. "They were really going to send you back to the brig—and they're the ones acting all high and mighty like they're the arbiters of justice in the Treaty of Aemon Cluster! The cocksuckers!"

"Settle down, Felix," Osborne told him. "We got what we wanted. Now come on, Captain. You need to spend the rest of your time before the inquiry in a conversion cycle."

Chapter 8

The elevator doors whisked aside and opened in front of Rhodes. A long corridor stretched out in front of him.

Dozens of Legion personnel of every rank strode back and forth in that corridor. They all carried out their duties as if he wasn't here.

He and the two Battalion 1 doctors stepped out of the elevator and the doors closed behind them. They entered the Ocao Space Station which of course orbited the planet Ocao in the Itriun system.

The system was conveniently far away from the Masks invasion. Everyone here from the Legion brass down to the lowest civilian janitor could continue to pretend that the war wasn't going on at all.

The corridor's glass sides curved upward from the floor and gave a view of the planet from orbit. The planet gleamed brilliant, verdant green down there. It was such a luxurious view—a view reserved for people who worked hard to get out into space and build a station like this.

Rhodes and the two doctors set off down the corridor as if, by some distant chance, they might be a normal part of the Legion just like the rest of these people.

Rhodes would never be a normal part of the Legion—not ever again. That became more obvious to him by the day—as if he hadn't already figured that out.

All these people around him right now—they all went about their business as if him being here was the most ordinary thing in the world. They didn't act like they knew what it meant.

Maybe they didn't know what it meant. Maybe none of them knew anything about him.

He and the two doctors passed down multiple corridors and took a few different elevators to the station's very highest deck—the administrative deck.

Rhodes had been in one long conversion cycle since his first meeting with the officers who wanted to hold him accountable for killing so many Legion soldiers.

Rhodes hadn't seen or spoken to anyone from Battalion 1 since Coulter left the conference room. Rhodes had been in his capsule ever since.

Dr. Osborne woke him up in the lab, waited a little while to make sure all Rhodes's systems were functioning, and then they came straight here.

Now Rhodes would face the inquiry—not to find out what he and the battalion did to those soldiers. Everyone already knew that.

Everyone already knew why they did it, too. Rhodes would hazard a guess and say the brass already knew that Fuentes wasn't under the Masks' control at the time, too.

The brass only held this inquiry to decide what to do with the battalion as a result. For all he knew, the brass had already decided what to do with the battalion. This inquiry was just a formality.

Dr. Osborne and Dr. Trudeau gave nothing away. Rhodes liked to think the doctors didn't know any more than he did.

He wouldn't have been surprised if the officers kept their decision from the doctors—and all the rest of their conversations. The two doctors had already made it perfectly plain that they supported the battalion.

Rhodes found it impossible to express his gratitude for their support. He should have. They did a lot more than support the battalion. They came with him right now. They stood by him.

Colonel Kraft, Colonel Neff, and General Hyde did, too. Rhodes would never forget that. He would never be able to repay it, either.

He could stay mad at people like General Brewster, Dr. Neiland, and Dr. Montague for doing this to him and the rest of the battalion. Rhodes couldn't stay mad at these people.

Fisher stayed visible in the corner of Rhodes's vision from the time he left his capsule, but Fisher didn't speak beyond the first routine pleasantries of greeting Rhodes and wishing him a good morning.

Rhodes got the same feeling of deep, almost painful gratitude for Fisher's presence and understanding. He knew as well as Rhodes did what was riding on this inquiry.

Fisher's existence hung on Rhodes. Fisher couldn't make the case on their behalf. He had to rely on Rhodes to do that for both of them.

He and the two doctors entered a different conference room—a much bigger, fancier conference room.

This one had more big windows offering another stunning view of Ocao floating in the darkness of space. That planet sure was beautiful, but Rhodes could only think one thing.

The Masks would reduce this beautiful green ball to a smoking black wreck the same way they reduced every other planet to a smoking black wreck.

They would kill everyone on this planet and raze every city. Why? Did their programming somehow make them want to take revenge on the people who created them?

Rhodes had to pay attention to the inquiry and not think about the fact that the Masks were still out there.

They were trying to wipe out the human race while these moronic officers sat around pointing the finger at Battalion 1.

Never mind. He didn't mind going through this charade if it gave someone some closure about all those soldiers dying.

The officers in charge of the inquiry sat in a line across a huge table set in front of the door. Rhodes walked in and faced all those officers staring at him.

Colonel Kraft, Colonel Neff, and General Hyde sat with the six officers Rhodes met last time.

The inquiry finally brought in General Brewster, Admiral Pulman, and Colonel LeClerc, too.

The three of them had such conflicting attitudes toward Battalion 1. This should get interesting.

The two doctors weren't under scrutiny here, but they planted themselves on either side of Rhodes and faced down the inquiry panel, too. That on its own counted for a lot.

"Welcome back, Captain," General Hyde began.

Rhodes replied, "Thank you, Ma'am," but everything that happened here was so automatic. He couldn't bring himself to care about much anymore.

"We've reviewed the Grid evidence from all Battalion 1's systems," Captain Lake went on. "We can confirm that you and Lieutenants Oakes, Lauer, and Rhinehart all resisted the Masks' control."

"I'd like to point out for the record that Sergeant Jairo Dietz resisted as well," Rhodes replied.

"Our concern is with Corporals Fuentes and Coulter and with Alyssa Thackery," Colonel Volk chimed in. "Each of them cooperated with the Masks at one point or another. Isn't that true?"

"The evidence also suggests that Fuentes wasn't under the Masks' control at all during the Battle of Keonus," Admiral Stabler added. "The evidence suggests he carried out the slaughter willingly and even enjoyed it—and that he was laughing during the Battle of Rono. Would you agree with that assessment, Captain?"

Rhodes felt himself squirming. "I would argue there were extenuating circumstances, Sir."

"What extenuating circumstances could possibly justify knowingly, willingly, and systematically slaughtering hundreds of Legion soldiers?" Captain Lake asked.

"For a start, the fact that the Masks kept us in a hallucinogenic state for almost the entirety of our captivity," Rhodes pointed out. "The Masks used drugs to induce a state of euphoria when we cooperated and fought on their side. They used these drug-induced hallucinogenic states to condition us to feel this euphoria during battle against their other enemies first. Then they turned us against the Legion expecting the same thing to happen. Some of us reacted differently than others. You can't tell me Fuentes just woke up one morning and decided to slaughter Legion soldiers. The Masks created the conditions to make him react that way. That was their plan all along. Surely you can all see that based on the evidence. I don't know why I have to explain this to you if you already know everything."

"That doesn't explain why he did what he did," Colonel Volk argued. "Fuentes wasn't under the influence of drugs or torture during the Battle of Rono. Then you, Rhinehart, Oakes, and Lauer all went through the same process of torture, drugs, hallucinations, and conditioning—yet all four of you resisted the control to kill Legion soldiers on Keonus. How do you explain that?"

"I can't explain it other than maybe the fact that all of us were officers in the Legion beforehand had something to do with it," Rhodes replied. "We're also older and more experienced than Fuentes. He's just a kid and not a very bright one." Rhodes opened his mouth to say something else and stopped himself in time.

"Do you have something to add, Captain?" Admiral Stabler asked "Whatever you have to say in your own defense, you better say it now. You won't get another chance to defend yourself and the battalion after this inquiry concludes."

Rhodes hesitated again, cast the briefest glance at General Brewster and the rest of the Battalion 1 governing body, and went for broke. What the hell did he have to lose?

"I would argue that the conditions of the Battalion 1 project prepared us for this and made us all more susceptible to the Masks' control," he blurted out. "I would argue that none of this would have happened without the conditions we suffered at Coleridge Station. I'm quite certain Fuentes wouldn't have flipped the way he did if we hadn't suffered the way we did."

"Suffered!" General Brewster snapped. "You and the battalion never suffered at Coleridge Station! I resent that implication! Do you have any idea how much trouble we went to over this project? We all worked our tails off to give you and the battalion every possible chance and opportunity."

"Every possible chance to survive, you mean?" Rhodes countered. "Our medical records will show that everyone in the battalion suffered from disorientation and distress, both physical and mental, severe enough to drive all nine of us to the brink of suicide. Fuentes was suicidal long before we ever went into combat against the Masks. He was a danger to himself and the rest of the battalion—and he wasn't the only one."

General Brewster shuffled in his seat. Colonel Volk glared at Brewster. "You never told us about this! You led us to believe the orientation process went smoothly for everyone in the battalion."

"Ask him how many people didn't survive even waking up from stasis," Rhodes went on."

"Those were just growing pains!" General Brewster blustered.

"I can personally testify that the physical pain alone would be enough to make anyone want to end their life," Rhodes added, "and that's not counting the distress of being ripped away from our families and them being told we were already dead."

"None of us knew anything about this, Captain," Admiral Stabler insisted.

"Colonel Kraft, Colonel Neff, and General Hyde did," Rhodes pointed out. "They should have told you."

"As a matter of fact, Captain," General Hyde replied. "We've been told since we first got here that your previous medical records weren't relevant to this investigation. The inquiry panel refused to accept any evidence from before your capture."

"It is very relevant." Rhodes turned back to the other officers. "The Masks offered us a way out of our pain and distress. These hallucinations offered us a way to live in comfort and happiness—a way to regain the pleasure and connection of human life—the pleasure and connection the Battalion 1 project robbed from all of us. The euphoria became addictive. I really don't blame Fuentes for getting swept away by it. I don't blame Thackery for betraying the battalion, either. The temptation to stay in the hallucination was overpowering. It took all our effort to resist it. So not everyone succeeded. So what? You can't blame them for that. I also don't blame Fuentes for resenting the Legion for putting us through all this. He wanted payback and he got it. The Masks didn't do this to us—the Legion did. None of this would have happened if not for the Battalion 1 project."

"Unfortunately, none of that absolves you of culpability in the deaths of all these soldiers," Captain Lake interjected. "Your argument only proves that you and the rest of the battalion are too unstable to function in battlefield conditions."

"I've been saying the same thing for weeks, Sir," Rhodes muttered.

"We can't run the risk of something like this happening again."

"It won't happen again because we aren't the Masks' prisoners anymore," Rhodes pointed out. "We've all withdrawn from the drugs."

"By your own argument, the orientation process integrating you back into the Legion ranks might be incomplete," Colonel Volk pointed out. "You might never completely reintegrate. Isn't that the point you're making? The risk would always remain that one of you might snap. Fuentes had a history of dangerous behavior before the Masks captured the battalion. He could snap on the battlefield and decide again that he wanted get payback against the Legion."

Rhodes shifted his weight again. "I don't say you're wrong, Sir."

"Then we have no choice but to discontinue the Battalion 1 project," Captain Lake announced.

Rhodes spun around fast. "Discontinue....."

"The remaining battalion members and their SAMs will be taken offline and rendered....."

"You can't do this!" General Brewster's voice started rising and he started to get out of his chair. "Do you know the investment we've put into this project? We finally have a fighting force strong enough to combat our enemies. If you take that away, the Masks will steamroll right over the regular Legion! We won't stand a chance!"

"At the moment, Battalion 1 is as much a threat to the Legion as the Masks are," Captain Lake pointed out.

"That is a bald-faced lie!" General Brewster countered. "Captain Rhodes and his subordinates saved more soldiers in numerous battles as they killed on Rono and Keonus combined. You all know this. Captain Rhodes even saved soldiers who were trying to hunt him down and kill him. If that doesn't prove his loyalty, nothing will."

"The fact that you hid how unstable these people are shows me that you aren't competent to run this project," Admiral Stabler fired back. "You knew these people were experiencing dangerous mental problems and you hid this, not just from us, but from the platoons who were supposed to fight alongside these people. This project is a menace to the Legion. The Battalion 1 project never should have started in the first place."

"Amen, Sir," Rhodes chimed in.

Admiral Stabler shot him a dirty look. "Don't you go agreeing with me. These officers are talking about taking you and your subordinates offline. Don't you even care about saving your own life? You might at least consider trying to save your subordinates' lives."

"I won't try to fool you into thinking we won't still suffer from malfunctions and problems," Rhodes replied, "but you might consider some other factors before you throw away everything we've already been through."

"What do you mean?" Colonel Neff asked.

"We've already suffered because of this project and from the Masks' captivity. I really don't blame you for wanting to end this project, but there might be a way to turn all of this around and make it into something good."

"Like what?" Captain Lake asked. "How could any of this possibly be something good?"

"When I was a prisoner of the Masks, I made up my mind to kill them all in revenge for what they did to me—to all of us. Some of us want to finish them for good. We might have our problems, but we're the ones most capable of doing that. Give us a chance to prove our loyalty and dedication to destroying the Legion's enemies. You have no other way to defeat the Masks. I'm not sure if we can, but we're the only ones who even stand a chance."

The officers exchanged glances again. General Brewster pointed at Rhodes. "Yes! That's right! That's what I was saying....."

"Sit down, Kenneth," Admiral Stabler snapped. "You aren't part of this. You're too attached to this project to think straight. None of us wants to hear from you again."

Rhodes got a sick little thrill listening to this. General Brewster was finally meeting some people of his own rank or higher. These officers all understood exactly what he'd been up to behind the Treaty of Aemon Cluster's taxpayers' backs.

Admiral Stabler glared at him. General Brewster sank back into his chair. He didn't look at anyone.

The admiral took extra long to straighten up and face front. "We need to consider this, Captain. I don't see how we can reverse our decision, but we thank you for your testimony. You're dismissed."

"I want to be returned to the battalion," Rhodes blurted out. "I want to see my people. If you're going to take all of us offline, I think I've earned the right to spend my last hours or days with them."

The panel went through another flurry of shifting in their seats. Rhodes didn't see why his request would cause them so much discomfort. What did they think—that he would let them keep him locked in a lab for the last hours of his miserable life?

Once again, Colonel Kraft spoke up for the first time and broke the awkward silence. "You can return to the battalion, Captain. We'll inform you of our decision in due course."

"Yes, Sir," Rhodes replied and left the conference room.

Chapter 9

Dr. Osborne and Dr. Trudeau stopped in the corridor outside the Ocao Space Station conference room.

Dr. Osborne sighed heavily. "I guess the decision isn't anything we didn't already expect. Still, it seems like a waste."

"Admiral Stabler is right," Rhodes replied. "This project never should have gotten off the drawing board."

"But you're already here," Dr. Trudeau pointed out. "It isn't perfect, but if you're functional enough to risk your life to save Legion soldiers, why waste that?"

"It doesn't matter because the panel won't reverse the decision," Dr. Osborne murmured. "Come on, Captain. I know your people are anxious to see you."

The three of them set off through the station's many corridors and elevators—back in the direction from which the three men had come.

It took a long time for them to get back to the *Ero*. The trip and the view of Ocao gave Rhodes plenty of time to think.

He didn't really mind the idea of the inquiry panel taking Battalion 1 offline. Rhodes himself had been thinking the same thing for weeks—maybe even months. How long had this been going on anyway? He lost track of time while he was with the Masks and while he was in so many conversion cycles.

Staying alive or going offline—what difference did it make in the end? He probably would have made the same decision if he'd been on the panel.

He couldn't even really pinpoint why he argued for them to keep him alive. It wasn't just a desire to take his revenge against the Masks.

Maybe he was just too stubborn to give up that easily. Maybe the primal will to survive kept him going even when his rational brain told him it wasn't a good idea.

Fisher didn't say a word all the way back to the *Ero*. He didn't comment positively or negatively on what Rhodes said to the officers.

Rhodes would have liked to talk to Fisher about all of this—now that the inquiry was over. Rhodes couldn't do that in front of the doctors. That would be a private conversation between him and Fisher—the way it should be.

The two doctors accompanied him back to the capsule hold that had always been the battalion's barracks on board this ship.

The doctors didn't enter with him. They left to go back to their lab. They left him to reunite with his subordinates on their own terms.

Everyone jumped up and made a big deal about Rhodes's return. "We thought they'd keep you in the brig forever," Thackery told him.

"We did not," Coulter countered. "They had to let him out so he could go through conversion cycles. They couldn't keep him there without risking his health."

"Is it true the brass is sending you to a disciplinary inquiry?" Oakes asked.

"They already did," Rhodes replied. "I just came from there."

Everyone jolted. "You did? What did they decide?"

"They're thinking about what to do with us. They're considering taking us offline."

A hush fell over the group. "They better not," Rhinehart snarled. "I'll fight back. I won't go willingly."

"You were the one who said you might do it yourself," Rhodes reminded him. "We've all been there."

"That was before," Rhinehart countered. "I didn't go through all that with the Masks for nothing. I didn't fight my way back here so I could get taken offline by my own people. Doing it to myself is one thing. That's my choice. No one is going to do it for me. Hell no."

"We should have stayed with the Masks," Fuentes muttered. "We could have stayed at Stonebridge."

"No, we couldn't have and we aren't having that conversation," Lauer fired back. "We're in this mess because they made us kill Legion soldiers. If we went back, they would do the same thing again and we would kill even more soldiers. We aren't even talking about that."

"What are we going to do, then?" Thackery asked. "What *can* we do?"

"We'll go on the run," Rhinehart suggested. "We'll steal our Strikers. Our SAMs will help us out. They won't want the Legion to take them offline, either."

"Don't do anything until you hear the panel's decision," Rhodes told them. "They might decide to keep us around for a while."

"That's even worse," Rhinehart sneered. "So a bunch of officers we don't even know get to decide if we live or die? This is no way to live. *We* decide if we live or die."

"They're worried we might do the same thing," Rhodes pointed out. "They're worried that one of us will snap in combat and turn a weapon on Legion soldiers again."

"Then why are they considering keeping us around?" Thackery asked.

"Because I told them that we all want to end the Masks for good. I told them we all want payback for what they did to us and there's no one else in the whole Treaty of Aemon Cluster that stands a chance of defeating the Masks."

Thackery gasped. "You told them that?! You said we wanted payback?"

"Of course. I do, at least. I don't know about the rest of you, but I want to make the Masks understand that capturing us was their first and last mistake. I don't care if I have to spend the rest of my life doing it. Them capturing us is going to be the beginning of the end of their whole stinking race."

Everyone stared at Rhodes in stunned shock when he finished speaking. He didn't see why they considered what he said so astounding or outrageous. He was only surprised the others weren't thinking the same thing.

Rhinehart sank down at the table and stared at his hands on top of it. "I guess that's it, then."

"What's it?" Rhodes asked. "They haven't come to their decision yet."

"I mean, if we're going for payback, we have to do it with the Legion, don't we? We have to sign ourselves up to be their dogs again."

"What's the alternative—going over to the Masks?" Rhodes countered.

"Yes," Fuentes interjected.

"Don't ever let me hear you say that again, Corporal," Rhodes snapped. "Not ever."

"What if he's right, though?" Thackery asked. "Why should we be loyal to the Legion if they could do something like this to us?"

"Compared to what the Masks did to us?"

Rhodes looked back and forth between Thackery and Fuentes. He couldn't decide which of them deserved a smackdown more.

In the end, he settled on Fuentes. "I just staked my life on proving to the Legion that we're still loyal. I just risked my ass to convince these people that the drugs and The Grid and all the Masks' treatment caused you to snap on the battlefield and kill those soldiers even when you knew exactly what you were doing."

Fuentes looked away. That one action shattered what little was left of Rhodes's patience.

He seized Fuentes and spun him around to confront him. "You look at me when I talk to you, Corporal. You were the one who signed up to join the Legion. No one made you do that. I just bet all our lives on you at least trying to put right what you did wrong. If you don't want to serve the Legion and protect your family anymore, you go right on ahead and take yourself offline right now. You don't have to wait for the brass to do it for you—but I swear to God, I will never let any of you go back to the Masks—not ever. I'll kill any of you before I let the Masks get their hands on you again. I can't risk the Masks using any of you against the Legion again."

Dead silence answered him. He felt his nerves nearing the breaking point.

That was the moment when Fisher finally spoke for the first time. "Well said, Captain," Fisher murmured.

Rhodes couldn't take it a second longer. He didn't know how long he'd been in a conversion cycle in Dr. Osborne's lab in between leaving the brig and going to the inquiry.

It wasn't nearly long enough to compensate for staying out of it for so long. He needed another one—maybe more than one.

He couldn't deal with his subordinates right now. He turned his back on them and walked over to his capsule. He hadn't entered it since he returned from the Masks' custody.

He tapped the controls to open the cover. Someone had modified the settings since he left. The toxin filtration system had been boosted with special emphasis on removing Epliothil, Kreandian, and Plianor metabolites from his blood.

Dr. Osborne must have prepared the capsule for Rhodes's return. Good.

The cover started to open when Oakes, Lauer, and Rhinehart came over to him. "We're still loyal to the Legion, Sir," Rhinehart murmured. "You don't have to worry about us."

"I know that, Lieutenant," Rhodes husked. "I never doubted any of the three of you."

"What about me?" Lauer growled. "I know you doubted me."

Rhodes had no choice but to face him. "A lot of bad shit happened to all of us while we were the Masks' prisoners, Lieutenant. The drugs, The Grid, and the torture played games with all our heads." Rhodes found himself gripping Lauer's shoulder. "I saw you during the battle, Lieutenant. I saw you resisting the control to fire on those soldiers. I'll never forget that."

Lauer lowered his eyes to the floor. His lips and cheeks spasmed all over the place and his voice cracked with buried emotion. "We should have done more. We should have resisted harder. We should have.....done something......We never should have let it happen....."

"They drugged us to make sure it happened, Lieutenant." Rhodes fought down a lump in his throat. He would never forget everything that happened during that battle, especially not his own part in it. "Whatever guilt you're carrying, I'm carrying it, too. We all are. Try to remember that. Now I gotta get some sleep before I fall over. I'll see you all when I wake up. Try not to worry about it too much. I know it's hard not to, but worrying about it won't change the outcome."

He stretched out on the mattress in his capsule. He tried not to look around at the others, but he wound up doing it anyway.

The last thing he saw before he locked into the prongs was Jairo Dietz sitting across the hold. He propped his hip against the table watching and listening to everything that went on between the rest of the battalion.

A question mark still hung over Dietz, but Rhodes didn't doubt any longer that Dietz was loyal to the Legion, too.

Rhodes would have liked to question Dietz about what exactly he experienced and didn't experience with the Masks, but that would have to wait.

Rhodes closed his capsule cover, shut his eyes.....and came face to face with Fisher.

Rhodes found himself shrinking under Fisher's unwavering gaze. Rhodes couldn't bring himself to open the dialogue he knew he needed to have with Fisher.

Fortunately, Fisher did it for him. "Do you think the battalion will try to run from the panel's decision?"

"None of us can run. We have nowhere to run to. It's the Legion for us or going offline. We don't have any other choices."

"Were you telling the truth about getting payback from the Masks?" Fisher asked.

Rhodes's eyes shot open. He opened his mouth to insist that Fisher already knew about that.

Then Rhodes remembered that Fisher didn't know. The connection between them had been so patchy while they were the Masks' prisoners.

Rhodes couldn't rely on Fisher knowing anything Rhodes had been thinking then. Fisher might even have dismissed Rhodes's outright threats against the Masks as the ravings of a tortured man in distress.

Fisher couldn't know about the other times—the times when cold, murderous determination took over Rhodes's soul. Fisher had been dead in the barn when Rhodes killed every last man, woman, and child in Stonebridge.

Rhodes shut his eyes, but he couldn't shut out Fisher. "Yes, I was telling the truth. Someone has to stop them. The battalion is the only force in the whole Cluster that might be able to do it."

"How will you do it when you can't fight them on your own? You're here now because you couldn't fight them."

"I don't know how I'll do it, but I have to find a way. This can't go on. Maybe this last trace of a connection between us will turn out to be useful in some way."

"The brass would take you offline for sure if they knew about it," Fisher remarked.

"They already know about it. You heard what General Hyde said when I first showed up to the inquiry. They want me to use the connection against the Masks. That might be the tipping point. It might give us some information about how they do things—some way we can defeat them."

"I sure hope you're right. We won't be able to defeat them the way things are going now. They're too powerful."

Rhodes didn't answer. He entered his conversion cycle as much to get out of the conversation as for any other reason.

He had no clue how to go about defeating the Masks, but he knew now that he had to do it. The process that started in Stonebridge already carried him forward onto another journey. He couldn't see the end of it, but he knew one thing for sure now.

That journey only ended one of two ways. Either he destroyed the Masks down the last individual and put a stop to their invasion forever....or he wound up dead.

There would be no middle ground, no compromise, and no negotiation in this. It was him or them with nothing in between.

Chapter 10

R hodes and his subordinates entered Dr. Osborne's lab on the *Ero*. "What are we doing here?" Rhodes asked.

"The inquiry panel ordered some more testing on all of you to see how well you're functioning since you finished your withdrawals."

"So...did they decide to keep us around a little longer?" Coulter asked.

"They still haven't decided," Dr. Osborne replied. "That's why they want these tests—so the panel can make its decision with all the latest information."

"Didn't they already have that?" Oakes asked. "We've been sitting around for a week waiting for their decision."

"I know. I don't know why they haven't made a definite decision yet."

"You must be able to take a guess, Doc," Coulter urged. "Give us some clue."

"If you really want me to guess, I'd say enough of them want to shut you down and enough of them want to keep you going. They balance each other out—which makes it impossible for anyone to come to any conclusion. Now if you'll all step over here......"

He waved across the room. Rhodes's stomach dropped when he saw a bunch of the Masks' standing conversion stations.

They'd been constructed into the lab wall where random collections of computer equipment had been before.

"What the hell is this?" Lauer snarled. "We are NOT going back into those again."

"They work the same way as reclining capsules," Dr. Osborne replied. "They're just more convenient because they don't have a closing cover."

"They aren't more convenient for us," Rhinehart snapped. "No way am I going into one of those."

"If you don't cooperate with the testing, the panel will shut you down for sure," Osborne replied. "You're only alive right now because Captain Rhodes gave the panel assurance that you all wanted to prove yourselves loyal to the Legion. Now's your chance. We won't be performing any tests you haven't already gone through at Coleridge Station."

Dietz, Coulter, and Oakes all glanced at Rhodes. He would have liked to glance at someone to give him a clue if he should go along with this.

He already knew he had to. He gave his word. Now he had to stick by it.

He crossed the lab getting closer to those stations. Cold dread spread all over his body just going near them. A thousand horrible memories rushed back to the surface just at the sight of the thing.

Dr. Trudeau followed him and stood waiting for Rhodes to turn around. It took all Rhodes's willpower to step back and lock into the prongs.

He stiffened and then they held him immobile. His every nerve and instinct told him to tear himself out of it and run for it.

He couldn't run anywhere. He was just as trapped here as he ever had been with the Masks.

Only Fisher's face in front of his eyes gave Rhodes the strength to go through with it. Fisher was still here—and not as some guy living across the road in Stonebridge.

This was the real Fisher. He blinked his bird eyes too fast, but his gaze never left Rhodes's face. Fisher's eyes brimmed over with compassion and understanding.

Dr. Trudeau started working on the station's controls. Rhodes didn't feel anything at first. He couldn't turn his head to either side to see what his subordinates were doing.

Nothing happened at first. Then a series of strange sensations coursed through Rhodes's veins and over what would have been his skin if he still had any.

"What are you feeling now?" Trudeau asked.

"Um..." Rhodes choked. "It feels.....like the wind....."

Trudeau changed something on the controls. "And now?"

"Um....." Rhodes fought another irresistible urge to struggle. "It feels.....uncomfortable...."

"Uncomfortable how?"

"I....I don't know....I can't explain it.....It just feels...."

Rhodes lost the battle and tried to squirm in the prongs. The feeling of being restrained and trapped made him burst into another fit of struggling.

"Is it painful?" Trudeau asked.

Rhodes couldn't answer. It wasn't painful—except that he couldn't stand this feeling. Something inside him raced under his skin, even on the mechanical parts of his body.

He had to get rid of that feeling. He had to stop it any way he could.

At that moment, Trudeau did something else. The feeling vanished and Rhodes found himself back in Stonebridge. It was nighttime and he sat at the table eating dinner with his family.

He knew he was still in the lab experiencing this memory through The Grid, but the rush of emotion never felt more real.

He almost burst into tears looking around the table at Ora and his children—except that they weren't his children. He remembered that, but he still felt everything as if it was real.

"What do you see?" Trudeau asked.

Rhodes opened his mouth and almost broke down completely. "I....." he croaked. "I see Stonebridge."

"What about now?"

The memory changed to another scene of the battalion sitting around the dinner table in the Fort Bastion barracks.

Rhodes suffered another crushing wave of emotion when he felt the aching affection for his subordinates. He never felt anything like that in real life. Would he ever?

"What do you see?" Trudeau asked.

Rhodes swallowed hard. "Fort Bastion."

"And now?"

Trudeau changed the memory a third time and Rhodes found himself standing at the window of the Masks' cityscape.

The smell of the ocean blew through the open window into his nostrils. He gazed out at the buildings and neighborhoods, but the heavy, ominous weight of hopeless despair no longer clouded the city.

The place radiated peace, prosperity, and community among all those beautiful, happy people. It was the most beautiful place in the world—the Masks' paradise.

Rhodes could have stayed there. He could have lived the rest of his life there. Instead, he came back here to be hunted and threatened by the people he most wanted to save. Why did he even bother to waste his time on the Legion?

A parade of other memories intruded on his mind faster than he could process them. He went through all the same terror and horror of killing Fisher in the barn and then the even greater nightmare of killing everyone in Stonebridge.

Then he switched back to the Battle of Keonus. He saw himself and his subordinates killing hundreds of Legion soldiers. He tried everything to stop it, but it happened anyway.

Just as fast, he found himself walking down the street in Preinea. He passed through his old neighborhood greeting and talking to everyone he knew—everyone he would never see again in this life.

He heard sobbing in the background. He couldn't tell which of his subordinates was doing the sobbing—like it mattered.

Trudeau did something else to the controls and the memory shut down. Rhodes was back in the lab on the *Ero* even though he'd never gone anywhere else.

"I'm going to do some basic neuromotor testing now, Captain," Trudeau told him.

Rhodes couldn't get his voice working to answer. The overwhelming emotion of reliving all those memories—it nearly destroyed his ability to cope with any of this.

Fisher didn't blink anymore. He sat there frozen without moving or responding to anything. Did the doctors take him offline for some reason?

Trudeau did something else to the controls and a different sensation flooded Rhodes all over. He knew this one only too well. It was the nauseating agony of withdrawing from the drugs.

He gritted his teeth and shut his eyes to endure whatever came—but he didn't know if he could endure it. In fact, he became more certain by the minute that he couldn't endure it.

The sensation built to an unimaginable torture a thousand times worse than anything he ever suffered with the Masks.

Lauer started bellowing in pain the way he did in the Masks' lab. Then Thackery started up, too.

Rhodes shut his lips and eyelid tight trying to block out that sound....and then the worst thing of all happened.

The image of Fisher sitting there frozen in the corner of Rhodes's field of view—it vanished. A different image took its place.

The new image wasn't the face of any SAM. Rhodes could have tolerated that.

The grid lines coiled out of nothing even though Rhodes wasn't in The Grid. The lines snaked together, converged to form an outline, and then became more distinct.

They made the full-length shape of a woman wearing a long dress ....and then the lines faded. Color took their place and Rhodes found himself glaring at Ora standing in front of him.

She looked down her nose at his suffering the way she did when the Masks used her to threaten him.

She didn't speak, thank God. Rhodes really would have lost it if she said a word to him.

He probably would have gone off on her the way he did the first time. He would have called her every foul name he could come up with.

He would have threatened the Masks all over again. He would have sworn on his mother's grave that he would kill every last single one of them.

He would have meant every damn word of it, too. He really hoped she said something so he could let loose on her. He needed to let loose on someone. Who better than her?

She didn't speak, though. She just stood there staring at him and watching him writhe in torment.

Her silence confirmed what Rhodes already knew. She wasn't here. This was a test and not a very good one.

Did the doctors conjure up this image to make him question his loyalty to the Legion?

Ora infuriated him. She personified everything he hated about the Masks.

He hated her even more than B—more than the illusion of Fisher as a man—even more than the mechanical Mask ground troops Rhodes had met and destroyed on the battlefield.

The excruciating agony built to an epic crescendo. Yelling, roaring, screaming voices echoed through the lab all around him, but Rhodes couldn't make a sound.

Who was doing this to him? Was it Dr. Osborne....or the inquiry panel? Were they the ones who ordered this test—for what?

What did they really hope to prove—that they could do something just as bad to the battalion as the Masks did?

Rhodes gritted his teeth willing himself to hold on and not start screaming the way he really wanted to—the way his subordinates were.

He thought he could pick out individual voices, but he might have been mistaken.

The sight of Ora standing in front of him hardened his resolve to hold on no matter what, but the pain and drilling rotten misery escalated past his limit. He couldn't hold on much longer.

Ora's lips curled up on either side. She sneered at him in superior disdain....and then Dr. Trudeau did something to the controls.

A catastrophic blast of some kind of electric charge hit Rhodes in the chest and he passed out.

Chapter 11

Rhodes woke up in his capsule in the *Ero's* hold—at least he assumed he was in the hold. He might have been asleep for a month while the *Ero* transported him and the battalion back to Coleridge Station.

He didn't think so, though. He couldn't explain why he thought this, but he didn't picture the inquiry panel ever sending him back to Coleridge Station. They would either take the whole battalion offline or send them back into battle against the Masks.

As soon as he thought that, he knew it in the marrow of his bones. The Legion needed Battalion 1 too badly.

If the inquiry panel could possibly see their way to clearing Rhodes and his subordinates for combat duty ever again, that's exactly where the panel would send the battalion.

If the panel couldn't see their way to sending the battalion back into combat, they wouldn't send Rhodes and his people back to Coleridge Station to live out their lives in peace and quiet. No way.

Fisher expanded himself in the corner of Rhodes's view as soon as Rhodes opened his eyes. "Good morning, Captain. I trust you had a good conversion cycle."

Rhodes bit back the urge to grin at Fisher for saying it was morning. The *Ero* was in space. There was no morning in space.

"Good morning, Fisher," Rhodes replied. "I'm glad you don't look like Ora anymore."

Fisher laughed. "So am I, Captain. I much prefer to be this." His smile slipped very slightly. "You sure do hate her. I wouldn't want you hating me like that."

"I could never hate you like that. I'm glad you're here."

"I'm relieved you feel that way after the rocky start we had at the beginning."

"Is anything going on out there I should know about?"

Fisher winced. "Apart from you and the battalion being slated for more testing? No, there is nothing else going on out there."

Rhodes shut his eyes. He hadn't unlocked from the prongs yet, so he couldn't move his head. "Are the others okay?"

"Their capsules are all reading normal life signs and brainwave patterns—as are yours."

"What exactly was supposed to be the point of that test?"

"I'm sure I couldn't tell you. Maybe Dr. Osborne knows. Why don't you ask him?"

"Hell no! I'm not asking him anything."

"Your test today is a Grid training session."

Rhodes raised his eyebrows. "Really? Do you know the scenario?"

"You should know better than to ask me that. The SAMs are considered part of the battalion. We're being tested the same way you are—as we'll be taken offline the same way you will be if the panel decides to take that course."

"I'm so sorry you got into this mess, Fisher," Rhodes croaked. "I would get you out of it if I could."

"I'm afraid we're even on that score, Captain," Fisher murmured back. "I'm sure I got you into just as much trouble in the Masks' custody if not more so. I wish I could take it back—all of it."

"Don't say that. They manipulated you as much as they did me."

Fisher looked away. "Perhaps. It doesn't make me feel better, though. Sometimes I agree with you that we would all be better taken offline."

"Then we're in the same boat. Anyway, as long as we're alive, we have to keep trying to fight the Masks. That's reason enough to stay alive—for now, at least."

Fisher turned around. "Dietz is awake, Captain. He's getting up."

"I better see how he's doing." Rhodes unlocked, opened his cover, and sat up just as Dietz did the same thing.

The two men eyed each other across the hold. "You okay?" Rhodes asked.

Dietz looked away and nodded. "I will be."

Rhodes gulped down the urge to apologize to Dietz, too, but that wouldn't accomplish anything.

Rhodes experienced another overpowering desire to grill Dietz on his experiences. How much did the Masks' drugs affect him? Did they affect him at all? Did he feel anything in Stonebridge?

Dietz had a family in Stonebridge just like everyone else. Did they remind him of his real family back in Preinea? Did Dietz even have a family back in Preinea?

Dietz did have family somewhere. He told the battalion he checked on them through the computer terminal.

Rhodes kicked himself for not finding out more about Dietz before now. Rhodes knew exactly zilch about Dietz apart from the fact that he had a criminal record.

Christ, how little that meant now! Why in the name of God did Rhodes put so much weight on that before?

Who the hell cared if Dietz had a criminal record? He could have gotten arrested for misdemeanor shoplifting when he was just a kid.

He could have used that experience to turn his life around. That could have been the catalyst that spurred him to join the Legion in the first place.

Who the hell was Rhodes to judge that? Who the hell was Rhodes to judge anything after all the sewage that passed under the battalion's bridge in the last few weeks?

Any of the others could have a criminal record, too. For Christ's sake, even Henshaw could have had a criminal record. What the hell difference did it make?

Rhodes couldn't bring himself to ask Dietz about any of that. It sounded so crass and rude to even think about asking about Dietz's former life.

Rhodes just hoped Dietz didn't think Rhodes held back because he didn't care. Rhodes would have given anything to show Dietz how much he valued him now.

Rhodes put Dietz in the same category as Oakes, Lauer, and Rhinehart. Dietz was one of those people Rhodes didn't have to worry about anymore.

If Dietz malfunctioned now, Rhodes would have seen it for what it was. He would put it down to one of those unavoidable consequences of this truly messed up situation.

Rhodes wouldn't even have minded Dietz aiming his weapon at one of his comrades or even threatening to kill them given the right circumstances.

Rhinehart had done it to Fuentes. Rhodes had been on the ragged edge of doing exactly the same thing more than once since this whole thing started.

Rhodes didn't get a chance to say anything else before Rhinehart sat up, rubbed his eye, ran his fingers through his hair, and scowled around the hold.

"So we're back here." He snorted. "I guess they fixed whatever they broke during their last play date."

Dietz cracked a grin.

"They plan to break something else today," Rhodes told them. "Fisher says we're scheduled for a training session as another test of our sanity."

"If they're testing us for sanity, I regret to inform them that they'll be sorely disappointed," Rhinehart snapped. "That horse left the barn a long time ago."

"Then I guess the sooner they figure that out the better," Rhodes replied.

"Are they going to let us interface for the training session?" Dietz asked. "It kinda defeats the purpose not to.....you know?"

"The great thinkers of history couldn't figure out how these shit-heads' brains work," Rhinehart snarled, got to his feet, and crossed the hold to the computer terminal.

He started working on it while the rest of the battalion woke up. Fuentes started out with a neutral expression on his face.

Then he saw Rhinehart occupying the computer terminal and immediately switched to glaring at everyone. That didn't bode well at all.

Rhodes tried to check on his subordinates' physical and mental state, but like Dietz said, checking was impossible without the interface.

Rhodes felt blind and deaf without being able to talk to the other SAMs. He made up his mind to ask Dr. Osborne about it and left the hold while the others were still getting out of their capsules.

"What do you hope to accomplish by talking to him?" Fisher asked. "He's working for the panel."

"Since when did you become so suspicious and hostile toward Dr. Osborne?" Rhodes countered. "He's treated us a damn sight better than Neiland, Montague, and Irvine ever did."

"I didn't say he didn't treat us well. I said he's working for the panel."

"What is that supposed to mean?" Rhodes demanded. "Just say whatever you have to say."

"He won't tell you what the training scenario is."

"That isn't why I'm going to see him."

"Why are you, then?"

Rhodes cocked his head to study Fisher in The Grid. "What's gotten into you?"

Fisher looked away again. He did that a lot more often now. "That last test....whatever you want to call it......"

Rhodes didn't answer right away. He never would have expected Osborne to inflict something like that on the battalion, but maybe Osborne had no choice about that.

"He did say that we had to undergo this testing for the panel to even consider keeping us around," Rhodes finally pointed out. "He had to test us just to keep us all alive."

"Why did he have to test us with that, then?" Fisher asked. "He could have done it some other way."

Fisher's tone startled Rhodes. He'd never heard Fisher so resentful.

"Are you going to ask him about it?" Fisher asked.

"About what?"

"About why he agreed to administer that test. Aren't you at least going to challenge him on the ethics of basically doing the same thing to us that the Masks did? He could get imprisoned for life under the Treaty of Aemon for torturing someone like that."

"No, I'm not going to ask him about it."

"Why not?" Fisher demanded. "How can you trust a man who would go through with something like that?"

"What do you think he should have done—quit in protest? We could have gotten someone like Neiland or Irvine again. That would have been way worse."

"Worse than your own people torturing you?"

"I'm not going to ask him about it," Rhodes countered. "We aren't people under the Treaty of Aemon, pal. I don't know what we are, but the rules that apply to everyone else under the Treaty of Aemon no longer apply to us. That might be the one thing in this whole catastrophe that I'm actually sure of."

Chapter 12

F ortunately for Rhodes's sanity, Fisher had to shut his trap when Rhodes got to Dr. Osborne's lab.

Rhodes didn't want to talk about the battalion's latest test or any of the other heinous shit the battalion had been through lately.

He wanted to forget it ever happened—but he couldn't. That was the problem.

Osborne blanched when Rhodes walked in. Trudeau stopped what he was doing and gaped across the lab in stark, staring horror at Rhodes trying to have a civil conversation with Dr. Osborne.

"We want to know when we're going to be allowed to interface with each other again," Rhodes began. "We're scheduled for a training scenario today. We won't be able to do it if we can't interface."

Osborne shut his mouth with difficulty. "I'm aware of that, Captain."

"So? Why aren't we allowed to interface with each other? The other SAMs are my subordinates just as much as the people are. I can't do my job without being able to communicate with them."

Osborne turned away and started busily tapping at his equipment. Trudeau stood rooted to the spot in frozen terror.

"I've been telling the panel that ever since the inquiry," Osborne went on over his shoulder. "I've been telling them that you aren't designed to function independently and that you're more likely to malfunction if you don't interface. The panel won't listen to me."

"Then I have no choice but to refuse the training session until we can interface," Rhodes told him.

Osborne spun around and opened his mouth to protest, but he wilted just as fast. "Yeah. I know."

"So are they going to take us offline for a simple, straightforward request like that? If they want to take us offline, why don't they just go ahead and do it? They don't need to justify it to anyone by making us jump through all these hoops."

"Don't you think I've been telling them that all this time?!" Osborne blurted out. "Trudeau, Kraft, Hyde, and everyone else has been telling them the same damn thing! Trust me."

"Well, there has to be a solution or a compromise or...or something."

Osborne threw up his hands. "God knows I've tried. I really have, man. You don't know the drama that's been going on behind the scenes."

Rhodes raised his eyebrows. "Really?"

Osborne rolled his eyes to heaven and turned back to his machines. "You don't want to know. You can tell everyone else in the battalion that we're pulling out all the stops just to get you the right to interface—and that's not talking about the right to exist. This whole thing is so complicated..."

"What's so complicated about it?" Rhodes asked. "The panel already knows everything that happened. Shit, they probably know more about what happened than we do."

"I know, Captain!" Osborne practically bellowed before he wrestled himself under control. "Trust me. I've seen the footage. I know."

Rhodes looked away. He didn't really want to be in the same room with someone who knew all that.

"Look," Osborne murmured. "I already told the panel that they couldn't expect you to go through with this test without interfacing. If they don't give you access to the interface by the time you get to the training room, just walk away. I honestly don't see how it can possibly make the situation any worse."

"Seriously?!" Rhodes gasped.

Osborne smacked his lips in exasperation again. "Don't ask. Really. Just go back to the capsule hold. I'll do what I can to restore the interface. If I don't.....Well, I don't know what it means."

Rhodes shut his mouth with difficulty. "All right, man. Thank you. I'm grateful for your support on this."

"For the love of God, don't thank me!" Osborne's face convulsed and he turned away to hide it. "Whatever you do, don't thank me."

Rhodes opened his mouth to thank Osborne again and stopped himself. That right there answered Rhodes's question for him.

No way would Osborne administer that test willingly—not unless it was a matter of life and death for the whole battalion.

Rhodes glanced over at Trudeau. He still hadn't moved. He didn't even seem to be blinking.

Rhodes resisted another urge to thank both of them again. He left the lab and headed back to the hold, but he didn't want to face his subordinates without answers.

They would be taking their lives in their hands by walking away from the training session. Things must be really bad with the panel if the negotiations had deteriorated as far as that.

Everyone was out of bed when Rhodes got back to the hold. They all turned around to face him when he walked in, and at that moment, the interface switched back on.

"Finally!" Wild growled.

"It's wonderful to see you all again," Van exclaimed.

"Now you can all enjoy my charming presence again," Murphy added.

"I was really starting to like the quiet," Fisher remarked and got a bunch of howls from the other SAMs.

"It looks like we're going through the training session after all," Dietz pointed out. "Here I thought we might be able to dodge it."

"We don't know if the panel will leave the interface active after the session ends," Rhodes told them all. "Enjoy it while it lasts."

"They wouldn't take it away from us, would they?" Koenig asked. "Doesn't the panel understand how important the interface is to our functioning as a unit?"

"They understand because Osborne, Trudeau, and the officers from the Battalion 1 governing body have been telling them all this time. The panel doesn't want to listen—or I should say the people who want to take us offline don't want to listen."

"Maybe they want us to fail," Zen suggested. "Maybe that's why they gave us that last test. They want to make us crack so they have a reason to take us offline."

"They don't need a reason to take us offline," Rhodes replied. "We're lucky we have a chance to maybe convince them otherwise. If we do, it will be a happy but unlikely turn of events."

He made sure to lay on plenty of sarcasm when he said it even though he partially meant it.

Thackery snorted and turned away. "I'll believe it when I see it."

"At least we can interface now." Dash turned to his fellow SAMs. "Life was getting so boring with only Oakes for company."

"Hey, pal!" Oakes snapped. "I can hear you, remember?"

"I need social stimulation," Dash countered.

"We all remember the social stimulation you need, chump," Wild growled. "You're the biggest whore in Stonebridge."

Dash turned away, but he couldn't hide in The Grid. "Then I guess it's a good thing I'm not in Stonebridge anymore."

Rhodes found himself laughing. "It might be your only chance to feel what it's like to be human. I'm glad someone enjoyed themselves there. I really wish I could have."

"You could have," Dash pointed out. "There was this one really nice girl named Luretis....."

"Stop right there!" Wild snapped. "You are NOT setting up the captain with some fictional girl in Stonebridge—or any of the rest of us."

Dash burst into a huge grin. "I had this really nice lady named Delora picked out for you, Wild."

Some of the others laughed. Wild glared at Dash and then at everyone else who laughed.

"The captain is too pure for that," Fisher interjected. "He never spent a single night with Ora the whole time he was in Stonebridge."

Everyone spun around to stare at Rhodes. Thackery gasped. "You didn't? No way!"

"What the hell did you have to go and tell them that for?" Rhodes fired back. "I thought we were friends."

"We are," Fisher replied. "That's why I told them."

"Keep my personal business to yourself. You shouldn't even be thinking about what I did or didn't do in Stonebridge."

Fisher turned to the other SAMs. "He slept in the barn."

"I won't interface with you at all if you don't shut up," Rhodes snapped. "Watch your mouth, Fisher."

Fisher grinned at him, but he didn't say another word. He beamed at Rhodes from the corner of The Grid.

Rhodes walked away and turned a deaf ear to the rest of his subordinates' conversation. They didn't talk about anything that concerned him.

At least Fisher didn't tell the others about Rhodes killing Fisher in the barn. Rhodes couldn't have tolerated that.

How much did everyone know about what Rhodes did that night? Did any of them know it was Rhodes who set fire to the eatery with Koenig and Van inside it?

Dash and Wild were probably inside it at the time, too. Thackery and her family were inside their house when Rhodes set it on fire. He already knew that.

He stayed out of everyone's way for the rest of the day until it was time to go to the training session.

The battalion fired a steady stream of shit talk, jokes, and general banter all the way there. The interface really was good for their souls.

Rhodes did his best to stay out of it, but he inevitably got pulled in when everyone started speculating about what their scenario would be and what the panel would do about the outcome good or bad.

"Just do your best," Rhodes told them. "We can't do anything better than that. Whatever they decide is out of our hands either way."

"You know it will be something from The Grid—the Masks' Grid," Rhinehart muttered under his breath. "It will be something they used on us. The panel wants to see if we react the same way."

"Then now's your chance to do it right," Rhodes replied. "We don't have the drugs and The Grid confusing us about what we're doing. We can all do the right thing this time and show the panel what we're really made of."

"Hell yeah," Oakes murmured. "This is our moment."

"Will the panel take some of us offline if we screw it up?" Thackery asked.

"They said it was all or nothing," Rhodes replied.

"So if one person messes up and makes a mistake, the whole battalion goes down?" Lauer countered. "Who's running this Mickey-Mouse outfit?"

"General Brewster," Dietz replied. "That tells you all you need to know."

"He isn't running the panel," Rhodes interjected. "The panel hates him and thinks he's an idiot."

"They got that part right, at least," Coulter added.

The group stepped into the training room. It sure looked strange after all this time. It had been so long and so much had happened since Rhodes entered this bare, white room.

It posed a startling contrast to the overstimulation of everything the Masks put the battalion through. Rhodes's senses weren't used to this total absence of all sensory input of every kind.

Rhodes pulled the door shut and the group gathered in a circle to face each other. "Remember what I said," he told them. "Just do your best. Don't worry about anything except getting through the session. We'll deal with whatever comes afterward."

"I wish I could be as confident as you, Captain," Coulter murmured.

"Me—confident?" Rhodes snorted. "I'm as scared as you are, Corporal. I don't know what we'll be facing on the other side, but I'm sure it will be something bad. I agree with Rhinehart. It will be something from our time with the Masks—probably something really bad—like maybe one of our sessions in the lab or maybe a repeat of the Battle of Keonus. I wouldn't be surprised if they make us relive it to see if we do anything differently."

"We will," Lauer growled. "We definitely will."

"Then now's our chance to show them. Let's go."

Rhodes dropped into The Grid. The rest of the battalion did the same thing.

He dropped into the black landscape with the green lines in squares all around him, but he found himself all alone.

He spun from right to left trying to see his subordinates. They weren't here. "Rhinehart!" Rhodes yelled. "Lauer!"

"The interface isn't connecting us anymore," Fisher pointed out. "I guess now we know why the panel didn't care too much about us interfacing with each other."

"What are we supposed to do here all by ourselves? Is this the test?"

"I don't know. Maybe you should start moving through The Grid and see where it takes you."

Chapter 13

Rhodes set off walking through The Grid. Then he started running and the landscape changed to gently rolling farmland.

The countryside didn't look that different from all the other training sessions he'd ever run at Coleridge Station—except that he was alone.

He'd gotten so used to having the whole battalion around him. The Grid didn't look right without them in it.

"Do you recognize this place, Captain?" Fisher asked.

"No, do you?" Rhodes fired his boosters to cover the terrain faster. "It doesn't look like any place I've ever seen before."

"You have seen it before. It's Stonebridge."

Rhodes almost stopped flying to stare at Fisher. "It is? Where's the town, then?"

"I'm not sure, but the contour of these hills matches Stonebridge exactly."

"That's weird. I wonder why we're here." He gunned his boosters, but the landscape remained just as empty as before.

He flew over a few dozen hills searching everywhere. He finally spotted the stream—the one that should have had a stone bridge crossing it. There was no bridge and definitely no town.

"Weird," Rhodes muttered. "This isn't even a training session. Am I just supposed to fly around and do nothing?"

"Something is bound to happen sooner or...." Fisher trailed off.

Rhodes saw the same bizarre landscape feature appear on The Grid at the same instant. Rhodes hackles stood up when he spotted a road ahead.

It wasn't the road leading to Stonebridge. The road didn't go near where the town ought to be.

A long convoy of vehicles passed down the road heading west. People of all ages crowded every vehicle, hung out of the windows and doors, sat on the roofs, and stood on the bumpers.

More men, women, children, and old people walked all around the vehicles. The vehicles had to move slowly so they didn't crush or bump into anyone.

The convoy migrated down the road at a snail's pace. Squads of armed soldiers guarded the convoy, but these weren't Legion soldiers.

The soldiers and refugees in that convoy were all human, but Rhodes didn't recognize the soldiers' uniforms. They didn't belong to any culture in the whole Treaty of Aemon Cluster.

Something about the people looked unfamiliar, too. Rhodes flew closer to get a better look.

Everyone in the convoy from the soldiers' officers to the smallest child—they all looked exhausted, emaciated, and barely on their feet. The soldiers dragged their heels. People stumbled every now and then.

"Who are they?" Rhodes whispered. "What's going on here?"

"I don't recognize them," Fisher murmured back. "They don't come up on any Treaty of Aemon Cluster database. This is some other world—some other sector of space."

"How is that possible if this is a Legion training scenario?"

Fisher didn't get a chance to answer. Rhodes circled the convoy for any sign of what he was supposed to do here.

None of the refugees or soldiers even looked up at him. Maybe they couldn't see him. Maybe he wasn't part of the scenario—or maybe they weren't.

He couldn't figure it out. He was just considering if he should land and check in with the officers in charge of the soldiers.

He made it to another set of hills. The convoy filed over it. When Rhodes got there, he saw that the line of people, soldiers, and vehicles snaked far away to the distant horizon. There must have been a million or more people in this convoy.

He paused there to take in the whole terrible sight. At that moment, a blast of fusion fire erupted from behind a different hill to the south.

The shot nearly hit him, sailed past him, and pounded down right onto one of the vehicles. The vehicle went up in smoke with a hundred people inside, on, and around it.

More shots exploded over the southern hills and bombarded the convoy up and down the road. Dozens of vehicles detonated with all their passengers meeting their fiery deaths.

The convoy disintegrated with everyone screaming and running for their lives, but they had nowhere to run.

Rhodes recognized those fusion shots instantly. He rocketed forward to defend the convoy, but he barely crossed the road before a tide of Legion platoons poured over the southern hills.

All those soldiers opened fire on the convoy with their Jackhammers. The soldiers that were supposed to guard the convoy rushed forward to defend the unarmed civilians.

The defenders were the first to go down under the Legion assault. More fusion blasts erupted from the hills and took out people all over the field.

Rhodes couldn't watch this. Those attacking platoons belonging to the Legion meant nothing to him.

He dropped from the sky, landed on the field between the Legion and the convoy, and opened fire with his lasers.

He couldn't think about anything other than doing the absolute most damage he possibly could. He had to stop those platoons no matter what.

His lasers covered a lot more ground than the Jackhammers. He sliced both beams back and forth laying down a solid of soldiers. He killed far more soldiers this time than he ever did at both Rono and Keonus, but he really didn't care.

He got another rush of exhilaration, especially when his assault started working. The refugees streamed west along the road and picked up speed when they saw him defending them.

More platoons charged over the hills, but they never made it within Jackhammer range.

Rhodes dropped all the soldiers coming from these hills. Then he fired his boosters, flew up there, and demolished all their big guns that they used to bombard the vehicles.

He finished them off and worked systematically up and down the road to completely wipe out every last Legion soldier.

The refugees shoved and pushed each other to go faster to get away from him. By the time he finished and landed back on the ground, a vast carpet of dead soldiers covered the fields from the road all the way south.

He stared out at them. Should he be worried that he killed a bunch of Legion soldiers?

It didn't bother him at all. He would do exactly the same thing again. He even scanned the landscape to see if any more platoons came out to attack these people. Should he stay here to make sure?

He was in The Grid. No one would die or even notice if he left.

"Is that the whole objective?" he asked Fisher.

"I honestly couldn't tell you, Captain," Fisher replied. "I don't know anything about this scenario."

"What kind of training session is it where they don't even tell me the objective?"

"Maybe it's a more subjective form of training—a scenario where the outcome isn't necessarily objective-based."

"I have no idea what that means, Fisher."

"Neither do I, Captain. I'm sorry I can't be more help."

Rhodes pursed his lips. Did everyone in the universe absolutely have to screw with him at every turn?

He waited another five minutes and left The Grid. He got back to the training room and found Rhinehart already there.

The interface reestablished instantly the minute Rhodes left The Grid. Rocky appeared on The Grid right next to Fisher.

Rhinehart clenched his jaws, narrowed his eyes, and shot hateful glares around the room. "I swear to Christ, if these jackasses think they're going to fuck with me by sending me into these ridiculous scenarios, I'll just keep killing Legion soldiers every goddamn day. I mean it, Sir!"

Rhodes bit back a grin. "I know, Lieutenant. So....did you kill them all?"

"You're damn right I did! Show me the platoon that attacks civilians and I'll kill them, too!" Rhinehart let out a shaky breath. "What do you think the others are doing?"

"I sure hope they're killing Legion soldiers, too."

"To hell with it," Rhinehart snarled. "If the panel decides to take us offline for defending unarmed civilians, then more power to them."

Rhodes clapped him on the shoulder. "It doesn't matter because it's over. You did the right thing."

"I know I did," Rhinehart fired again. "No one can tell me I didn't."

"I guess we just go back to the hold and wait for the....."

Rhodes broke off when Dietz and Coulter returned at the same time.

Dietz appeared out of The Grid as calmly as if he was taking a walk through the park. Coulter dropped from above and stumbled before he caught his balance.

He glanced right and left panting hard. "Were we supposed to stick around and defend those people? Murphy couldn't even tell me what the objective was."

"I don't think there was one," Rhodes replied.

"So we were just supposed to defend the civilians?" Dietz asked.

"I don't know. Maybe the panel wanted to see what we would do in that scenario."

"In other words, it was another mind game," Rhinehart spat. "Run through this maze, little mouse, and you might get a piece of cheese."

Dietz laughed just as Thackery, Lauer, and Oakes returned. The interface with them and all their SAMs switched back on, too.

"Where's Fuentes?" Rhodes asked.

"We were by ourselves," Oakes replied. "I was the only person there."

Rhodes checked with Fisher. "Can I go into whatever part of The Grid where Fuentes was being tested?"

"I don't see how we can. The Grid was programmed to take you directly to the training session. If you couldn't get to the same part of The Grid he was using before, you won't be able to do it now."

"He could be in trouble in there," Thackery pointed out. "He could have gotten shot down."

"Dr. Osborne will be able to locate him." Rhodes turned away to leave the training room just as Fuentes came back.

"Are you okay, Rudy?" Thackery asked. "Did anything go wrong with the scenario?"

"What scenario?" Fuentes asked. "There was no scenario."

"What do you mean?" Oakes demanded. "Didn't you see the refugees.....and the soldiers....and everything?"

"I didn't see a thing. I went into The Grid and wound up in a landscape that Van said looked like Stonebridge, but the town wasn't there."

"Yeah?" Oakes prompted. "Didn't you find the convoy?"

"What convoy? I was out in the fields by myself. I didn't see anyone else."

"So you....you didn't fight the Legion?"

"The Legion wasn't there. I'm telling you I was the only person in the whole landscape. I looked. I didn't see anyone, so I just stayed there. I didn't figure I was supposed to stay there forever, so I came back here."

Rhodes and his subordinates exchanged glances, but there was nothing else to do. He led the way back to the capsule hold.

"When do we find out if we passed the test?" Murphy asked.

"I'm pretty sure we all know we didn't pass," Rhinehart cut in. "The test was to see if we would kill Legion soldiers and we did."

"Did we?" Thackery asked and she looked from one face to another. "Did we all kill Legion soldiers—except for Rudy, I mean?"

"You killed Legion soldiers—again?" Fuentes gasped. "That was the test—to kill Legion soldiers? I'm glad I didn't find them, then."

"Did *you* kill the soldiers, Alyssa?" Coulter asked.

"Damn straight I did. I couldn't let them kill all those women and kids and old people."

"Did the rest of you kill the soldiers?" Dietz asked.

Lauer nodded. "I tried to drive them off, but they just kept attacking. They left me no choice."

"Then I guess we just sit around enjoying our last few hours alive." Coulter sat down at the table and looked around at nothing. "It would be nice if they gave us a last meal. At least we had that at Fort Bastion."

"We can't even play The Ship, The Captain, and the Crew," Oakes grumbled. "These jokers really know how to take all the fun out of everything."

Rhodes found himself studying each of his people in detail. His connection to each of them bordered on the kind of heartfelt affection for them that he felt at Fort Bastion, but it didn't go quite that far—not yet.

Maybe the Battalion 1 project robbed him of that, too. Maybe he would never feel any of those strong emotions for anyone ever again.

Maybe he really was turning into a robot who couldn't love or care about anyone but himself.

He felt plenty when it came to murderous rage, resentment, and revulsion for what he'd become. He sure cared when it came to hating the people who did this to him.

He would never feel the deep bond of admiration and camaraderie for his subordinates—not the way he felt at Fort Bastion and at Stonebridge. Why not?

Did his own hatred and fury stop him from feeling that way about anyone—or was it just them?

Did the way they met have something to do with it? Would the circumstances taint their relationships for the rest of their lives?

Chapter 14

R hodes wavered between joining his subordinates at the table and making himself one of them for the last few hours of their lives or......what was the alternative? He didn't even know if he was allowed to go off by himself to another part of the ship.

He would have to break the interface if he did that. He didn't dare to insult his people by doing that—not after all this time of not being allowed to interface.

He took a few steps toward the table when Colonel Kraft walked into the hold. He stopped just inside the threshold and didn't come any farther in.

Everyone turned around to stare at him. No one greeted him. He stared back at them and didn't say a word to explain why he was here.

That moment of hostile silence might have gone on for the rest of eternity. Rhodes eventually crossed the floor. "Can I help you, Sir?" Rhodes asked.

"Do you mind taking a walk with me?" Kraft asked. "I want to talk to you."

Rhodes glanced over his shoulder at his subordinates. He didn't have to because he could see all of them through the interface.

He thanked the stars now that he *was* interfacing with them. They would be able to see and hear everything Kraft did and said.

Did Kraft realize that? Did he understand that anything he said to Rhodes privately would transmit to the rest of the battalion? What was the point of taking a walk at all?

Rhodes shrugged. "I guess I'm not doing anything else."

Kraft inclined his head toward the door and Rhodes followed him outside. They walked in silence for a while, but Kraft still didn't open the dialogue.

"What's going on?" Rhodes finally blurted out. "Did the panel come to its decision about whether to take us offline?"

"They haven't come to a decision," Kraft replied without looking at Rhodes. "Or, to put it another way, some of us have come to one decision while the others have come to a different decision. We can't agree on what decision to come to as a group."

"Why did you want to see me, then?" Rhodes asked.

Kraft kept walking for a while. He faced front without looking at Rhodes.

"Colonel?" Rhodes prompted. "What did you want to talk to me about?"

"I....I'm actually not sure why I wanted to see you. I guess.....I guess I owed it to you if the panel decides to take you offline. I guess....I just felt like I had to see you and talk to you one last time if it really is going to come to that."

Kraft stopped in the middle of the corridor and turned to face Rhodes at last.

Rhodes studied Kraft waiting for the colonel to say something, but Kraft didn't say anything.

He scrutinized Rhodes with those intense black eyes. Kraft studied Rhodes much more closely than Kraft ever studied Rhodes at Coleridge Station.

"Is something wrong, Sir?" Rhodes asked.

"You are. You're what's wrong with this—all of you. Everything about you is wrong. You never should have existed, and yet you're some of the most honorable soldiers I've ever met."

Rhodes made a face. "Maybe not all of us are."

Kraft turned away and kept walking. "Every part of me tells me to agree with the other panel members about taking you offline. I know rationally that shutting down the Battalion 1 project is the right thing to do and that we'll all be much better off without some psycho, power-hungry general playing God by joining men and machines. I know all that, but I just can't bring myself to go along with shutting you down even though I know it's the right thing to do."

Now it was Rhodes's turn to face front without looking at or talking to Kraft. Every word out of Kraft's mouth rang out of Rhodes's own mind. He'd been thinking exactly the same thing.

"I don't see how there is ever any way I can do right by you," Kraft went on. "Shutting you down is right and it's also wrong. Keeping you around is right and it's also wrong. There is no winning solution to all this. I guess that's why I thought I had to see you. Maybe I thought seeing you would clarify things for me, but it doesn't. It only makes it harder."

"I wish I could help you," Rhodes murmured. "I don't know what to say."

Kraft stopped again and drilled Rhodes with another deep stare of unrelenting attention. "You really don't have anything to say in your own defense? You're just going to let them take you offline?"

"I already said everything at the inquiry. What did you think I would do—fall on my knees and beg for my life? Why have you been defending us all this time if you think keeping us around is so bad?"

"I really don't know. That's what I'm saying. I don't know. Maybe I think taking you offline is too drastic a step. It's an irrevocable step.

We wouldn't be able to take it back later. Maybe we should keep you around just in case we discovered something or changed something later that would improve the situation."

"Things might change for the worse," Rhodes pointed out.

Kraft nodded. "You're right—in which case it would be glaringly obvious to everyone that taking you offline was the right thing to do. It isn't glaringly obvious right now—not to me, at least. As long as that doubt remains, as long as there's even the tiniest chance that keeping you online could be a good thing, then I don't see how we can justify taking you offline."

Rhodes frowned. "Why are you telling me all this? Haven't you been telling the panel all this time?"

"Yes, I've told them a million times."

"Why tell me, then? You don't need to justify your decisions to me. You're my superior officer."

"I don't think I need to justify my decisions to you. I guess I just felt like I had to see you one more time. I thought seeing you might clarify things and tip the scales one way or the other. It doesn't, but I still felt I needed to see you—at least to face you if I'm going to participate in making this decision on behalf of you and the whole battalion."

Rhodes waited for Kraft to say something else. "Well, here I am. Now you've seen me."

Kraft's eyes bored into Rhodes and left nowhere to hide. "Yeah. I've seen you."

Rhodes hesitated. The intensity of Kraft's gaze started to make Rhodes uncomfortable, so he started walking without waiting for Kraft to do it first.

Kraft walked by his side in silence for a long time. Rhodes really wished he could go back to the capsule hold. He didn't want to spend his last hours alive with Colonel Paxton Kraft.

"I've seen the footage of your time with the Masks," Kraft finally murmured. "I couldn't have done what you did."

"You might have," Rhodes mumbled back. "You might have gotten yourself into a situation where you had no choice."

"I doubt it. I would have stayed in that world. I would have given anything to get back even a little of what they took from me. Fuentes .....I would have done exactly the same thing he did. I'm certain of it."

"Don't sell yourself short," Rhodes replied. "You're tougher than you look. Everyone is."

"But not him? I knew you were the best of them when you first woke up from statis."

"I'm not the best of them—not at all," Rhodes countered. "I'm just as screwed up as they are. Anyway, I killed Legion soldiers during that last training session so I guess I'll go down with the others, too. At least the panel will do the same thing to all of us. I won't have to worry about sticking around without them."

Kraft didn't say anything else. He kept strolling through the *Ero's* many corridors in no particular direction.

Rhodes waited until he could politely excuse himself and go back to the capsule hold. Kraft eventually got tired of all this and turned his footsteps in that direction.

"It's strange that even the inquiry panel and the Battalion 1 governing body are suffering from the same doubts as we are," Fisher remarked on the way back there. "It makes them somehow....more human. I didn't expect that."

Chapter 15

Rhodes re-entered the Ocao Space Station conference room and faced the inquiry panel.

Drs. Osborne and Trudeau went with him. They stood on either side of him in support the way they did before.

Their presence didn't offer the same assurance that it did last time. Rhodes faced the panel alone—which on its own was a massive insult as far as he was concerned.

These numbskulls didn't even have the decency to call in the whole battalion before they passed a death sentence on everyone.

That proved more than anything that no one in the battalion was a citizen under the Treaty of Aemon anymore. They were things—property of the Legion.

The panel didn't have to treat the battalion as human beings because they weren't. They had no rights. The panel didn't have to dignify anyone in the battalion with the decency of looking them in the eye.

Rhodes wouldn't have been even marginally surprised if the panel passed a death sentence on the battalion without even facing him.

They could have. They could have ordered Osbourne and Trudeau to take the whole battalion offline during their next conversion cycle.

The two doctors could have made sure no one in the battalion ever woke up. None of them would have known what hit them.

Rhodes supposed he should feel grateful for this small courtesy of facing the people who passed judgment on him.

He didn't feel grateful. He felt absolutely nothing at all.

His conversation with Kraft might not have clarified things for Kraft, but it did clarify things for Rhodes.

The outcome didn't matter anymore.

Kraft seemed to think that neither course of action would be right. Taking the battalion offline would be wrong. Keeping them online would be wrong.

Rhodes saw it differently. Taking the battalion offline would be right. It would correct the catastrophic error General Brewster made when he started this project.

On the other hand, keeping the battalion alive and active would also be right. It was the Legion's only chance to defeat the Masks even if Rhodes didn't know how yet.

Admiral Stabler straightened up behind the big table and then, amazingly, he actually got to his feet. Rhodes definitely didn't expect that.

"The inquiry panel has come to its decision, Captain," Stabler announced.

Rhodes left the interface active. The rest of the battalion listened from the capsule hold. All the SAMs remained silent to hear the panel's decision, too.

"It is our decision to place Battalion 1 on disciplinary probation for the time being," Stabler went on. "We've decided to give you all one last sudden-death chance. We'll send you back to the front to fight the Masks the way you said. If you can find a way to defeat them, I'm sure the whole Treaty of Aemon Cluster will owe you a debt of gratitude."

Rhodes heard his mouth say, "Thank you, Sir," but Rhodes's heart wasn't in it. He didn't feel grateful for this—or anything else.

"Don't thank me, Captain. If you make one mistake—and by that, I mean if even one person on your battalion makes a single mistake or screws up or shows any sign of disloyalty, you'll all be taken offline immediately. There will be no second inquiry. There will be no discussion or explanation at all. It will be over—for all of you."

"I understand, Sir," Rhodes replied.

He probably should have offered his assurance that none of his people wouldn't screw up or act disloyal ever again.

He didn't offer any such assurance. Did it make any difference in the end?

Stabler finally said, "You're dismissed, Captain. I'm sure you can communicate our intentions to the rest of the battalion."

"Yes, Sir," Rhodes replied and left the room.

The two doctors accompanied him as far as the capsule hold before they split off.

The battalion started talking over the decision long before Rhodes got back.

"Those cocksuckers better keep us online," Rhinehart growled. "How dare they even suggest taking us offline after the shit we've gone through for this Legion?"

"We'll just have to prove ourselves," Oakes added. "It's as simple as that."

"I guess we did the right thing by killing those soldiers in the training session," Dietz remarked. "I didn't expect that."

"Of course we did the right thing," Rhinehart snapped. "We defended the refugees. To hell with the Legion."

"That isn't a very loyal thing to say," Thackery pointed out. "You better not let the panel officers hear you talking like that."

"I don't give a shit. I'll tell them to their faces."

No one answered him. Rhinehart had been becoming more and more aggressive in his expressions of dissatisfaction with everything the Legion did.

He vocalized these sentiments much more freely than Fuentes or anyone else. Rhodes didn't know what to think.

Rhodes should have stepped in as Rhinehart's commanding officer. Rhodes should have put more pressure on Rhinehart to keep his attitude on a leash.

Rhodes felt that slipping away from him, too. Rhinehart didn't say anything Rhodes and the rest of the battalion wasn't already thinking.

He just said it more forcefully and added a lot more profanities when he did say it. In essence, he didn't say anything Colonel Kraft didn't say.

Rhodes got back to the hold and the battalion spent the rest of the day talking about the decision. No one could decide if it was good or bad—because it was neither.

Rhodes entered his conversion cycle early to get out of the conversation. It didn't accomplish anything or illuminate anything because there was nothing to illuminate. The whole subject remained as muddy and nebulous as before.

He woke up before everyone else. "Good morning, Captain," Fisher greeted him. "We got orders to deploy back to the front."

Rhodes sighed. "That was quick. I knew the Legion needed us. I didn't think they were that desperate."

"We're deploying to the planet Katera in the Bigleos system." Fisher brought up a chart of the area on The Grid.

Rhodes nodded. "I know Katera."

"It isn't what you remember. The Masks have taken over half the planet. They're making steady progress on the rest of it."

Fisher zoomed in on the Bigleos solar system. The Grid angled past a few other planets to show the Legion fleet in orbit around Katera.

The *Ero* glided into the Legion ranks to join the other Ravagers stationed there. The battalion must have stayed in their conversion cycle while the ship traveled here.

The Grid revolved around the planet to show more than half of it scorched, torched, and leveled. Legion Ravagers scrambled to evacuate a few population centers on the opposite side.

The Ravagers didn't make very much headway, though. The Legion didn't assign enough of them to do the job quickly enough. All the remaining Ravagers were tied up fighting the Masks and trying to slow them down.

The invasion ships would have been here by now if not for the Ravagers' defense. The platoons certainly couldn't stop the Masks ground troops from advancing anywhere they wanted.

"What the hell are we supposed to do about that?" Rhodes murmured.

"Maybe this is the panel's way of shutting us down anyway," Fisher remarked. "Maybe they think it won't matter in the end because we'll die along with the platoons."

Rhodes looked away from the battle. "Turn it off. I don't want to see that."

Fisher switched The Grid back to Rhodes's normal view of the capsule hold, but there was nothing to do but wait for the order to deploy.

A heavy silence hung over the hold. No one talked. The SAMs didn't interrupt the funereal silence.

Rhodes didn't keep track of what his subordinates did to occupy their time. He had as much as he could handle just mentally preparing himself to go back into combat against the Masks.

He already knew what to expect. At the same time, none of his previous experience would prepare him for what might happen.

He couldn't imagine what would happen—except that he could. The Masks would pull out every dirty trick in the book to try to defeat the battalion.

That was the rub, wasn't it? The battalion couldn't defeat the Masks in open combat any more than the regular Legion could.

Rhodes would have to come up with some strategy to defeat them—something other than just fighting them by force.

That strategy must be something he learned while he was their prisoner. General Hyde asked him about that when he first met with the inquiry panel, but he didn't have any more answers then than he did now.

He didn't want to think about what he learned while he was the Masks' prisoner. He didn't want to remember it at all, much less study his memories and experiences in the kind of detail he would need to get that information.

Facing them in combat would be much easier—and futile. He shouldn't even be deploying on Katera—not until he had some better plan for how to deal with them.

He couldn't exactly tell the inquiry panel that—or whoever was giving the battalion orders now.

Rhodes didn't ask Fisher who that was. Rhodes didn't ask if anyone from the Battalion 1 project was even still involved in making decisions about the battalion.

The inquiry panel or Captain Ackerman or someone else might have taken over. It didn't really matter in the end. Rhodes and the battalion just had to fight the Masks.

Rhodes shouldn't even be thinking about how to defeat them. That was someone else's job—but wasn't that the argument he used to convince the panel to keep the battalion active?

His own determination to defeat the Masks kept him going. He could accept just about anything else as long as he kept fighting them—in any capacity.

This would be his only mission as long as he was still alive. He might not be able to do anything else related to human life, but he could do this.

That on its own gave him all the motivation he needed to think about his captivity with the Masks. Something in those memories would give him the clue he needed to defeat them.

He told himself that before. Now he knew it was true. Capturing the battalion was the Masks' biggest mistake.

They thought they did it to learn from the battalion. The Masks thought they could integrate the battalion's technology and improve the Masks' own systems.

The Masks didn't realize that, by capturing the battalion, they were actually handing him the evidence he needed to find their ultimate weakness—the weakness he would use to destroy them.

He just had to find it...so where should he even start looking?

He spent the rest of the day crashing wildly back and forth between an insatiable desire to search his memories and revulsion over the same memories.

His desire to defeat the Masks made him want to pore over them in minute detail. Once he started, they repelled him and made him sick. He always wound up pushing them away so he didn't have to relive those nightmares.

Chapter 15

T he order came down for the battalion to assemble in the *Ero's* landing bay. "Are we taking Strikers?" Dietz asked. "How are we supposed to do anything from the ground?"

"Strikers won't help us. We saw that last time," Rhodes replied. "The invasion ships will only drive the Strikers off."

"So what are our orders?" Thackery asked. "There are only eight of us against the whole Masks army."

Rhodes interfaced with his people and shared The Grid layout of the Masks' position. "They've already torched the city of Onaevis. The Legion is trying to stop the Masks from leaving and moving on to the next city. The platoons are holding the line...here.....We'll flank the Masks on this side...."

"To make sure we don't go near any regular Legion platoons," Rhinehart added. "In case something should happen to go wrong."

"Of course," Rhodes replied.

"And something always goes wrong," Oakes muttered.

"Listen up," Rhodes interjected. "Here's the deal. We're going down there to try to defeat these things. We're going to end this war. Our only mission is to find something that gives us the edge—something that tips the battle in our favor."

"What would that be?" Thackery asked.

"Something we found out while we were with them—something no one else in the Legion knows about. This is our chance to find some critical vulnerability."

"The Masks don't have any vulnerabilities," Coulter countered.

"They must. Everyone does. Fighting them won't defeat them. Whatever we use to destroy them has to be something else."

That killed the conversation. Rhinehart furrowed his brow in concentration. Thackery's eyes went out of focus and she stared off into space.

Rhodes saw them all drifting off into their memories of their captivity. Just seeing them do it made Rhodes shudder. He shook himself back to the present.

"We're deploying in a few minutes. Just remember what I said. Think of this as a fact-finding mission. We're here to annihilate these cocksuckers. We just have to find out how. We can't do it with guns."

The battalion fell silent. Rhodes saw his own internal conflict playing out on every face.

He didn't like being the one to throw them all back into those bad memories. What would it accomplish?

If anything, it would make them less effective in combat. It would make them more susceptible to the Masks' influence if they decided to use it.

The Masks *would* try to use their influence. Rhodes already knew that. They would be stupid not to exploit their advantage over the battalion.

He had to make his people think about it the same way he had to think about it. He didn't let himself off the hook.

Maybe someone in the battalion saw or experienced something Rhodes didn't know about. Any one of these people might be the one carrying the clue right now.

The *Ero* descended into the atmosphere, but the ship didn't go near enough to the battle to put itself in danger. Rhodes and his people launched out of the landing bay and soared across the landscape toward the city in the distance.

The battalion approached the torched landscape from the south. Mountains of rubble covered the ground from all the city's destroyed buildings.

They obscured any roads leading into or out of the city. Rhodes didn't see how the platoons would be able to retreat once the Legion inevitably gave up on this city, too.

The whole landscape brought up all the memories of Rhodes's previous encounters with the Masks, but he couldn't think about that right now.

He and the battalion banked westward and dropped from above.

"We should be attacking from the air," Lauer muttered. "No way should we be on the ground anywhere near these assholes."

"We're following orders." Rhodes fired his boosters toward the ground and lowered himself to one of the side streets.

The Masks weren't here. They were too busy assaulting the platoons farther south.

"They'll notice us soon enough," Rhodes told his subordinates. "Let's get over there and engage before they decide to come after us themselves."

"Isn't that the point—to take the pressure off the platoons?" Thackery asked.

"Don't confuse the captain with facts," Rhinehart interrupted.

Rhodes chose to laugh that off and set off through the streets closing on the Masks' position.

The Grid measured the surroundings in time with his movements. Nothing moved in this disaster zone. The Masks had razed the whole city to the ground.

The piles of debris everywhere looked exactly the same as his last encounter with the Masks except with a lot fewer destroyed robots lying around.

The Legion wasn't doing as much damage to their enemies here—not as much as the Masks were doing to the Legion.

Rhodes tried not to notice all the dead soldiers' bodies in the jumbled wreckage.

The noise of gunfire and explosions got louder as the battalion approached the front line. Rhodes brought up his lasers. He always fell back on them when he wanted to really slaughter some people.

He got ready to fire as many Vipers as he could. He only made it ten blocks before the Masks wheeled in the battalion's direction.

He saw them on The Grid first. The noise didn't slacken.

Without warning, from some silent signal amongst themselves, the Masks pivoted out of line, broke off their assault against the platoons, and the whole Masks front line diverted to intercept the battalion instead.

"Here they come!" Rhodes called to his subordinates. "Spread out to cover more of the line!"

His subordinates fired their boosters to put as much distance between themselves as they could. Coulter and Oakes sailed into a different side street to the left. Dietz and Rhinehart went off to the right.

Fuentes turned away to the left, too, but he didn't make it more than fifteen feet before the Masks rushed into view.

They flooded out of streets and around buildings. The Masks fired their fusion rifles at the battalion.

Rhodes returned fire with his lasers and unleashed his Vipers. He stood his ground to cut down as many Masks as he could.

Even then, he knew in the back corner of his mind that none of this would make any difference. This wouldn't defeat the Masks' war machine. There never had been any form of gunfire invented that could accomplish that.

Fuentes used lasers, too. He sidestepped to get away from Rhodes, but Fuentes only separated himself a few more feet from Rhodes.

They fanned their lasers back and forth and Fuentes's arcs joined up with Rhodes's. The combination of all four lasers covered the most possible ground to take out as much of the Masks' line as the two men could cover.

Rhodes kept up that steady stream of laser fire. The Masks couldn't get past it.

He bombarded them with dozens of Vipers. They exploded behind the line, but more Masks kept rushing in behind those he killed. Was there any limit to how many Masks they could send into battle to do their dirty work?

Rhodes went into another battle trance. Killing meant nothing to him in this quiet place. He could keep this up all day. He didn't feel the slightest guilt about killing hundreds or thousands of Masks.

A scream jolted him back to his senses. He spun around to check on Fuentes.

Fuentes still stood there passing his lasers back and forth across the Masks. Rhodes didn't see anything wrong with Fuentes. That scream didn't come from him.

Another piercing scream set Rhodes's nerves on end....and then he realized that the scream *did* come from Fuentes.

Grid lines snaked out of the surrounding terrain, twined themselves into Fuentes's grid lines, and wove their way into The Grid.

They surrounded Van, tied their lines into hers, and started twisting her out of her normal shape.

Rhodes stared in shocked horror as the grid lines surrounded Fuentes, tangled themselves among the grid lines of his body, and started maneuvering his arms where they wanted him to shoot.

Fuentes fought back this time. He really must have been under the Masks' control during the Battle of Keonus even if he didn't seem to be.

He grimaced at something in The Grid, straightened his arms, and marshaled all his effort to keep shooting his lasers at the oncoming Masks.

Rhodes opened his mouth to say something when Fisher yelled out, "Captain! Help me!"

Rhodes spun around. He barely managed to keep shooting when he saw more grid lines weaving their way around Fisher's face.

The lines twined into Fisher's grid lines and started wrenching him out of shape, too. Fisher thrashed and writhed in The Grid, but the invading grid lines kept advancing.

Rhodes froze trying to remember what he should do about this. In that moment of hesitation, he felt thin, crawling lines of some otherworldly substance creeping up his legs.

In a split second, more grid lines sprouted out of the ground, crawled inside the grid lines surrounding his body, and took over his being.

The invading lines twisted and pulled him out of shape....and then they took control of his weapons.

He had half a second to see the same thing happening to the rest of the battalion. These strange lines took over everyone until the lines inevitably pulled every battalion weapon away from shooting at the Masks.

Fisher yelled again, but he couldn't call out for Rhodes to help him. Fisher couldn't form words anymore at all.

The grid lines burrowed into his mouth and contorted his cheeks, jaw, and skull out of shape. He gave one last strangled cry before the grid lines muffled him.

Rhodes raised his weapon one more time. A dozen thoughts raced through his mind.

He wanted to shoot at his enemy, but that meant shooting at the grid lines or maybe even his own head to get them off him.

He took another instant of hesitation before he remembered. Seeing Fisher in danger flipped a switch in Rhodes's head. He couldn't use a weapon against these lines, either.

He dropped into a different part of his own awareness. He went into The Grid—the part of The Grid he entered for training sessions.

He took control of the lines he usually used to alter his own shape or the configuration of his weapons.

He surrounded himself with lines—his own lines. They twisted and slithered all over him the same way these alien lines did.

The two sets of lines fought each other for control of Rhodes's limbs until something gave. He didn't understand any of this even to realize what he was doing.

He thrust out dozens of lines, surrounded Fisher's head, and Rhodes started using his own lines to tear away the web of fibers from around Fisher's head.

"Fight back, Fisher! Use your grid lines to fight back!" Rhodes interfaced with the rest of the battalion. "Use your grid lines to fight back! You can stop them! Save your SAMs and yourselves!"

Rhodes kept ripping the lines away from Fisher's head, but that one moment of clarity gave Rhodes all the control he needed. He swung his lasers back toward the Masks and opened fire.

As soon as Rhodes started to expose Fisher's face, Fisher recovered, too. Grid lines sprouted from the outer rim of his face.

He sent his own lines to finish tearing the enemy lines away. Then Fisher started working on Rhodes.

He was too out of his mind with battle fury gunning down the Masks. He didn't pay attention to what Fisher was doing.

Rhodes did notice the lines taking control of Fuentes. The lines hauled his weapons away from the Masks against his best efforts to stop them.

Fuentes bellowed in rage trying to control his own guns, but his lasers eventually rotated in Rhodes's direction.

"Fight back, Rudy!" Rhodes yelled again, but Fuentes was already fighting back the only way he knew how.

The lines overcame his strength. They completely covered Van. Rhodes couldn't see her at all.

Fuentes tried one last hopeless time to force his own arms away. One of his lasers fired while it was aiming straight at Rhodes.

Rhodes gave it up and sent his own lines through the interface to untangle Fuentes. Rhodes tore the lines away from Fuentes's arms and he turned on the enemy raging at the top of his lungs.

Rhodes didn't even know where to start with Van or if she was even still online under there.

"You fight the enemy, Captain!" Fisher told him. "I'll take care of her."

"I hope she's all right."

Rhodes and Fuentes went back to passing their lasers back and forth across the Masks' line. Rhodes's warning gave the rest of the battalion the boost they needed to free themselves from the grid lines, too.

Fisher attacked Van, but it took him a long time to get her free from all the lines covering her face.

In a few seconds, the Masks broke off their assault, wheeled south, and surged away. They left the battalion standing there with nothing to shoot at.

Rhodes interfaced with everyone in the battalion. "Is everyone all right? Are you all right, Van?"

One of her eyes showed from under a mass of lines. So many of them surrounded her head that Rhodes couldn't see any squares between them.

Fisher finished tearing the lines off. What was left of the attacking lines sank back into The Grid.

Chapter 16

The Grid surrounding Rhodes, the lines covering his body, and the squares marking out the landscape returned to normal.

That's when Rhodes saw why the Masks just left the way they did.

The Masks might have just been toying with the Legion platoons before. Now the Masks charged the Legion position. Instead of attacking head on, the Masks curved their line on both sides to surround the platoons.

Rhodes didn't even finish checking to make sure all the SAMs got free from the attacking grid lines. They still covered half of Van's face.

In a split second, the Masks rushed back to their original position and encircled the platoons. They tried to retreat, but not fast enough.

"Hell no," Rhinehart snarled. "I don't think so, puppies."

"Let's go," Rhodes replied and ignited his boosters.

He took off much faster than he planned to, but he didn't come out here to stand aside and watch the Masks cut down even more Legion soldiers.

Rhodes streaked south and then cut eastward. The battalion surrounded him. Fisher couldn't even see The Grid to give Rhodes any information. Fisher was still too busy unwrapping Van from her cocoon of lines.

Rhodes didn't need any information. He already knew where he was, where the enemy was, and what he had to do.

He veered south, east, and then north to charge the platoons from the south. He opened fire before he got anywhere near them, hammered the Masks with Vipers, and then blasted his way into them with every weapon in his arsenal.

He could have changed into some fancy shape, gone down there, and slaughtered them from the ground.

He stayed airborne and the battalion widened their formation to join their gunfire with his. The battalion formed an inner ring right on top of the platoons to drive the Masks back.

The platoons took advantage of the battalion's sudden arrival. Rhodes heard officers yelling down on the ground.

As soon as the battalion opened fire, the platoons surged back out of the trap and retreated farther south.

Rhodes unloaded on the Masks even harder and forced them to open the two curved sides of their formation. Their line straightened out under the battalion's onslaught.

Rhinehart bellowed a string of curses at the enemy, sailed a little farther forward, and cut the Masks' line in half. He dove into the gap and turned left to push the two flanks farther apart.

His actions electrified the battalion. The others scattered and each person concentrated on a different part of the enemy swarm.

The battalion worked itself deep into the Masks' horde, split it apart, and drove the sections away from each other.

Rhodes wound up at the far righthand edge of the Masks' position. He worked around behind a group of fifty Masks all shooting up at him.

He angled his back toward Lauer who attacked the Masks right next to Rhodes. Rhodes showed no mercy and leveled the Masks by the dozen.

By the time he finished with that bunch, the surviving Masks of other, larger groups were already falling back before the battalion.

Rhinehart started forward to pursue them. "Fall back, Lieutenant," Rhodes ordered. "They might be trying to lure us into a trap."

Fisher rotated The Grid in a different direction. "The platoons are regrouping farther south. They're reestablishing another defensive blockade to stop the Masks from leaving town."

"Let's fall back with them," Rhodes replied. "The brass might not want us to flank the Masks a second time."

"How are you going to explain why we're here?" Oakes asked.

"I'll explain it to them with my mouth," Rhodes clipped over his shoulder. "Let's go."

He could have flown south to the Legion's new defensive position, but Rhodes chose to walk instead. He wanted to be in the right place to defend the platoons in case the Masks came back.

All the SAMs kept manipulating The Grid in different directions, but the Masks didn't make another push to engage.

"It looks like they know we're here," Dietz pointed out. "I guess it's asking too much to hope that they're afraid of us."

"They aren't afraid of shit," Rhinehart countered. "They're planning how to recapture us and defeat the platoons into the bargain. Their little trick with those grid lines didn't work so the Masks are working out their contingency plan."

"What are we gonna do about that, Captain?" Coulter asked.

"He can't do anything about it because he doesn't know their contingency plan," Lauer muttered. "They can't know what their contingency plan is yet because they haven't worked it out. Once they pull it, then we'll know what to do."

"Those lines were terrible," Van breathed. "I really thought they had me that time."

"The Masks might try to control us another way," Rhodes remarked. "I'm surprised they went for that instead of whatever they used on Keonus."

"That just means they'll try something else next time," Oakes pointed out. "It proves they're still trying to retake us and use us against the Legion."

"We'll have to make sure that doesn't happen," Rhodes replied.

Fuentes spoke up for the first time. "What if we can't stop it? What if something happens and they really do take control of us? We could get recaptured and there would be nothing we could do to stop it."

"Then it isn't your fault, is it?" Rhinehart countered.

"I don't think that will happen," Rhodes replied.

"What makes you so certain?" Fuentes looked away. "I wish I could be as sure about everything as you are."

"I'm only sure about it because I'm going to do everything in my power to make sure it doesn't happen. We're onto them now. We know their methods. We know more about them than anyone else in the whole Legion. Forewarned is forearmed. We know their tricks and we're prepared. They haven't had a chance to soften us up with drugs and torture. That will make it harder for them to take us a second time."

Fuentes sighed. "I wish I could believe that."

"You better start believing it, boy," Lauer snapped. "If you really believe they'll retake you, you'll find a way to make it come true. You listen to the captain and make up your mind that you will never let them retake you no matter what they do. I'm with Captain Rhodes. I'll die before I go back to them."

Everyone had to stop talking when they got to the Legion blockade. Lauer squinted at the platoons taking up their placements behind fortified concrete barricades. "We probably shouldn't go over there. We'll only make the soldiers uncomfortable."

"We'll stay out here." Rhodes halted fifty yards away from the barricade. "We'll meet the Masks first whenever they decide to come."

The Masks didn't come—not right away. They held off for over an hour.

Dietz finally gave it up and sat down on a chunk of broken concrete that must have split off from one of the ruined buildings. "Wake me up when they start serving breakfast."

Rhinehart snorted. "You're gonna be sleeping a long time before that happens, pal."

Dietz grinned at him. "Do you remember the waffles at Fort Bastion?"

"Do NOT start talking about food," Lauer cut in.

Dietz laughed. "You just don't want me to talk about how you always got whipped cream in your beard." He shut his eyes and smiled in blissful ecstasy. "I'll cherish that memory for the rest of my life."

"It will be a very short life if you don't shut up about food," Lauer fired back.

"What about the...." Thackery began, but Fisher interrupted.

"There's a message coming in for you from the *Ero,* Captain. Colonel Kraft is hailing you."

"That's unusual. It isn't like him to contact us in battle."

Rhodes connected the interface to the *Ero.* Colonel Kraft appeared standing full length in The Grid.

"Can I help you, Colonel?" Rhodes asked.

"Only if you can explain to me why you disobeyed a direct order by changing your position in the middle of that battle."

Rhodes lost what little patience he had left. He actually rolled his eyes at the colonel. "Please, Colonel. If you know that much, you know the Masks encircled the platoons and would have wiped them out. What did you think—that we would just stand there on the western side and watch?"

"No, but....."

"Who the hell is making decisions for the battalion now?" Rhodes snapped. "It better not be you. Who gave the order that we should flank the Masks from the west side?"

"The panel is assuming decision-making authority over Battalion 1 as long as you're in...."

"Then tell the panel to actually decide what they want us to do. Do they want us to knowingly put Legion platoons in harm's way or not? It sure looks from where I'm standing that the panel is trying to frame us into a situation where they have an excuse to take us offline."

"No, no," Kraft exclaimed. "It isn't like that."

"Then you can tell them to keep their noses out of my business. I'm down here doing a job. If they think what I did by saving those soldiers is so bad, tell them to just pull the plug and leave me the hell alone."

Rhodes would have liked to cut the interface then and there, but he couldn't do that to Kraft—not after Kraft went to so much trouble to get the battalion this extra chance.

Rhodes's words sank in, though. Kraft mumbled. "All right, Captain. I'll tell them you said that." Then he cut the interface.

"Damn, Captain!" Rhinehart murmured after Kraft disappeared. "That was one ballsy thing to say."

"To hell with them," Rhodes muttered. "I'm sick of them playing games with us. We can't win for losing."

"So....we could just be walking along minding our own business, and the next minute, we would go offline right there on the sidewalk?" Coulter asked.

"That won't happen," Oakes replied. "We're here because the Legion needs us. I mean, look at this place. The Legion is on its last legs. We're it. We're the only thing standing between the Masks and the whole Treaty of Aemon Cluster."

"I agree," Dietz added. "The Legion will never take us offline. That's just a hollow threat to make us cower in meek submission."

"Do you really think so?" Thackery asked. "That's kinda harsh, isn't it?"

"The Legion already knows they can't control us. They wouldn't be trying so hard if they weren't worried about us going rogue and throwing off all command authority. That's their worst fear."

Oakes cocked his head. "You sure have given this a lot of thought for someone who pretends not to care about any of it."

Dietz only shrugged. "It's pretty obvious, isn't it? The panel is bending over backward to exert every ounce of control it can over us. That transmission from Colonel Kraft just now proves it. We didn't do anything wrong, but they keep sticking their noses in to say we did and to threaten to take us offline. They're trying to reassert control."

"I sure hope you're wrong," Thackery remarked.

"Why would you hope that?" Dietz asked. "They can't control us either way. They can squawk 'til the cows come home. If we did decide to go off the reservation, they wouldn't be able to do a thing to stop us."

"They could take us offline," Coulter pointed out. "They can do that with the press of a button."

"Are you sure about that? When have they ever taken anyone offline?" Dietz turned to Rhodes. "Have you ever seen them take anyone offline?"

"Not permanently, no. The doctors took some of us offline when we malfunctioned and attacked each other."

"Don't forget that one time when Dr. Irvine took Legacy offline," Oakes pointed out.

"That was a SAM," Rhodes argued. "All he had to do was delete Legacy's program files."

"So why couldn't they do the same thing to a person?" Oakes asked. "The doctors could delete someone's entire neural core."

"You don't know that," Dietz countered. "None of us knows how much of our original neural network is still intact. The doctors might disconnect us from The Grid and the whole Battalion 1 mainframe, but we have no proof that doing so would actually kill the person."

"It could wipe their whole neural core," Thackery chimed in. "The person would be reduced to a vegetative state."

"It *might* wipe their whole neural core and it *might* reduce them to a vegetative state. We don't know for sure."

"Why are we even talking about this?" Lauer growled.

"We're talking about it because the Legion is using the threat of being taken offline to coerce us into obedience," Dietz returned. "If they're going as far as that, then it's in our interest to find out if they even *can* take us offline. If they can't, then the whole threat is hollow."

"But by that logic, you're saying they don't need to threaten us because they can't control us either way," Oakes pointed out. "You're saying we could do whatever we wanted and go completely rogue and they still wouldn't take us offline—assuming they have the power to."

"They won't," Dietz replied. "They're afraid of us."

"Then why haven't they taken us offline already?" Thackery asked. "They should have taken us offline by now if we're such a threat."

"That's exactly my point," Dietz returned. "I would have done it a long time ago if I was in their position—which leads me to believe that they can't take anyone offline."

Rhinehart rubbed his chin. "It's an interesting idea. I don't know that it changes anything, though."

"Think about it," Dietz went on. "The whole Battalion 1 project has been geared from the beginning to getting as many of us through the process as possible. The doctors and officers have been so worked up about protecting anyone who survives the process. I personally don't see General Brewster taking anyone offline—ever—no matter how badly they malfunction. It probably never once crossed his mind to implant any kind of safety failsafe like a shut-off switch to take us offline in case something went disastrously wrong—which it already has."

Now it was Oakes's turn to frown. "You're right about that. He should have shut *you* down when you malfunctioned if he was going to shut anyone down."

The group fell into a thoughtful silence. Rhodes didn't get involved in the conversation.

Dietz's argument made a scary kind of sense. Rhodes didn't picture General Brewster taking anyone offline, either.

He treated everyone who survived the Battalion 1 project long enough to wake up like his own baby.

He got irrationally attached to each person no matter how messed up or dangerous they turned out to be.

Rhodes found himself gazing across the landscape while he thought about it. What would he do if he knew for certain that the inquiry panel couldn't shut him down whenever they pleased?

He might have gone on a killing rampage just for the thrill of spiraling completely out of control.

He doubted he would do anything differently, though. The threat of being taken offline long since ceased to hold any power over him.

He no longer feared death. Maybe he never did. He definitely didn't fear death since he woke up from stasis.

No one else in the battalion did, either. Each of these people had flirted with the darkness too many times already.

The inquiry panel couldn't threaten them with anything worse than what the battalion had already gone through.

Chapter 17

R hodes sat on the ground talking to his subordinates and their SAMs. The landscape in this city offered plenty of places to sit while the battalion waited for something to happen.

Wild startled everyone out of their trance. "The Masks are making their move again, Captain."

Rhodes shot to his feet, but the Masks were nowhere in sight.

They *were* in sight on The Grid, though. They left their retreated position and advanced slowly and steadily toward the Legion's fortifications.

The platoons must have been scanning the Masks, too. The soldiers behind the barricades all jumped up, propped their weapons on top of the fortifications, and aimed north where the Masks would come from.

The battalion stood between the platoons and the Masks. Rhodes braced himself for the coming onslaught, but he still wasn't prepared for it when it did come.

The Masks trooped through the streets and then rushed south much quicker than they usually did. How the hell did they move so fast?

They charged the battalion's position in a swarm of thousands. They no longer used the single-file line they used during their first engagements on Bao and Rono.

Rhodes and his subordinates all used The Grid to change themselves into different fighting machines.

Rhodes started out using his lasers to mow down Masks all around him, but they overran the battalion and kept going to assault the Legion defenses.

Enough Masks surrounded Rhodes that they protected others to get past him. They threw hundreds of Masks at him to block his weapons from hitting the others.

His subordinates faced the same problem. The Masks' desire to keep the battalion intact played against Rhodes this time.

The Masks ignored the battalion except to neutralize their weapons. The Masks could get as many of their numbers as possible to the barricades.

The Masks threw hundreds of their numbers at the soldiers, too, took heavy losses on the fortifications, and used the fallen Masks to climb over the barricades.

Masks streamed behind the fortifications, leveled all the defending platoons, and kept flowing south with nothing to stand in their way.

As usual, the Legion had set up a staging area south of the city. Ravagers brought in supplies there, lifted off wounded, and organized troops coming and going from the battle zone.

Now nothing stood between the Masks and the staging area. The last surviving soldiers got trapped there fighting a few straggler Masks.

The same thing happened to the battalion. Rhodes tried his hardest to break away from the Masks surrounding him. They effectively neutralized him just by fighting him—and not fighting him very hard.

He scrambled to find a way to stop the disaster looming over the staging area. The Legion hadn't set up any defenses that far back. The brass relied on the platoons to hold the Masks off just a little longer.

Rhodes kept shooting as fast as he could at the Masks nearest him while he cast his mind over The Grid. There had to be a way....

In that moment, the residual connection still linking him to the Masks kicked back into gear. Nothing more than a vague subconscious inkling of what they planned to do crept into his brain, but the connection was still there.

In that split second, he saw their whole contingency plan—the contingency plan Dietz said the Masks would come up with to trap the battalion on this planet.

The bulk of the Masks' horde charged straight south without turning aside once, but they didn't plan to keep going like that.

Word spread through the staging area that the Masks were on the way. Ravagers that had been landing extra platoons and taking on wounded for evacuation now fired their engines to lift off and defend the staging area from the impending assault.

All those ships and the platoons who were ready to fight—they all trained their attention north. They thought the Masks would come from there. That was the contingency plan.

At the last second, the Masks planned to split their formation, flank the surrounding rubble mounds, and surprise the Legion by attacking the staging area on both sides.

The rubble piles hid the Masks from both directions. They planned to leave just enough Masks attacking from the south to distract the Legion forces from seeing anything else.

The Ravagers and platoons would all be facing the wrong way. They would be sitting ducks for the Masks' maneuver....unless Rhodes could stop it somehow.

All this information poured into his head in the blink of an eye even as he still gunned down as many Masks as came within range.

The Masks were already approaching the place where they would divide into two flanks.

He reacted on pure instinct, transmitted all that information to his subordinates through the interface, and fired his boosters to take off into the air.

The Masks tried to grab him and hold him back. He even sensed them trying some of their old tricks to control him through The Grid, but he broke away too fast.

He veered south and cut wide to the west. He didn't have time to explain anything to his subordinates, so he showed them through The Grid. He didn't have to say a word.

Dietz, Fuentes, and Thackery went with him. Coulter, Oakes, Lauer, and Rhinehart served east.

The two groups rushed the Masks from both sides. Rhodes didn't decide until the last second what he would do.

Lasers wouldn't stop this. Vipers wouldn't make a dent in the Masks' numbers.

He had to come up with something else—some other weapon to flatten these machines for good—or at least for today.

He had to make sure they didn't launch another assault, but he already knew they would. They had too many Masks on the planet already. Nothing would stop their relentless advance.

That didn't matter right now. He sent a silent signal to Zen, Van, and Koenig. Rhodes and Thackery landed behind one of the rubble piles—one of the rubble piles the Masks planned to use to ambush the Legion.

Dietz and Fuentes landed directly opposite behind another mound.

Rhodes cast one backward glance at The Grid. Rhinehart and the others were just dropping into place when the Masks split their formation, streamed around the piles, and passed directly between the battalion's positions.

Rhodes opened fire with his thermal cannon this time. The heat wave hit the Masks and melted their metal housing. They slumped and then collapsed in puddles.

More advancing Masks marched into the molten metal and the thermal cannons hit them, too.

The Masks coming in behind turned around to confront their attackers only to fall to the battalion's weapons. If the Masks faced Rhodes and Thackery, Dietz and Fuentes hit the enemy from the other side.

The Masks melted before they could mount any defense. The first lines of Masks entered the staging area.

The platoons and Ravagers opened fire, but the Masks fell easily without the two side flanks to support the assault.

Rhodes and his people stayed where they were just to make sure no more Masks came out of the woodwork to cause any trouble.

Rhodes tried to reestablish the connection to find out what the Masks were doing and what they might be planning next.

He extended his awareness northward, and in that moment, a sudden feeling of cold emptiness gripped his heart.

There was nothing there. He couldn't connect to the Masks anymore. They must have broken the connection at last. It took them long enough to figure it out.

Thackery gasped next to him. "No!!" she choked. "No!!"

Rhodes couldn't answer. This feeling.....this feeling of being utterly, hopelessly alone in the world....

He didn't realize until this moment that he even still had that connection to the Masks. He thought he got away from them when he withdrew from the drugs.

He turned away and swallowed hard. He lost something today—something he didn't even know he had—something more painful than anything that happened to him in the Masks' custody.

He and Thackery were still standing there when a few platoons of soldiers advanced up the street to check the area. They had to divert away from the river of melted metal.

A few soldiers spotted Rhodes and his people hiding behind the mounds. Rhodes didn't want to talk to any of them.

"Let's get out of here," he told his subordinates. "Get into the atmosphere and let's rendezvous with the *Ero.*"

He launched and all his subordinates followed him into orbit where they landed in the bay on board the *Ero.* The same oppressive cloud hung over the whole battalion, but no one spoke about it.

They returned to the capsule hold where Thackery went over to the table, sat down, buried her face in her arms, and burst into tears.

Rhinehart went straight to his capsule, locked himself into it, and shut the cover. Everyone stayed away from each other.

Rhodes couldn't tell if breaking that connection meant anything to the SAMs. He didn't ask. He would have expected Fisher to say something, but Fisher remained as silent as the others.

Rhodes milled around the hold for a while at loose ends. He really needed to do something, but he had nothing to do.

In the end, he just couldn't stand it a second longer. He went down to the *Ero's* recreation department, got himself some pencils and blank paper, took them back to the hold, and sat down at the table.

He started drawing and let his pencil float over the page. He didn't think about what he was drawing....until he got halfway through filling the page with lines.

As soon as he realized what he was drawing, he gave in and kept going. He made the outlines more distinct, sketched out hills, trees, houses, roofs, roads, and finally, a stone bridge crossing the stream.

The road led east from the town and vanished behind the hills. He drew children playing among the stepping stones, livestock grazing in the fields, and women hanging their laundry outside the houses.

He allowed his mind to relax into that scene for the first time. He let himself vanish into it in ways he never let himself when he actually lived there.

Thackery heard him sketching, looked up, and burst into another flood of tears when she saw what he was drawing.

She almost kicked over the bench when she leapt to her feet and ran away. She sat down on her capsule with her back to him and didn't come near him again.

He didn't care if he upset everyone by drawing this. He added more and more detail to make the picture as accurate and lifelike as possible.

Every detail made it stand out and swept him deeper into the illusion that he really was there. He could smell the wildflowers and woodsmoke on the breeze. He smelled the sun baking the long grass out in the fields.

He even smelled the food cooking in Koenig's eatery. He smelled sweat and tobacco smoke and food and the woodsmoke coming from the fireplace.

He also smelled the hay in the barn...and then another smell flooded his senses. It was Ora's smell—the way she smelled when she kissed him that one time.

Her smell overwhelmed him with emotion—the emotion he should have felt for her but didn't.

That emotion was part of the illusion. The Grid made him feel something for her the same way it made him feel something for their children—the children they never had.

He stopped in mid pencil stroke and stared down at the picture in front of him. It was a perfect representation of Stonebridge the way he remembered it.

He tried to remember his wife and children—his real wife and children that he left behind on Preinea. He had to struggle to remember that photograph he destroyed.

This picture of Stonebridge seemed like such an insult to their memory. The very existence of Stonebridge was an insult to his family's memory.

He snatched the paper, squashed it between his fingers, crumpled it into a ball, and threw it on the floor. He never wanted to see Stonebridge again, not even in his own memories. What an insult it was that he even had to remember it at all.

He started sketching again. This time, he drew the backyard of his own house in Preinea. He definitely remembered that.

He was still working on it when Thackery glanced over her shoulder, saw him, and got to her feet. She inched across the hold and picked up the crumpled piece of paper.

Rhodes pretended not to see her take it back to her capsule, unfold it, smooth it out, and stare at it for a long time.

He fought down a surge of sadistic rage when she stretched out on her mattress, shut her capsule cover, and stuck the picture to the underside the way Lauer stuck the picture of his family riding horses.

Rhodes concentrated on his new drawing so he wouldn't completely blow his stack. Thackery better not be planning to spend the rest of her time in this battalion mooning over Stonebridge.

How dare she?! How did she have the nerve to mourn over such a stinking, rotten, foul insult to everything he held dear?

She was an orphan with no home and no family in the world, but that was no excuse.

He had to fight the urge to go over there and get in her face about it right now. If she ever acted even slightly upset about losing Stonebridge, he didn't trust himself to handle it rationally.

He did his best to focus on his current drawing. Lauer came over to sit next to Rhodes.

A little while later, Oakes sat down opposite Rhodes and Oakes started drawing, too. It was just like old times except that it wasn't.

Lauer didn't comment on Rhodes's drawing. Oakes kept shooting sidelong glances at it.

He didn't make any remark until Rhodes got closer to finishing. He added his children practicing sports, playing basketball, or just running around in the backyard while Rhodes's wife lounged in the hammock.

Rhodes added every detail he could remember out of his memory. The more he added, the more he remembered.

He still didn't remember their faces, though, so he left them blank. He could imagine them smiling and laughing.

His imagination added every detail of their eyes sparkling and their cheeks glowing. He didn't need to remember the exact details of what they looked like. They were just as happy in his memory.

He spent a lot longer working on that picture than he spent on the picture of Stonebridge. He made this one as true to life as he could.

He could definitely vanish into this. He could drift back to that day and feel how much he loved and cared for each person in the scene.

Oakes raised his eyebrow at the picture. "It isn't like you—drawing something like that."

Rhodes stared down at the picture. It brought up so many memories—memories of happy afternoons spent in that yard—memories of spending long nights in his house with his wife—memories of taking his children on trips and watching them compete in sports—memories of the person he used to be before all this.

He wasn't that person anymore.

He wasn't the person who would stick this picture to the inside of his capsule cover. He wasn't the person who would drift off to sleep every night thinking about his old life.

He definitely wasn't the person who wanted to think about his old life every morning when he woke up. Starting his day like that would be an unimaginable torture far worse than anything the Masks did to him.

How interesting that they didn't use memories of his old life to torment him. They could have. They could have tormented him much more that way than by inflicting any physical pain.

He put the picture aside and left it there at his elbow while he drew a bunch of other stuff. Oakes drew a few pictures from Stonebridge, too, but they were much more general in their subject matter.

He drew trees standing in open fields and a few houses. He didn't draw any people.

Rhodes kept drawing until everyone in the battalion entered their conversion cycles.

Coulter got into his capsule last. "Don't stay up too late, Sir," he called across the hold.

"I won't. Good night, Corporal."

"Good night, Sir."

Coulter stretched out and shut the cover. Only then, after everyone else was gone and Rhodes sat alone at the table, he pulled the picture forward and stared at it for a long, long time.

"They look very happy," Fisher remarked.

"They were," Rhodes replied. "We had a nice life."

"What will you do with this?" Fisher asked. "Will you keep it the way the others do?"

Rhodes answered by aiming his thermal cannon at the picture and firing. He burned that picture to a cinder, too.

"Why are you doing this?" Fisher murmured. "Why did you go to so much trouble to draw this picture of your family only to destroy it? I don't understand."

"I guess I just needed to see them—just once. I needed something to make me stop thinking about Stonebridge. I don't need to see them anymore."

"Maybe you do," Fisher remarked.

Rhodes didn't answer. He gathered up his other drawings, tapped them into a neat stack, put his pencils into a pile with Oakes's, and went to his capsule.

He locked into the prongs and shut the cover thanking Almighty God he didn't have a picture of his family around to look at or think about. That was the last thing he needed right now.

It was the last thing the battalion needed right now. He wouldn't be able to function as their commanding officer if he had that memory distracting him day and night.

Chapter 18

R hodes reentered the conference room on the *Ero's* administrative deck. He didn't realize until now that the inquiry panel had traveled to Katera with Battalion 1.

He should have figured it out when Colonel Kraft said the inquiry panel was taking over decision-making authority for the battalion. Did the panel plan to stay on board so they could scrutinize the battalion's every move from now on?

The two doctors didn't come with Rhodes this time. They'd been working around the clock to collate the data from non-stop testing on the battalion since the Battle of Katera.

Neither of the doctors would tell Rhodes if the battalion was in trouble for disobeying orders—or for not taking the time to receive them in the first place.

The panel should have taken the battalion offline if Rhodes and his people were in trouble.

Dietz must be right about that. Either the battalion wasn't in trouble or the panel couldn't take the battalion offline at all. Maybe no one could.

Rhodes was about to find out which it was right now. He straightened up in front of the panel, but his tolerance for these formalities had long since come to an end.

He saw no reason to be polite to them anymore even though he planned to be. He could be the bigger person here.

"We're delighted to inform you, Captain, that we've decided to take Battalion 1 off probation," Admiral Stabler began. "You'll be returned to regular duty from now on."

Rhodes should have thanked the panel for their generosity, but instead, he just said, "Yes, Sir," as stiffly as he could.

"We would also like to extend our gratitude on behalf of the Legion for your intervention on Katera," Colonel Volk added. "You've proven your worth to our efforts against the Masks. We hope you'll continue to help the Legion defeat this enemy."

Rhodes replied, "Yes, Sir," and left it at that. What more was there to say? He already told these people that he planned to fight the Masks.

"Is there any way you could use your intelligence from the Masks to anticipate their next move?" General Hyde asked.

"I'm afraid not, Ma'am," Rhodes replied. "I don't have any control over my connection with the Masks....and I think they probably cut the connection on their end. I doubt I'll get any more information from them—not in that way, at least."

"Would you be willing to give us some recommendation on how to defeat them?" Admiral Stabler asked.

"I would be very willing if I had some recommendation to give, but I don't. I've been racking my brain to come up with some way, but I haven't yet. I would tell you if I saw a way to do it."

"We'd like you to continue working out a strategy—even a strategy that might work for the entire Legion," Colonel Volk added.

Rhodes just said, "Yes, Sir." He'd already been trying to work out a strategy for the whole Legion.

"The battalion will be assigned to the Drion campaign from now on," Captain Lake chimed in.

Rhodes's head shot up. "Drion....?"

"You're familiar with the planet, aren't you?" Lake asked. "You served there once before."

"Twice before," Rhodes muttered.

"Then you understand that the planet's heavy cloud cover makes air assault much less viable," Colonel Volk added. "Drion is a ground game. We hope the cloud cover will somewhat mitigate the invasion ships' advantage."

Rhodes only nodded. Drion's cloud cover might mitigate the invasion ships' advantage. Then again, it might not mitigate anything. It might work in the Masks' favor.

"If there's nothing else, you're dismissed, Captain," Admiral Stabler finished. "You and the battalion will disembark from the *Ero* and deploy with the 765th platoon to land on the planet."

"Will the *Ero* continue to act as our support vessel?" Rhodes asked. "We'll still need somewhere to go through conversion cycles."

"We're still working out the logistics," Colonel Volk replied. "We'll inform you where to go for conversion cycles and any other support functions you need. You're dismissed, Captain."

Rhodes said, "Yes, Sir," again and left.

"This sounds like the most poorly planned military campaign in history," Fisher murmured on the way back to the capsule hold.

"More poorly planned than Katera?" Wild asked through the interface.

"They don't even know where we're supposed to go through conversion cycles," Fisher went on. "What are we supposed to do if one or more of us gets injured? Dr. Osborne and Dr. Trudeau won't be around to repair us. It isn't the smartest way to protect your most valuable assets in this war."

"At least we'll get away from this stupid inquiry panel," Zen pointed out. "They won't be close enough to call up the captain over every little decision he makes, even the ones that work in their favor."

"Drion is going to be a nightmare," Lauer grumbled. "I served on that shithole. I never thought I'd live long enough to go back there."

"What's wrong with it?" Thackery asked.

"Besides the fact that it has no sunshine?" Oakes asked. "The atmosphere makes air travel impossible. We'll be lucky if we can use boosters—and forget about bringing Ravagers to provide air support or evacuate any platoons that get trapped."

"Fantastic," Thackery mumbled.

"You have no idea," Lauer replied. "This is gonna get hectic."

"More hectic than our other battles?" she asked.

"Considering we won't have boosters or Ravagers, I'd say yeah, more hectic than our other battles."

"We'll just have to get creative," Rhinehart chimed in. "That's one thing these Masks don't have. They aren't very bright."

"They seem to strategize pretty well," Dietz pointed out. "I don't see them having any problem outsmarting the platoons."

"Then we'll just have to outsmart them," Rhinehart replied. "Right, Captain?"

Rhodes barely heard them. "I guess we'll see what conditions are like once we get down there. If Drion does give the Legion an advantage, this could be the tipping point we're looking for."

"You're delusional," Lauer told him.

Rhodes chuckled. "Probably."

"At least no one in the 765th is trying to kill us," Coulter pointed out.

"That we know about," Oakes corrected.

"It doesn't matter if they are," Rhodes replied. "We have a job to do. What the platoons do doesn't concern us except where we're responsible for protecting them. That will be the best way to convince them not to kill us."

"So....does your order about defending ourselves apply to the platoons?" Rhinehart asked. "If one of them aims a weapon at us and tries to kill us, do we have your permission to defend ourselves?"

Rhodes found himself squirming. "I guess so."

"Why should we protect people who are trying to kill us?" Coulter asked.

"Because they're ignorant," Rhodes replied.

"Because they're scared of us," Dietz added. "They're more scared of us than the panel—or the brass."

"You should protect them because they're human," Rhodes replied. "They're our own people. We aren't robots even if the platoons think we are. These are our people and we're going to protect them if we can. Heaven knows they have enough enemies as it is without us becoming more of them."

"Do you know what our orders are for when we deploy?" Coulter asked.

"If I knew that, I would already have told you."

That ended the conversation, but a few hours later, the battalion got called down to the landing bay where they boarded a Duster. The ship took them to another Ravager called the *Rapho* carrying the 765th to Drion.

"So....this ship doesn't have a single capsule on it for us to go through conversion cycles," Rhinehart remarked. "Fisher is right. This operation stinks."

"What's your solution—that we all resign from the Legion and go home to our couches?" Rhodes countered. "Grow a pair and deal with it."

The Duster set down in the landing bay. The battalion disembarked into a bay crowded with other Dusters and a bunch of crewmen working on them.

Plenty of regular Legion soldiers worked around the Dusters, too. Rhodes checked the *Rapho's* duty roster and located the captain in command of the 765th.

His name was Emanuel Blackwell and Rhodes knew nothing about him except what appeared in Blackwell's service record.

The roster said Blackwell was in the supply store adjacent to the landing bay along with his two lieutenants, Nikolai Edgecombe and Devin Lohr.

Captain Blackwell turned out to be a burly, gruff, hard character like Lauer, but younger, stockier, and clean-shaven.

Blackwell kept every detail of his personal presentation immaculately groomed. Rhodes had never met any officer anywhere, not even in the highest ranks of the Legion brass, who kept their uniforms this neat.

The fact that Blackwell was about to deploy into combat and wore fatigues only made his meticulous appearance even more striking.

He narrowed his eyes at Rhodes the minute Rhodes walked into the supply store. Then Blackwell compressed his lips. Rhodes read in Blackwell's granite features exactly how this deployment would go.

Lieutenant Edgecombe was a tall, beefy, brutal guy with short-buzzed white-blonde hair. Rhodes could see Edgecombe's ivory-white scalp straight through his hair.

He also gave Rhodes and his people a flinty glance and immediately looked away.

Lieutenant Lohr did not look away. He didn't harden his features at all. He showed no emotion at all—not even the slightest glimmer of surprise or acknowledgment that Battalion 1 meant anything to him or the wider battle.

Rhodes stuck out his hand to Blackwell. "Captain Corban Rhodes of Battalion 1. My crew is ordered to deploy with you."

Blackwell glanced down at Rhodes's hand and hesitated for a split second before Blackwell decided to shake it. "Welcome aboard," Blackwell replied.

"Do you want any help loading the Dusters?" Rhodes asked. "We don't have any orders apart from deploying on the planet. If you need help, we're happy to pitch in."

Blackwell leveled him with another direct stare and then said, "I think it would be better if you didn't mix with my platoon, Captain. Not everyone here is thrilled about deploying with you—for obvious reasons."

"Oh." Rhodes frowned at the men around him. Everyone in the supply store had magically stopped working to listen to the conversation. "Well, while we're making ourselves scarce, you might want to inform your men that we'll be fighting side by side once we get down on the surface. They don't have a choice about deploying with us—just like we don't have a choice about deploying with you. Tell them they better get over themselves pretty quick or we'll all be in trouble."

Rhodes walked out of the supply store and then out of the landing bay. He had nothing else to do and no capsule hold to go to.

If the Legion brass wanted to ostracize Battalion 1 and make them feel like outsiders, the brass wasn't doing a very good job of it.

Now the battalion had no choice but to go where all the other regular Legion personnel spent their time.

Rhodes threw caution to the wind and went to one of the *Rapho's* crew lounges. The sixty people sitting around talking in there all fell silent and stared when the battalion walked in.

Rhodes didn't give a shit anymore if he made people uncomfortable. They could take it up with their officers if they didn't like it.

The brass had kept the battalion hidden away in the *Ero's* capsule hold like the dirty little secret Battalion 1 was.

All of that was coming to an end by the brass's own staggering incompetence at planning this campaign.

Now every single goddamn member of the regular Legion could get used to having Battalion 1 around whether they liked it or not.

Rhodes sat down on one of the couches. Five people were already sitting there. They all sprang up and evacuated in a hurry to get out of his way.

Rhodes and his people sat down in their places. Three of the crewmen had been playing cards. They abandoned their game, so Rhodes picked up the deck and started shuffling it.

"Who wants to play Slaughter Power?" he asked.

"I'm in." Rhinehart leaned forward, scooped up the crewmen's chips, and started to rearrange them in stacks according to color. "Come on, Oakes. You know you want to play."

"I'm in, too," Dietz chimed in. "I'll skin every last one of you."

"Keep dreaming, squirt," Rhinehart sneered.

"How do you play?" Thackery asked.

"If you don't know, you're too inexperienced to play against us," Rhinehart told her.

Rhodes finished shuffling and started dealing. Dead silence hung over the lounge. Everyone gaped at the battalion in shocked horror.

Rhodes ignored them. "What about it, Lauer? Do you want to lose epically?"

Lauer didn't turn around. He picked up a magazine one of the crewmen had been reading and started flipping the pages. "You remember how things went when you got me playing The Ship, The Captain, and The Crew. I win all the games. I'll sit this one out and give you all a chance."

"How do we know you really win all the games if you don't win all the games?" Rhinehart asked.

Lauer didn't look up. "Take my word for it, son. I'm doing you a favor."

Rhinehart laughed and distributed the chips between himself, Dietz, Oakes, and Rhodes.

They started playing the game while the *Rapho* crew watched in horrified silence.

The rest of the battalion slotted right into the routine of pretending the *Rapho* crew wasn't there. Thackery picked up a different crewman's book and started reading that instead.

Another crewman had been looking at pictures of his family on a remote device. Coulter picked up the device and started flipping through the family photographs as if they were his own.

Fuentes perched on the arm of the couch next to Rhinehart, looked over Rhinehart's shoulder at his cards, and watched the game.

The group lounged at their ease for half an hour before Lieutenant Edgecombe came in with five of his men from the 765th.

He scowled at Battalion 1 from across the room, tried unsuccessfully to go about his business as if Battalion 1 wasn't here, and finally stormed over to the table where Rhodes and his men were playing cards.

"What the hell are you doing here?" Edgecombe demanded. "Captain Blackwell told you to keep your distance from the crew."

"Mind your manners in front of the captain, Lieutenant," Lauer snapped from the other end of the couch. "You might not like Captain Rhodes, but he's still your superior officer."

Edgecombe opened his mouth to say something else and stopped himself in time.

Rhodes decided to take pity on the guy. "I offered to help your platoon get ready to deploy. Blackwell turned us down and we have nowhere else on this ship to wait for the order—so we came here." He looked up just then and locked eyes on Edgecombe. "Did you think we were going to hide in a closet or something?"

"Captain Blackwell told you to keep a low profile," Edgecombe growled. "He told you it wasn't a good idea for you to fraternize with the crew or the platoon."

"Fortunately for me, Captain Blackwell and I are the same rank, so whatever he said was just a suggestion. Anyway, as you can see, we aren't fraternizing with the crew or the platoon."

"Unless you want to sit down and get your balls crushed by Rhinehart here," Oakes added.

Rhinehart laughed loudly and tossed five chips into the center pile. "I'll see your two hundred and raise you three hundred."

Oakes dumped another five on top of Rhinehart's. "I call."

Rhodes tossed his cards down on the table. "I'm out."

Oakes and Rhinehart turned to Dietz. He pierced them both with an eagle eye and pushed a large stack of chips into the center. "I'll see your five hundred and raise you another five."

Rhinehart's already pale skin turned grey. "You're insane." He tossed his cards down. "I'm never playing against you again."

Dietz faced Oakes. "What'll it be, Lieutenant?"

Oakes clenched his jaw. "You're bluffing, Corporal." He pushed in the rest of his chips. "Call."

Dietz laid down his cards to reveal four aces and a king. "Don't ever call me a liar again, Lieutenant."

"Jesus Christ!" Rhinehart muttered and threw up both hands. "Unbelievable."

Oakes tossed his cards face down. "Great way to end the game, pal. Now what are supposed to do?"

Dietz only grinned at him and stacked up the chips. "If you fellas are all too chickenshit to play against me, I guess my title as reigning champion will stand uncontested for all time. You can all go home and cry into your pillows."

Rhodes looked up. Edgecombe and his men still stood there scowling down at Rhodes and his men. "Are you still here, Lieutenant? Don't you have anything better to do than stand around staring at us?"

Just then, Coulter turned to Thackery who was sitting next to him. He showed her something on the crewman's device and she exploded in laughter. She almost fell off the couch.

Coulter grinned at her reaction. Then he looked up like he just happened to notice Edgecombe standing there.

Edgecombe snapped around when Thackery started laughing. He glared at her and Coulter....until Coulter held up the device and showed Edgecombe whatever was on it.

He struggled to keep his composure for a second, furrowed his brow in consternation, and then compressed his lips to stifle laughter. A few of his men standing close enough to see the device burst out laughing, too.

Edgecombe bumped one of them in the shoulder. "Let's get out of here."

Chapter 19

R hodes and the battalion returned to the *Rapho's* landing bay. The 765th Platoon was already there loading into the Dusters that would take them down to Drion.

"You said aircraft didn't function on the planet," Thackery reminded Lauer. "How can Dusters get in and out?"

"They won't have navigation. We'll be flying blind. We'll be lucky to land at all without crashing and burning with all hands."

"Spectacular," she muttered. "Who's running this operation?"

Just then, Captain Blackwell came over to Rhodes and pointed to a Duster near the sidewall. "You and your crew can take that Duster over there. Some of my guys are on board, but they'll make room for you."

"Thanks," Rhodes replied and waved his people over to the ship.

They climbed on board and found Lieutenant Edgecombe in there with ten of his men. They crowded against the walls to make room for Battalion 1.

"Who's flying this crate?" Lauer yelled over the escalating engine noise.

"Our boy Jonovich is supposed to take us down to the surface!" Edgecombe hollered back. "He's the best pilot we got...but he isn't here yet."

"I'll take us down, Lieutenant," Dietz offered. "I can get us onto the surface."

Lauer gave him a hard look. No one else volunteered.

"Wait two more minutes," Edgecombe added. "If he doesn't show, you can take us."

Jonovich didn't show. A few more men from the 765th jammed into the Duster's rear. They shoved against Rhodes's people who in turn had to shove against Edgecombe's men.

Even then, everyone had to stand body to body just to fit inside the vessel.

"Get up there and take over!" Lauer yelled to Dietz. "If you crash the ship, I'm gonna kick your ass."

"Yes, Sir!" Dietz yelled and started elbowing his way between the other men.

He vanished into the cockpit. The engine noise howled to an epic pitch and the ship lifted off the landing bay floor.

Rhodes shut his eyes. He couldn't see where the ship was going.

He wouldn't have been able to see even if he'd been sitting in the cockpit himself. The Drion cloud cover would be too thick to see a damn thing.

The Grid showed him more than enough. Dietz would use The Grid to get the Duster onto the ground.

If everything went sideways, this would be the only Duster to land on Drion. Then the 765th wouldn't be there to fight the Masks at all.

Rhodes interfaced with the other SAMs on the way down to the planet. They all interfaced with Zen and watched Dietz fly the ship.

He flew better than Rhodes ever thought possible. Why was he even surprised that Dietz could handle himself like this?

He worked all the controls with expert precision, dropped out of the *Rapho's* bay, and plummeted into the atmosphere. He lost sight of the other Dusters and pulled up the landing coordinates on the cockpit controls.

The other Duster pilots navigated the cloud cover with no problem, too. They assembled on a remote airfield outside another city ravaged by the Masks. The Grid said the city's name was Ypra.

The Duster's hatch popped and all the men of the 765th streamed outside. Rhodes and his people went with them to an assembly point on the other side of the airfield.

Captain Blackwell gave orders to his men. "Edgecombe, take your squad up the western avenue over there. Lohr and I will circle from the west and converge on the enemy at the central greenway."

"You got it, Sir," Edgecombe replied.

Blackwell narrowed his eyes at Rhodes and the battalion. "What are you people going to do?"

"Why are you taking the western avenue?" Rhodes asked. "It's a death trap of Masks."

Blackwell's head shot up. "It is?"

Rhodes had to remind himself that these people couldn't see a thing about the enemy position. None of their technology worked on this planet.

Rhodes bent over and scratched a crude outline in the dirt at his feet. "The Masks are all stationed here—along the eastern bank of the river. They have the avenue covered. If you really want to circle and flank them, you should go farther east and then cut north—here. The greenway is too far out of range. Edgecombe's men would get pinned down and your two squads would be nowhere nearby to help them out."

Blackwell started to scowl and stopped himself. "So you're saying we should circle east, then north, and hit the enemy from behind? Are you willing to put your money on that by coming with us?"

"That's why I suggested it," Rhodes replied. "Your squad and the battalion will hit the enemy from here—from the east. Edgecombe's and Lohr's squads can come directly from the south. As soon as the enemy faces us, the two squads can move in and flank them from here."

Blackwell shrugged. "All right. Sounds good."

"How do we know the enemy won't see us coming?" Lohr asked. "If your technology works down here, theirs will work, too."

"I don't know how well their technology works down here," Rhodes replied. "Ground game is all we have. We can't get near the enemy from any other side except the west and that's too heavily defended, especially with the river in the way."

"We have only your word on that," one of Lohr's men chimed in.

Rhodes shrugged. "Don't take my word for it, then. Go your own way and get your ass shot off. I really don't care."

The guy pulled his head in quick. No one else argued. "Let's move out," Blackwell ordered. "You two take your squads in from the south like he said."

Lohr muttered, "Yes, Sir," and the squads split up.

Rhodes scanned The Grid on the way farther east. "The Masks don't seem to be using any scanning technology, either, Captain," Fisher reported. "They aren't adjusting their formation to compensate for our movements."

"They're facing west, so it looks like they expect something to come across the river from there," Dash pointed out. "The other platoons that have been on the planet all this time are all west of the river. The Masks might expect those platoons to make a move."

"The Masks aren't stupid enough to fall for that," Oakes replied.

Blackwell whipped around fast. "Who is your guy talking to?" he asked Rhodes.

"We're in communication with another squad that is taking readings on the enemy position," Rhodes lied. "We're communicating through our helmets in different parts of the city."

"How did your guys get onto the planet if they didn't come down with our platoon?"

Rhodes tried to shrug it away. "Like I said, they're with another unit, but they have information on the enemy position. They say the Masks aren't adjusting their position to compensate for our presence. It looks like the enemy isn't using scanning technology after all."

"What else can you tell us about the battlefield? We can't see shit out here."

"Just what I already told you. The Masks are lined up along the river facing west."

"Why?" Blackwell asked. "What's on the west side that's so important to them?"

"The other squad thinks the Masks are responding to earlier platoon activity. These guys are speculating that the Masks are preparing for more maneuvers coming from that direction."

"Are any of the Masks facing east?"

"Not that I can see," Rhodes replied.

Blackwell jolted again. "You can see that?"

"My helmet gives me a view of the landscape and the enemy position."

Blackwell looked away. "The Legion should give all of us that."

"You don't want this," Rhodes muttered. "Trust me."

"It would be nice to be able to see what's going on in the battle zone."

"It wouldn't be nice—ever." Rhodes let the matter drop. "Edgecombe and Lohr are in position. They're just waiting on us."

"How are they supposed to know when to attack?"

"Hopefully one or both of them will be smart enough to wait until we attack. Then the Masks will turn away from the river to defend themselves. Then the other two squads can move in."

Blackwell gave Rhodes another hard look, compressed his lips, and turned away. Rhodes didn't ask what was on the captain's mind.

The platoon inched through town covering every possible angle and corner where the Masks might be hiding.

The planet's cloud cover cast the whole city in perpetual darkness. A few surviving lights in the surrounding buildings gave the only light to see anything.

Most of the buildings had been bombed out of existence. Others stood partially destroyed or with half their structures blown off.

The usual carpet of broken walls, dead bodies, destroyed vehicles, and twisted wreckage covered the ground.

The platoon had to wind its way with painstaking slowness through this lawn of trash and ruins. The soldiers kept jerking their Jackhammers into every deserted alley and corner.

Rhodes kept a close eye on The Grid. The fact that no one in the battalion raised a weapon even to ready themselves for battle seemed to unnerve the platoon soldiers even more than they already were.

They cast suspicious glances at Rhodes and his people walking normally through the battle zone. Some of the soldiers outright glared.

Rhodes was too used to it to pay much attention.

"We've traveled far enough east, Captain," Fisher reported. "We should start heading north."

Rhodes got Blackwell's attention. "We've traveled far enough east. We should start heading north."

"Is there an echo in here?" Dash teased.

"Don't let them hear you talking," Zen chimed in. "One of them might get trigger-happy and shoot at you."

Some of the other SAMs laughed. Rhodes had to bite his cheek to stop himself from smirking. It must be nice to hold a conversation no one else could hear.

Rhodes indicated to Blackwell where the platoon and the battalion should stop and turn westward to make their assault. Rhodes had to wait while Blackwell went through his squad and make sure everyone was armed and ready.

Blackwell finally made his way to the front, took his place next to Rhodes, and eyed the battalion. "It must be nice not to have to deal with all your guys getting geared up every time."

Rhodes didn't tell him again that there was nothing nice about being in Battalion 1. Rhodes didn't want anyone envying the battalion for anything.

Blackwell squinted into the distance. The Masks' position cast a glow into the sky. They had light—more light than they needed. It gave the platoons more than enough of a target to aim for.

"I guess we just launch the assault whenever we..." Blackwell began.

At that moment, a gunshot went off behind Rhodes's back. Actually, it was about four gunshots, but he couldn't be certain of the number.

Jackhammers erupted from the squad standing behind Rhodes and Blackwell. All those shots hit Rhodes in the back. Stray fusion fire also hit Oakes who stood closest to Rhodes at the time.

He stumbled under the barrage. Blackwell dove out of the way yelling in surprise.

The rest of the battalion reacted instantly, spun around, and opened fire on the gunmen. Seven platoon soldiers held their weapons jammed into their shoulders. The barrels smoked from the shots they just unloaded on Rhodes.

Dietz, Rhinehart, Lauer, and Coulter dropped the soldiers in a heartbeat, but Rhodes didn't have time to deal with the aftermath.

He staggered a few steps forward from the blows. He'd been so focused on The Grid until right that moment.

It gave him more of a view than he ever wanted of the Masks' position farther west. They responded to the attack on Rhodes with unbelievable ferocity.

The Masks wheeled backward and surged at the platoon so fast that no one in Blackwell's party had time to prepare themselves. The traitors who shot Rhodes completely obliterated the platoon's element of surprise and turned the tables in the Masks' favor.

Rhodes tripped over his own feet and wound up farthest forward of the whole party. That put him in a prime position to meet the Masks first.

Dietz, Rhinehart, Lauer, Coulter, and Captain Blackwell all had their backs turned to hold the platoon at gunpoint. The five men got caught backfooted before they turned around to face the enemy.

The rest of Blackwell's squad were also so focused on those soldiers shooting Rhodes and Oakes that the Masks caught everyone by surprise.

Rhodes raised his weapons first and unloaded his thermal cannons, but melting the Masks didn't work fast enough to cope with their numbers.

He switched to lasers and cut them down, but it was already too late. They rushed the platoon. The soldiers all fumbled to raise their Jackhammers.

The whole disaster positioned the squad behind Battalion 1. The soldiers' Jackhammer fire put the battalion in just as much danger as the Masks.

It took way too long for everyone to figure out where their enemies were, where their friends were, and which direction they should be shooting.

By that time, the Masks charged far enough east to get past Rhodes and half the battalion. Nothing stood between the platoon and the enemy.

Confusion reigned. Rhodes found himself too far away from the rest of the squad. Masks surrounded him on all sides, but that only made them easier to target. He didn't have to worry about hitting anyone friendly—or supposedly friendly.

He concentrated his laser fire toward the west to stem the tide of Masks coming from that direction.

It seemed to work. The rush slowed down and he didn't see any more Masks advancing through The Grid.

He did see Edgecombe and Lohr moving in, though. They approached the battle from the south.

Their trajectory would lead them to open fire on the confused jumble of their own men fighting hand to hand against the Masks.

Rhodes made a split second decision, altered his grid lines to change his shape, dropped under the pavement, and released a powerful electric charge from his fusion generator.

The charge electrified the ground for a fraction of a second and conducted up the Masks' legs through the metal housing of their feet.

The soldiers' rubber boots insulated them and the Masks wrapped up in the battle collapsed at once.

Chapter 20

The soldiers of the 765th platoon jerked their weapons right and left and in all directions trying to find an enemy to shoot at.

Rhodes straightened up on the pavement and they all spun around to hold him at gunpoint.

Oakes rushed over to him. "Are you all right, Captain? Did they hit any of your organic tissue?"

"I'm fine, Lieutenant." Rhodes turned his gaze to the platoon.

Blackwell had gotten hit by stray fusion fire when the traitors opened fire on Rhodes. Rhodes's subordinates had already killed the people who attacked him.

Blackwell staggered over cradling one wounded arm. "Don't....do n't retaliate....against the whole platoon....Captain...." he gasped.

"I didn't plan to retaliate against anyone. Maybe now you and your guys will see that we're all on the same side here."

Blackwell's eyes swiveled to the rest of his squad, and just then, Edgecombe's and Lohr's squads raced around a corner and charged their position.

The soldiers slowed when they saw Blackwell's squad and Battalion 1 standing there surrounded by a bunch of dead Masks.

Edgecombe's eyes widened and he opened and closed his mouth a few times before he managed to get his voice working. "Sir....what the......what happened?"

"It's complicated, Lieutenant." Blackwell turned to Rhodes. "Any clue on where the enemy is and where they're going next? It would help if we could coordinate with the other platoons in the area."

"There are no other platoons on this side of the river," Rhodes replied. "We're the only ones over here. If we wanted to make an assault on the enemy, we could try driving them toward the river. Maybe that would give the platoons on the west side a chance to attack from their side....but that's just an idea."

"You want to....assault the Masks....." Lohr stammered. "As in....we charge them instead of them charging us?"

"Why not? Isn't that what we're here for?" Rhodes asked.

Blackwell started to say, "Maybe that isn't such a....." when Lauer snapped, "Captain!"

Rhodes jolted to alert just in time to see the Masks change their position in The Grid. They'd been lined up along the river the same way they had been when Rhodes's party landed on this planet.

Now the Masks clustered together and burst out into the city—heading straight for the 765th.

"Close ranks!" Rhodes bellowed. "Stand fast and close ranks!"

Edgecombe and his squad rushed forward to join up with Blackwell's men. Lohr hesitated to follow Rhodes's order.

Rhodes made an executive decision not to pay any attention to what any of Blackwell's men did. If they didn't close ranks, they would die out here. He couldn't help that if they didn't follow orders. He was still a captain even if he wasn't their captain.

The battalion spun around to face west just in time. Once again, the battalion wound up getting pushed to the front to block the Masks from getting near the 765th.

Lohr and his men finally pulled their heads out of their asses and rejoined the other squads. The platoon packed together and everyone trained their weapons toward the west just as the Masks surged out of the darkness.

Their glowing eye slits made them look extra menacing in the shadows. The faint light in the sky glimmered off their metal bodies.

Their feet made an extra loud tramping noise on the ground. They closed on the platoon with frightening speed.

Rhodes reacted instantly and launched a dozen Vipers into their midst. The rest of the battalion did the same thing.

The platoon fell back from the explosions. That little extra space between them and the battalion put the soldiers more at risk.

Rhodes backed up to defend the platoon. The Masks stretched their formation northward trying to encircle the platoon again.

"They're flanking us!" Rhodes bellowed. "Fall back to the south! Wheel to the south and fall back!"

Enough of the soldiers followed his orders that they prevented the Masks from cutting the platoon off completely.

It couldn't last, though. Rhodes cast a frantic glance at The Grid. "Find us some cover, Fisher!" he roared above the noise. "Find us somewhere we can defend ourselves."

"There's the Astronomical Observatory!" Fisher countered. "It's a defensible position, but it's north of here. We would have to fight our way through this group of Masks—and more are moving in!"

He adjusted The Grid in front of Rhodes so he could see the surrounding city. Fisher was right about the observatory being defensible.

It had been built like a fortified castle on top of a hill in the center of the city.

Hundreds of Masks blocked the 765th from getting near the observatory. More Masks advanced from the river to flank the platoon on the west side.

The battalion's presence must have tripped something with the Masks. Other flanks who'd been fighting the Legion in other parts of the city now broke off to converge on the 765th.

The 765th wouldn't be able to hold its own out here in the open. Once those other groups of Masks showed up, the platoon would need a defensible spot even more than they did now.

Rhodes made up his mind. "Follow me and head north!" he yelled to the platoon. To the battalion, he called, "Switch to thermals and blast your way north!"

Fisher transmitted the route to the observatory to all the other SAMs. Rhodes switched to thermal cannons and the rest of the battalion joined in.

The battalion still stood at the front with nothing but a wall of Masks blocking the way to the observatory.

The Masks had been slowly pushing the platoon farther and farther south. The platoon resisted, which brought the battalion face to face with the Masks.

The Masks didn't anticipate the battalion using thermal cannons. Rhodes opened fire and the Masks nearest him started to melt.

"Push north!!" he yelled to the soldiers behind him. "Punch through and head north!"

The soldiers didn't respond right away—not until the battalion succeeded in melting enough Masks to open a gap between them.

Rhodes and his people forced the Masks apart and back. Rhodes, Rhinehart, and Lauer wheeled part of the Masks to the left. Dietz,

Fuentes, Thackery, and Coulter drove the rest of the Masks to the right.

Blackwell and Edgecombe realized first what the battalion was trying to do. Rhodes's continued yells for the soldiers to head north finally got through their heads.

Blackwell and Edgecombe waved their men forward. "Come on! MOVE!!"

The soldiers had to tiptoe through puddles of melted Masks. The platoons darted past the battalion still locked in battle against the Masks.

Rhodes shifted a little farther to the left and turned his back to the observatory in the distance. All the soldiers retreated behind him.

Now he and the battalion stood between the Masks and the platoon facing the other way. The Masks tried again and again to push past the battalion to pursue the fleeing platoon, but the battalion stood strong.

The Masks' efforts only brought them deeper inside the battalion's thermal cannon range.

Rhodes was just starting to enjoy the sweet taste of victory when a different crowd of Masks crossed the river farther north. They crossed level with the platoon's position. The platoon couldn't see the enemy closing in.

The platoon wasn't close enough to take refuge at the observatory, either—not without the battalion's protection.

"Break off!!" Rhodes ordered. "Fall back to defend the platoon!"

He fired his boosters and launched away from all the Masks trying to get past him. His boosters coughed and barely held him aloft.

They carried him three blocks before they failed. He hit the ground and took off running, but he couldn't catch up with the platoon fast enough to avert the disaster.

The rest of the battalion tried to follow him. He didn't have time to explain everything to them, but they could already see the problem on The Grid.

Rhodes altered his grid lines, transformed himself into a fast-moving ground vehicle with giant, all-terrain tires, and raced away over the rubble fields gaining speed as he went.

His subordinates followed him and launched one Viper barrage after another at the advancing Masks.

The Vipers detonated at the very front of the Masks' formation. The bombardment slowed them down and it also alerted the platoon of the advancing enemy.

The platoon started moving faster, but the Vipers didn't stop the Masks completely. Those behind charged through the explosions to close on the platoon.

Rhodes bounded over the rough terrain as fast as he could go. The Grid gave him a perfectly clear view of the Masks about to overrun the platoon just a few blocks from the observatory.

The Masks surged through one more street and flooded toward the platoon in an unbroken wave. The soldiers spun around and raised their Jackhammers to defend themselves.

Rhodes blasted over the last mound spitting debris and rubble from under his tires. He pushed his engines to the limit and hit the last rise so fast that he sailed over it into cloudy sky.

The Masks looked up and so did the soldiers. The two sides forgot to shoot at each other.

Rhodes plummeted into the Masks' formation gunning for doomsday. He took down as many Masks as he could until the rest of the battalion caught up.

"Get to the observatory!" he yelled to Blackwell.

Blackwell stood there in stunned shock trying to figure out why Rhodes's voice was coming from this bizarre vehicle.

Rhodes bellowed one more time. "Take cover in the observatory! Get your men off the street!"

Blackwell finally snapped out of his trance and got his men moving again. The battalion's sudden arrival distracted the Masks into going after the battalion instead.

Rhodes fired his lasers, thermal cannons, and Vipers as fast as he could.

He didn't try so hard to shoot them far enough away not to put himself in danger. Neither did the rest of the battalion.

Stray laser fire skittered across his shoulder and then a Viper went off too close to him.

The impact snapped him out of The Grid and he morphed back into his normal shape. He and the battalion were stranded out here alone against the Masks.

All the 765th's life signs showed up inside the observatory. The soldiers aimed their Jackhammers out into the night, but they didn't have to fire with the enemy so far away.

"Fall back!" Rhodes ordered through the interface. "Fall back to the observatory!"

The battalion pivoted and backed away. Rhodes and his people had taken down enough Masks that they no longer had the numbers to put the battalion in danger.

Rhodes kept unloading Vipers by the dozen into the Masks' formation. The Masks tightened together. They really weren't that smart at all.

The battalion carved out another little gap of space between themselves and the Masks. Rhodes fired his Vipers into this space and then Oakes and Dietz added their Vipers to the same defensive line.

Dozens of explosions went off and forced the two groups farther apart. A few more seconds of heavy Viper fire bought the battalion enough breathing room to break away and run for the shelter of the observatory.

Chapter 21

R hodes and his people collapsed behind the wall panting hard. The soldiers of the 765th platoon fired their Jackhammers down the hill to drive the Masks off. The enemy couldn't climb high enough to put the platoon in danger.

Rhodes interfaced with his subordinates. None of them took any damage in that last battle.

"Are you hurt, Captain?" Wild asked him. "Those soldiers' Jackhammers damaged your shoulder implant."

"The damage is superficial," Fisher replied. "All the captain's systems are functioning normally."

"The bastards!" Van husked in her deep undertone. "I'm glad they're dead or we might have to kill them a second time."

"You didn't kill them," Zen pointed out.

"Stop arguing!" Koenig snapped and turned to Rhodes and Fisher in the interface. "I'm afraid the same can't be said for Captain Blackwell. His own men injured him badly."

Rhodes searched the observatory until he found Blackwell. He sat on the ground while one of his medics wrapped gauze around the captain's injured arm.

Rhodes crawled over to him. A waist-high wall surrounded the observatory's outer gallery. The soldiers hunkered behind the wall to cover the surrounding hill down to the Masks' position in the city streets.

The observatory building had been almost completely obliterated in the Masks' bombardment. The building wouldn't offer much shelter, especially since the platoon had to guard the wall non-stop to prevent the Masks from storming the hill.

Rhodes squatted down in front of Blackwell. "How bad is it?"

"Captain...I'm sorry....about...my men...." Blackwell choked.

"Stop it. You didn't do anything."

"I should have....I should have been stricter with them....before.....I should have stopped them....from talking about you....after you came on board...."

Rhodes waved that away. "That's water under the bridge. The question is what to do, now that we have this place. Do you have any orders about our objective in this city?"

"Our orders are to secure the city—or as much of it as possible. Aarrrggghh!" Blackwell roared and bared his teeth at the medic when the guy did something to his arm.

Rhodes watched the medic finish bandaging the rest of Blackwell's arm and most of his shoulder. The fusion burn must have been severe.

"What were you supposed to do after you secured it?" Rhodes asked after the noise settled down.

"Hold it," Blackwell snapped and compressed his lips to hold back another groan of agony. "I guess we're holding it now."

Rhodes chuckled before he thought to stop himself.

"Can you find out what they're doing?" Blackwell asked. "You can see where they are....but some people say you know their thoughts. Some people say you knew ahead of time what they were going to do."

Rhodes stopped himself from telling Blackwell all the gory details of how it all worked out.

Rhodes also didn't tell Blackwell that the Masks had taken steps to make sure Rhodes didn't anticipate their movements again. Blackwell didn't need to know that.

Rhodes surveyed The Grid. The Masks were regrouping on the riverbank. They pulled their numbers back from surrounding the observatory, but that didn't put Rhodes's mind at ease.

The Masks obviously didn't choose to assemble on the riverbank because they were worried about the platoons attacking from the west. He saw that now.

The Masks chose that spot because it gave them a perfect position to launch strikes into any part of the city.

That part of the riverbank let them penetrate in any direction quickly. They didn't have to cover extra territory.

They would be able to get to the observatory just as quickly whenever they wanted to. No one from the platoon would be able to show his face off this hill without running straight into the Masks.

The Masks could send out an overwhelming force to the east or to the south to stop the platoon from retreating to any place the soldiers might be able to evacuate.

The 765th was trapped here. The soldiers were prisoners here as much as if the Masks actually surrounded the observatory itself and held the soldiers at gunpoint.

Rhodes shook himself out of his trance and noticed Blackwell eyeing him more closely. "What is it? What do you see out there?"

Rhodes got to his feet. He didn't have to worry about the Masks shooting him over the wall. The Masks weren't there anymore.

"Stay here," he told Blackwell. "Keep your men alert for any sign of the Masks coming back."

"Where are you going?" Blackwell asked.

"I'm going to see about finding a way out of here—and to see if there's another way to hack the Masks' plans. That will be a lot more help to us than anything we can do with guns."

He walked off, but he headed in a different direction. He didn't return to the battalion. He didn't want any of his subordinates to try to talk him out of what he knew he had to do.

"I'm going to search the observatory and see if I can find anything useful to us," Rhodes told everyone. "I'm breaking the interface for a while. I need to think."

"Are you sure you aren't injured, Captain?" Koenig asked. "You took some heavy hits that time."

"Fisher already said the captain was fine," Zen countered. "We can all read his systems through the interface. He's...."

Rhodes cut the interface. He didn't want to talk about it with anyone. He wished he could stop Fisher from seeing, but that would be taking this too far.

He strode down the wall checking on the soldiers. They started to relax, now that the Masks no longer surrounded the hill.

They didn't lower their Jackhammers, though. The soldiers kept the observatory under constant guard. Rhodes wouldn't have felt comfortable leaving if they didn't.

He went into the destroyed observatory building and found a bunch of dead bodies of people wearing white lab coats.

These must be the astronomers—though Rhodes couldn't fathom why they would wear lab coats.

That didn't concern Rhodes. He kept searching and finally found what he was looking for.

The wreckage of a few more ruined buildings covered the other side of the hill. The wall surrounding the upper levels didn't extend this far.

The soldiers didn't guard this side of the observatory. That would have to change. They couldn't leave this side completely exposed to a Masks assault.

Rhodes climbed down the hill. The street passed in front of the pathway leading up to the observatory.

The remains of an intense battle lay all over this street. Dead Legion soldiers, crashed vehicles, and the torn remnants of destroyed Masks lay jumbled together in heaps all over the street.

Rhodes hunted in the ruins until he found a Mask torn apart by seeker missiles. Its body had been completely obliterated.

Only its head, neck, and one shoulder remained intact. Wires and broken rods hung from its chest, shoulder socket, and the lowest part of its neck.

Rhodes picked it up. This was the first time he'd ever touched a Mask in anything other than battle.

Touching it, holding it like this, turning it over in his hands, and studying it felt oddly intimate.

The eye slit no longer glowed with any light coming from under the helmet. The thing was completely devoid of power. It was dead.

It wasn't dead because it had never been alive. It was just offline.

How strange it felt to hold this thing in its utterly vulnerable state. It would have been totally at his mercy if it had still been online.

What would he have done then—torture it?

He didn't come here to torture it. He just wanted information—but how could he get that if it was offline?

He adjusted his hands to clasp either side of the head. He extended his grid lines into the metal housing, jacked into the machine's neural core, and sent a surge of power into it through his fusion generator.

The Mask head switched on immediately. The eye slit started glowing whitish green the way it would if the thing was still fully functional.

The head jerked back and forth and a male voice came from inside the helmet. "I'll meet you....I'll meet you....at the eatery.....tell Ora..... I'm going down the road....tell Ora....tell Ora....tell Ora.....I'll be home late...."

The Mask talked fast and repeated itself every time its head jerked to the side. It was exactly the kind of behavior Rhodes had seen from the SAMs when they malfunctioned.

"What do you know about Ora?" Rhodes demanded.

"Tell Ora....tell Ora....tell Ora....."

"Tell Ora what?" Rhodes heard his voice rising. He might even have shaken the Mask to make it make sense.

"Tell Ora...I'll be home late...I'll meet you...I'll meet you....at the eatery....." The Mask turned its head again and looked straight at Rhodes. "Are you coming with us? Will Thara let you go?"

"Thara....." Rhodes croaked.

"Tell Ora I'll be home late....come and get something to eat......You never come anymore.....Thara has to let you get out sometimes....."

Rhodes opened his mouth to ask again what this machine new about Ora....and Thara....None of this made sense.

It was talking about Stonebridge. This machine was talking about people who lived in Stonebridge.

Rhodes's heart pounded. He had to find out what this thing knew about Stonebridge—and anything else he could find out.

Rhodes extended his grid lines a little deeper into the head and jacked directly into the Mask's neural core. He jolted when a rush of memories flooded into his brain.

He snapped back to Stonebridge, but this wasn't the Stonebridge he remembered. He saw himself moving through the town the way he used to, but at the same time, he saw himself standing outside the observatory in Ypra.

He knew where he was and he knew he wasn't in Stonebridge—and yet he was. He walked through all the memories of his life there—except that they weren't his memories.

He walked into the house he shared with Ora and the children—except that he was one of the children. He was the little boy.

He sat down at the table while his mother served him a bowl of soup. His sister sat opposite him and talked about her activities that day.

The firelight glowed on his mother's skin. Everything looked exactly the same way Rhodes remembered from his time in Stonebridge.

A few minutes later, the father came in, sat down at the table, and the mother served him a bowl of soup, too, before she sat down on the bench next to the boy.

All four of them sat around the table exactly the way Rhodes remembered.

He would never be able to mistake what was missing, though. The four members of that family glanced, gazed, and talked to each other exactly the way Rhodes remembered, but none of those faces or eyes communicated any feeling, intimacy, love, or affection at all.

Rhodes felt nothing for these people. The boy didn't realize he *should* feel anything for them. He didn't know anything different.

Rhodes's outside awareness overlaid a dozen different realities on top of each other even as he saw himself standing outside the observatory.

He went through the whole process as the boy and as the man simultaneously. His awareness overlaid the image of each person as a

Mask in a metal helmet with electronic components instead of organs and mechanical rods for joints.

They went through the motions of eating at the table. The mother put the children to bed and then the mother and father went to bed together.

Rhodes felt nothing for the woman next to him—no desire, no bond, no affection, no admiration, or even any respect.

He accompanied the man across the road to the eatery by the bridge. They sat at the table with their fellow townspeople. They talked and shared the conviviality of being neighbors.

All the same people occupied the places that Rhodes remembered. The man in leather clothes with the knife in his boot sat by the stairs with two scantily clad girls on his knees.

The old man sat smoking a pipe by the fire with his back to the room. The red-haired young man entered with his friends, sat apart, and they talked about their own business.

The same people lived in the same houses all over town. The aging man and his older, grey-haired wife ran the eatery. The woman who lived across the road from the eatery wasn't Thackery, but she looked just like her.

Rhodes's other awareness overlaid a Mask's helmet on each of them. Each person went through the hollow actions playing their part.

The same dull sense of apathy and disconnection poisoned the whole landscape. Each person labored under a heavy weight of hopeless despair that hung over the whole town.

That agony stabbed Rhodes in the heart. It stabbed each person in the heart, but they had no way of finding the one thing they were missing. They couldn't. They were machines.

His awareness expanded—or maybe the Mask whose head he jacked into was already aware of it.

The reality of the city machine overlaid the illusion of Stonebridge. All the banks and banks of millions and billions of Masks he'd seen locked into their conversion stations—they all lived in the Stonebridge landscape.

They spent their stasis there, living their lives and talking to their friends, families, and neighbors. They lived in the most beautiful town in the world.

None of them could enjoy it because nothing bonded them to each other. He felt absolutely nothing when he looked around the table at his wife and children. He felt nothing for the man across the road. He didn't even feel any attachment to Stonebridge itself.

He felt no tactile sensation when he touched anything. His fingers didn't pick up the texture of his walking stick when he went out to herd livestock in the fields. He didn't smell the scent of the wind or feel the sun on his face.

He didn't taste the food he put in his mouth. He went through the actions of putting it in his mouth because the scenario called for that.

He'd been programmed to eat it, but The Grid didn't provide any taste, texture, or even the sensation of him swallowing it or the fullness in his stomach afterward.

Lying down in his bed at night after a long, hard day of work—he felt nothing. Drifting off meant nothing to him and neither did his wife at his side. None of those emotions or sensations existed in this version of Stonebridge.

It became torture to always ache for something he could never have. He searched and searched, but the part of his awareness that lived as a Mask didn't even understand what was missing.

All those billions of Masks went through the charade of human life, but with that one crucial element missing from their existence. They all knew something was missing—something important.

Only Rhodes understood that—the real Rhodes standing outside the observatory.

Mask technicians, doctors, and officials wandered the halls checking the conversion cycle readings on all those Masks. Rhodes's other awareness overlaid B's face on one of the doctors.

"It's always the same," he murmured to one of his technicians. "We've tried everything."

"Isn't there anything we can do to fix it?" his female technician asked. "This can't go on. We can't live like this."

"We just have to keep searching," B replied. "We have to find a solution. It's the only way. We should capture some humans, study them, and figure out how they work. Maybe then we can figure out what's missing from this program."

The hopeless desperation infected everything here, too. This had been going on for years—maybe even decades or centuries. Billions of Masks had been living this way all this time.

The misery coming from all those people living empty, meaningless, pleasureless lives revolted Rhodes. He tried to take his hands off the Mask head, but he couldn't unwind his grid lines fast enough.

He scrambled to get away from that feeling, but it was too late. It crept into his heart and chilled him to the bone. These people....they couldn't be living like that.

They were people—inside the scenario, at least. The only thing they felt was this tormented ache for something—something missing—something that would make all of this mean something.

He shook his grid lines free and yanked his hands away from the Mask head. It fell on the ground and the light vanished from behind its eye slit. It lost power and became just another piece of trash lying on the pavement.

Rhodes backed away, stumbled over more destroyed Masks, and finally turned to stagger back up the hill.

He couldn't shake that feeling, though. The gnawing agony of all those people....it ate away at him from the inside.

This was so much worse than anything he suffered at Coleridge Station. He could have lived with any of that as long as he still felt ....something.

What kind of life were all those people living where they couldn't feel anything—no tactile sensations, no emotion, no connection? It wasn't a life at all.

It wasn't a life because it was just a computer program. It was a paper cutout of human life with no substance.

They knew, too. That was the most horrible part of the whole disaster.

Each of them knew it wasn't real. Each of them longed for that one undeniable element that would make it all mean something—that would give it substance.

Rhodes blundered back up the hill to the observatory, but he didn't dare to go back to the battalion or even near the soldiers.

He stopped outside the observatory building, let his back fall against the wall, and shut his eyes. His heart pounded and he fought for every breath. He had to compose himself before he saw anyone—anyone human.

All those soldiers—they were all human.

They bled. They felt the ache of comradeship with their fellow soldiers.

They suffered pain when they got injured. They longed for their families and overflowed with joy and painful love when they went home to their wives and children.

Fisher hovered there in front of Rhodes's eyes, but Fisher didn't talk or question Rhodes about what he saw inside that Mask's head.

Did Fisher even understand? Did Fisher experience Stonebridge the way the Masks did?

Now Rhodes understood his own reaction to meeting Fisher as a man. He wasn't real, either. He was a facsimile of the main character's best friend.

The Mask Rhodes jacked into—that man's best friend lived across the road. Every Mask living as a man in Stonebridge had a best friend who lived across the road.

He remembered that picture of his family—the photograph he burned when he first woke up from stasis.

He struggled to remember exactly what his family looked like. Even drawing that picture last night didn't completely bring the memories back.

All those emotions flooded him even now just from thinking about the photograph. He didn't have to be on the same side of the galaxy with them to feel how much he loved them—each one of them.

The sensation of eating food at Koenig's place—of lying in his own bed after a long day of work—of walking through the long, sunbaked grass—of smelling the wind....

Those sensations were the only things that made Stonebridge even marginally appealing. Stonebridge held no temptation for him at all without those.

He and the battalion had spent weeks at Coleridge Station without food or beer or the feeling of clothes on their skin.

Rhodes gasped in ecstasy even now when he remembered gulping that first sip of beer into his mouth. What was Stonebridge without that?

His stomach plummeted all over again when he remembered the banks and banks of conversion stations. Each one held some person suffering the worst torture he could possibly imagine.

He definitely would have ended it if he thought he could never feel anything ever again. He would have no reason to live if he didn't feel some attachment to his family or his comrades or....or anyone.

These poor people didn't even know enough to end it. They knew their lives were hopeless, meaningless wastes, but they didn't know how hopeless their lives were. They couldn't know because they'd never experienced what they were missing.

Dear God, what a nightmare they must have been living all this time! Who in their right mind would want to live like that?

They didn't want to live like that, but they had no choice. They had to keep going. They had no way out.

Chapter 22

R hodes strode back through the observatory to the wall. The soldiers stood upright behind it, paced up and down, and kept the surroundings under constant watch.

Captain Blackwell was back on his feet with his arm in a sling. He went through his men checking on everyone and giving them orders.

He brightened up when Rhodes showed up. "Did you find anything that could help us?"

"No," Rhodes replied and kept on walking. He couldn't explain to anyone what he saw inside that Mask's head.

He returned to the battalion. His people sat on the ground behind the wall waiting for him to show up.

He had forgotten to reestablish the interface when he came back, so he reestablished it now. The others all stared at him. "Is something wrong, Captain?" Rhinehart asked.

Rhodes threw himself on the ground next to Lauer, shut his eyes, and rested his head back against the observatory building. "No," he mumbled. "I'm fine."

They could all see that he wasn't, but he couldn't talk about it—to anyone. He couldn't even talk about it to Fisher even though Fisher saw everything Rhodes saw.

"How long are we supposed to stay here?" Oakes asked.

Rhodes didn't open his eyes. "The platoon has orders to take control of as much of the city as possible and hold it no matter what. I guess that's what we're doing."

"So we just have to stay here forever?" Coulter asked. "What's the point of that?"

Rhodes didn't answer. The unbearable oppressive blanket of bleak desperation didn't go away, now that he was back with normal people.

Every word out of their mouths confirmed that they were still human. They felt.

They went through the same ecstasy just from putting food and drink in their mouths. They still ached for their families even if none of these people could see their families again.

"Captain?" Dietz asked. "Are we making a move against the Masks or what? Or are we just going to stay here until they make a move on us?"

Rhodes opened his eyes and looked around at nothing. What was he supposed to do with this information? Did it change anything?

He got to his feet and walked back down the wall. He used The Grid to survey the whole city.

The Masks along the riverbank stayed where they were, but they weren't the only Masks in this city.

Invasion ships landed to the north and disgorged thousands more Masks. The invasion ships didn't have any problem navigating through the dense atmosphere. The ground troops streamed south clearing everything before them.

He didn't stay jacked into that Mask head long enough to find out why the Masks invaded the Treaty of Aemon Cluster. He could only speculate.

He thought at first that the Masks wanted revenge on the Legion that spawned their original technology.

Now he saw their motivations more clearly. Maybe this obsessive desire to study human beings somehow spun out of control and turned into this invasion.

Maybe some error in their program caused them to equate conquering humans with studying them.

The Masks advanced through the streets and engaged with any Legion platoons they found.

The Masks' numbers gave them an overwhelming advantage. They cleared those platoons easily and continued their inevitable march south.

Most of the Masks still gathered on the west side of the river. They made better progress there.

Their collective understanding of their relative positions gave them a global picture of where every other Mask was in the city.

They didn't need to cross to the east side of the river. They already had plenty of ground troops stationed there.

They didn't come after the observatory to eliminate the 765th...but the Masks would come here eventually. They would raze the whole city and kill every single human being they found.

The Masks advanced closer to the airfield. The platoons couldn't stop the Masks from overrunning that, too.

Dusters descended through the atmosphere by the dozen to evacuate fleeing platoons, but the Dusters couldn't get here fast enough.

They could only carry twenty-five people at a time. It took too long for the Dusters to rendezvous with the Ravagers in the atmosphere, unload their passengers, and then return to the airfield.

Rhodes spun around fast and rushed back to Captain Blackwell. "Get your men ready to move! We're pulling out!"

Blackwell jolted. "What?! We just got here! You were the one who got us to fight our way here!"

"I know!" Rhodes fired back. "Get your men ready to go. We're evacuating back to the airfield—NOW!! Hurry! We don't have much time."

The platoon didn't have any time at all as far as Rhodes knew. It might already be too late.

He interfaced with the battalion and informed them of the same thing. "Get outside the wall and get ready to defend the soldiers' retreat. We can expect the Masks to come at us from the riverbank. That's what they're there for."

Coulter stood up. "At least we don't have to spend the rest of our careers here."

Rhodes didn't remind him how desperate the situation was. The Legion might decide it was too dangerous to send any more Dusters down to this planet.

The brass might decide to abandon the platoons here while the fleet pulled out to the next battle zone.

Rhodes would have liked to hustle the soldiers out of the observatory faster. Even moving at their top speed might be too slow.

Edgecombe's squad climbed over the wall first. "Let's move!" he called to his men. "We gotta make tracks! We're pulling out for the airfield."

Rhodes found himself migrating toward Edgecombe. At least someone here understood the need for urgency.

One glance at The Grid made Rhodes's stomach seize in knots. "The Masks are already moving!" he called to the soldiers. "Get as far south as you can! MOVE!!"

He and the rest of the battalion pivoted to the west side of the platoon. The soldiers started forward heading south under the battalion's protection, but the platoon still didn't move fast enough.

Rhodes would have liked to tell them to run for it. Blackwell's squad took way too long to leave the observatory.

Rhodes went through another pang of uncertainty when he watched the Masks advancing through The Grid. Each of those Masks lived the Stonebridge nightmare every day.

They just wanted answers. They wanted hope. How could Rhodes take that away by killing them?

He would have given anything to somehow transmit what he knew into each of their heads.

He would have willingly volunteered to hook up his brain to their vast banks of conversion stations so they could program all their people with the emotions, sensations, and connections that would give them peace.

It wouldn't work. He already knew that. He and the battalion had already been plugged into The Grid in the Stonebridge landscape.

This was the very reason the Masks captured the battalion in the first place. B told Rhodes so point blank.

The Masks kept the battalion in their lab and hooked Rhodes and his people up to the Masks' program. The Masks did it to try to transfer what the battalion knew to the rest of the Masks living the same program.

It didn't work. It would never work. The Masks didn't possess the hardware to process emotions, human attachments, or biological sensations.

The whole project was all so brutally, excruciatingly hopeless.

The Masks didn't even realize that it was hopeless. Their desperation drove them to endlessly search and search and search for a solution they would never find.

If they understood that they weren't capable of it, they would have given up. They could have disconnected all those Masks from the

Stonebridge landscape. The Masks could have just lived their lives doing whatever it was the Masks did.

This whole war.....it all hinged on this endless obsession with finding the one secret clue that would fix what was wrong with them. The Legion would never be able to give them that. No one could.

Unbearable pity clenched Rhodes's heart watching the Masks come closer through The Grid.

Could he really kill these people? Could he kill that boy—the boy who ached for nothing but his mother's love—a gleam of pride and affection in his father's eyes?

Could Rhodes kill the man—or the woman across the road—or Ora—or any of them?

In that moment, he suffered a rush of such powerful love and compassion for them that it almost knocked him over.

He would do anything to give them peace. He would have paid absolutely any price to make that boy feel the love and warmth that Rhodes felt for his own parents—or to make the man feel the pride and protective affection that Rhodes felt for his own children.

A gunshot snapped him out of his stupor. He spun around to see the Masks attacking Edgecombe's squad.

Rhodes didn't react fast enough. The Stonebridge landscape distracted him for a split second.

Lauer, Oakes, Dietz, and Coulter got to Edgecombe's squad first. The four men used their boosters to fly between the squad and the enemy.

Rhodes raised his arms to aim his weapons at the Masks, but he still hesitated—right up until the moment that the Masks opened fire on the battalion.

A blast erupted from one of the Masks' rifles. The four men combined their fire the way the battalion usually did, but the Masks' numbers made it impossible to hit all of them.

That shot hit Lauer and sent him stumbling backward into Edgecombe's squad. The men caught him and propped Lauer back on his feet. The soldiers pushed him back toward his comrades and he went on fighting.

That one gunshot brought Rhodes back to reality. He spurted his lasers into the Masks from the side. He stood farther north than the others and he made a sizeable dent in the Masks' numbers.

He bought the platoon enough time for Blackwell to catch up with Lohr's squad. The 765th rejoined. They could defend themselves better this way, but the situation didn't improve as the minutes ticked by.

Rhodes rotated into formation with the rest of the battalion. Fuentes, Thackery, and Rhinehart battled their way from even farther north.

The three of them had been defending Blackwell's and Lohr's squads leaving the observatory.

Now the whole party gathered in one clump, but that only slowed them down.

"RUN FOR IT!!" Rhodes bellowed. "MOVE OUT!! RUN FOR THE AIRFIELD!!"

The platoon set off a little faster. Jesus, what would it take to get these men to realize the danger?

They couldn't see what the battalion saw on The Grid. More fleeing soldiers swarmed the airfield trying to escape the Masks' advance. The Dusters couldn't keep up with the evacuation.

The soldiers had to wait there and defend the airfield against the Masks' assault. The Masks didn't take long to figure out that the soldiers were trying to get away.

The Masks targeted the Dusters and blew five of them. The Dusters had to set down in another part of town, which meant the soldiers had to leave the airfield.

A few platoons stayed behind trying to stem the tide of Masks so other platoons could evacuate. Rhodes tried not to watch the catastrophe unfold, but he had to.

Edgecombe urged his men forward faster. His squad picked up speed and then the men broke into a run the way Rhodes told them to.

Edgecombe's squad separated from the others. Edgecombe turned back to see if Blackwell approved.

"KEEP GOING!!" Rhodes ordered. "DON'T STOP FOR ANY-THING!"

Edgecombe turned away. His men started to disappear into the dark city. Separating them from the platoon and the battalion might make Edgecombe's squad more vulnerable to Masks attack.

Rhodes knew it would, but anything would be better than getting stranded on this planet with no way off it. Everything depended on getting to the airfield in time.

Rhodes and the battalion spread out to cover as many of the soldiers as possible. The wounded slowed down Blackwell's and Lohr's squads, but the wounded alone couldn't explain why these men were traveling so slowly.

Rhodes turned back to help them in any way he could, but right then, Edgecombe's squad ran into a Masks ambush. Masks crossed the river from the west side and came at Edgecombe's squad too fast.

Rhodes's first instinct told him to use his boosters to fly there to help defend the squad, but boosters didn't work in this atmosphere.

He altered his grid lines to turn himself into another all-terrain vehicle. "Stay here and defend the platoon!" he told his people. "Get them to the airfield no matter what!"

Chapter 23

R hodes plowed over hills, bounced off the hulks of crashed buildings, and revved his engines closing on Edgecombe's squad.

The soldiers hunkered against a different building unloading their Jackhammers at the enemy. The squad just had to carve out a little circle of breathing space around their position.

Rhodes barreled straight into the Masks shooting everywhere in sight. He broadcast his voice over the noise of gunfire. "Get out of here, Lieutenant! Take your men and run!!"

Edgecombe kept firing for a minute until the Masks turned away to deal with the fighting vehicle in their midst.

Rhodes started out by spraying his lasers everywhere and unloading Vipers as fast as he could shoot them.

He had to keep up a steady barrage of Vipers on more flocks of Masks crossing the river. That was the only way to stop them from overrunning the squad.

In the end, he fired his thermal cannon into the Masks closest to them. They started to melt into puddles around his tires.

He winced when he saw their bodies crumple and smear out of shape. Was he really killing these people? Was he really robbing them of their only hope that their lives might get better?

Their lives would never get better. He already knew that, but he still hated to put them in their graves. What if.....What if somewhere, someday, someone found a solution? What if Rhodes was the one who stopped that from happening even for one of them?

He found himself looking into their eye slits even as their faces melted right in front of him.

Did they recognize him? Did they see that he was the one killing them?

Did they recognize that he might have been their friend, their neighbor, or even a member of their own family?

They were his family. Each of them was the boy or the father or the best friend living in the house across the road. Each of them was Ora or Wild or Thackery. How could he be the one killing them?

Thinking that almost made him stop shooting—almost. Another blast of fusion fire hit the building above Lieutenant Edgecombe's head. Mortar chips peppered him in the face and he yelled out in alarm.

Every assault against the platoon spurred Rhodes to keep shooting, but the guilt didn't fade. He was the one killing these people. He was the one snatching away their last hope.

They still had a chance as long as even one of them remained alive. That must be why they stayed locked into the Stonebridge world all these years. They just kept hoping....and praying....and wishing....and longing....

Rhodes had to stop thinking like that. He motored south to keep pace with Edgecombe's squad and hold the Masks off.

Edgecombe turned west and headed for the airfield. The rest of the platoon fell farther behind.

Rhodes changed back into a person for part of the journey. He rejoined the squad to urge them all to run faster. "Get to the airfield and get on board the Dusters! Evacuate the planet immediately! Don't wait for Blackwell and the others! That's an order, Lieutenant!"

"Yes, Sir!" Edgecombe called back. He didn't need any extra encouragement.

Rhodes faced outward to confront the Masks just as a Duster broke through the heavy atmosphere. It was nowhere near the airfield.

That Duster came in too far east, but that worked in the platoon's favor. The Duster diverted and lowered into the middle of the street where the platoon could get to it.

Edgecombe yelled to his men and they all charged for the Duster. The Masks tried to intercept, but Rhodes stood his ground until all the men got on board.

The Masks surrounded him on all sides falling to every weapon he could lay into them. He couldn't rest, not even when the Duster took off into the clouds with Edgecombe's squad on board.

Rhodes changed back into a vehicle, bumped over dozens of Masks, and burned rubber heading northeast to meet up with the rest of the platoon.

The battalion surrounded the fleeing soldiers and defended the platoon's retreat against a growing onslaught of Masks. The platoon couldn't last much longer.

More Dusters lowered through the cloud. They no longer even tried to land at the airfield.

They landed in the outlying areas where the platoons could get on board more easily. Five Dusters descended behind the 765th.

Battalion 1 surrounded the platoon in a half-circle of guns. The Masks kept making rush after rush to cut the platoon down.

Rhodes spun his wheels in mountains of debris, blasted over hilltops, and soared down to land in the middle of all those Masks.

Their obsession with getting near anything human drove them toward the platoon no matter what. They barely noticed Rhodes, the battalion, or their weapons.

Even their mindless drive to overtake the soldiers stabbed Rhodes in the heart. He couldn't hate them. He couldn't hate anyone suffering the tortures they were going through—all of them.

His mind staggered at the sheer scale of misery infecting their entire race. Every single one of them buckled under the load. That anguish would have driven any normal human being to suicide.

They would have killed themselves en masse long ago if they'd only been human enough to realize how bad their lives were.

That was the problem. They weren't human enough to realize it. That was the double bind that made their existence such a colossal tragedy.

Rhodes saw all of that even as he cut them to pieces with his weapons. He felt it even more acutely every time one of the Masks fell under his guns.

Three Dusters touched down. Lohr's squad broke away and then Blackwell's did the same thing.

The soldiers jammed inside, the doors slammed shut, and all three Dusters lifted off.

The battalion backed off just a little as two more Dusters dropped toward the street. Rhodes took a few more steps away and herded his people, stragglers, and wounded toward the ships.

Everyone piled on board. Rhodes was the last person left on the ground. "Come on, Captain!" Dietz yelled. "Come on!"

Rhodes cast one last pathetic glance at the Masks. They still clambered over their fallen comrades trying to get near the battalion.

The Masks raised their fusion rifles to fire at the Dusters. Rhinehart and Oakes released Vipers from the Duster's back end to pulverize the Masks.

The Vipers leveled as many of them as possible to clear a space for the Duster to lift off.

Rhodes only looked for a split second before he leapt on board. The doors slammed in front of his face and he lost sight of the Masks, but they were still out there coming toward the battalion in a steady, unwavering march.

Even raising their rifles to shoot at him looked like the Masks were stretching out their arms to him for help. It looked like the desperate plea of a dying man begging for someone to throw him a lifeline.

He couldn't get that image out of his mind, not even when the doors blocked his view of the city flooded with thousands or even millions of Masks.

Each of them was his friend, his loved one, his heart's companion. How could he abandon them?

He had no choice but to keep killing them. The outside awareness that watched all this from the hillside near the observatory—that part of him understood this.

He was a soldier in the Aemon Legion. His duty demanded that he fight and kill the enemies of the Treaty of Aemon Cluster.

The battalion, wounded, and the last soldiers crowded inside the Duster. Rhodes got jammed against the wall, but he wanted to be there.

He didn't want anyone to see him collapse shaking against the wall and shut his eyes. He fought back an overwhelming desire to break down completely.

Those memories wouldn't stop. They plagued him no matter how far away he got from the Masks.

His subordinates and their SAMs watched him in concern. That was nothing compared to the way Fisher was looking at him. How could he ever explain any of this to them? He couldn't even explain it to himself.

He kept silent all the way back to the *Rapho*. The rest of the battalion could see he wasn't injured.

They could also see through the interface whatever emotional or stress response he was having to this....whatever it was.

Captain Blackwell met the battalion in the landing bay. Rhodes supervised the wounded going to the infirmary and the soldiers returned to the 765th.

He avoided anyone from the 765th who tried to thank him, especially Lieutenant Edgecombe and his men.

Rhodes felt himself shaking by the time the whole process came to an end. He really needed to go into a conversion cycle, but the *Rapho* didn't have any capsules on board or even any standing stations.

The rest of the battalion held up better than he did. He stumbled through the group making sure they were all okay.

Lauer had superficial damage to his chest implant from the Masks' rifle fire. No one in the battalion besides Rhodes appeared to be suffering from the need to go through a conversion cycle.

Just when he thought he might lose his mind completely, he received an order to go to the bridge where he met up with *Rapho* Captain Miguel Ortego.

Captain Ortega informed Rhodes that the *Rapho* was on course to rendezvous with the *Ero*. Ortega informed Rhodes that he was ordered to report to the inquiry panel as soon as humanly possible.

Rhodes only nodded, left the bridge as politely as he could, and cut the interface so he could walk around the *Rapho* in solitude.

He made sure to tell the rest of the battalion before he broke the interface, but they could all see something bothering him.

Walking around by himself didn't help much. Fisher kept staring at Rhodes with that all-knowing gaze that made Fisher's presence so maddening.

Rhodes didn't mind Fisher staring at him—or Rhodes wouldn't have minded Fisher staring at him.

These memories from Stonebridge wouldn't leave Rhodes alone. It wasn't even the memories that bothered him so much.

The feelings behind them made him want to die. All those people wanted to die. That was the worst part. They all wanted to destroy themselves to end their own misery.

They couldn't even do that because, like everything else, they didn't understand that destroying themselves would end their misery. Their programming didn't include killing themselves.

Rhodes had to stop more than once, prop his arm against the ship's corridor walls, shut his eyes, and catch his breath.

Every breath hurt. Everything hurt. Just existing hurt with this pain stabbing him in the guts. How was he supposed to live like this? How *could* he live with this? How could anybody?

He shared that Mask's thoughts and feelings. He was that Mask. He was all of them at all times and all places. He was all of them simultaneously.

The journey to rendezvous with the *Ero* never took so long. Every minute tormented Rhodes beyond all endurance.

He eventually went back to the battalion, but he didn't talk to anyone. He just stood near them and waited for the hammer to come down.

He couldn't fathom what the inquiry panel wanted to talk to him about. He sure as hell hoped it didn't have anything to do with this.

The Grid fed all his sensations, actions, and experiences back to the Legion database. Was anyone watching when he accessed that Mask's memories?

Did anyone on the *Ero* understand what it meant? How much of the Mask's emotions—or lack of emotion—translated through The Grid?

Dr. Osborne or Captain Lake or Colonel Kraft might just have seen another replay of Stonebridge. They might not have felt what Rhodes felt.

The two ships rendezvoused and the battalion transferred back to *Ero*. Rhodes took Lauer to Osborne's lab to get Lauer's chest implants repaired. Then Rhodes dragged his feet upstairs to meet the panel.

He walked into the conference room....and stopped. Admiral Stabler was the only person in here.

Admiral Stabler turned away from the window to face Rhodes. "Come on in, Captain. Welcome back."

Rhodes glanced around at nothing. "Sir? My orders were to meet the panel."

"You're looking at it, son." The old man's eyebrows wiggled when he smiled. All the deep lines on his face etched even deeper into his papery skin. "You're only meeting me today."

"Um....why am I meeting you?"

"Come over here and talk to me." Admiral Stabler turned toward the window and looked out it. The *Rapho* hovered off the Ero's bow.

Rhodes crossed the room to stand at the old man's side, but Rhodes studied the admiral, not the view. "What did you want to see me about, Sir?"

"Some of the soldiers are reporting that you hesitated to attack the Masks to defend the platoon," Admiral Stabler asked.

Rhodes didn't turn around. "I wouldn't contradict them if that's what they're saying."

"Is it true? Did you hesitate?"

Rhodes shrugged. "I guess I did."

"The panel would like to once again express its gratitude to you for your actions during that battle. You're proving an asset to the Legion."

Rhodes only mumbled, "Yes, Sir."

"Was there some reason you hesitated to engage with the Masks?" Admiral Stabler asked. "Did the attachment you developed during your captivity cause you to hesitate?"

"No, Sir," Rhodes replied. "It had nothing to do with my captivity."

"I'd like to think you could tell me if you had a problem we needed to resolve. One of your men got injured because you hesitated."

"He didn't get injured, Sir."

"You know what I mean. If you're suffering from any malfunctio n....."

"I'm not suffering from any malfunction, Sir."

Admiral Stabler frowned at him. Rhodes barely knew this guy at all, but Admiral Stabler had a way of looking straight through Rhodes. "What's bothering you, then?"

Rhodes looked away. "Nothing, Sir."

Admiral Stabler made a few more noises about the war and the battalion and the whole Drion disaster—as if any encounter with the Masks could be anything else.

He eventually dismissed Rhodes back to the capsule hold. Everyone jumped when Rhodes returned. He didn't remember until right then that he still hadn't reestablished the interface with the rest of the battalion.

He didn't do it now, either. He went straight to his capsule, locked himself in, and shut his eyes.

Fisher finally broke the silence between them. "Are you going to talk to me now?"

"I guess I have to," Rhodes husked.

"You don't have to if you don't want to. I suppose we can just keep giving each other the silent treatment the way Van and Fuentes do."

"No, I need to talk to someone. I just....I don't know what to say. I can't imagine a fate worse than what the Masks are going through. I can't imagine anything worse than not feeling those feelings of intimacy and connection. I can't help feeling the agony of what it must be like to want something so badly—to yearn for something they can never have."

"Do you feel that way about Ora and your family in Stonebridge?"

"Not for them. I feel it for my original family—my real family. That feeling of sitting around the table with them—the feeling like I belong to them and they belong to me—I don't know if I'll ever feel that way again about anyone, but at least I remember it. That's why I hated the Stonebridge landscape so much. It was fake. It was an insult to the way I feel about real people and real events. The Masks manipulated me into feeling that way when it wasn't real."

"It's interesting," Fisher murmured. "All this time, we've been wondering why the Masks do what they do. Now we know....and yet it might almost be better not to know. Sympathizing with them won't make it any easier to fight them."

Rhodes blurted out the question that had been gnawing at him all day. "Is it like this for you and the other SAMs? Do you feel any loss or that something is missing because you aren't human?"

"I don't feel anything," Fisher replied. "I don't miss anything about being human. I never have been human. I suppose I never had any desire to be anything other than what I am. I don't long for something

I can never have. This is what I am. I'm satisfied with that even if I'm not human."

"Did you envy anything about the Fisher that lives in Stonebridge?" Rhodes asked. "He was such a vibrant, human version of you."

"He wasn't me. The Masks used his face to try to manipulate you into confiding in him and trusting him the way you confide and trust in me."

"I know. I just wondered.....You used that body to communicate with me....a few times....."

"I did it because I thought it would help get you out. I never lived in Stonebridge."

"Not at all? Not even for a few minutes?"

"Not the way you did. It didn't tempt me the way it tempted you. It couldn't since I don't experience the sensations and emotions that made it so tempting. It was more a veil to confuse us and stop us from thinking about our problems."

Rhodes looked away. "All those people...." His voice failed him again. "I just can't wrap my head around all those people suffering like that."

"Do you still doubt your humanity? Did seeing the Masks as similar to you make you doubt that you're fully human?"

"No, not at all—not anymore. I know I'm human because I can still feel that. I always will be human as long as I can feel that way about other people, even people that are far away. The Masks can't."

"It's interesting," Fisher murmured again. "I never thought we'd discover anything like this about the Masks."

"Maybe they're human because they want it," Rhodes suggested. "Maybe that's what makes them human. They realize that this is what they need and they're searching for it. Maybe that's all it takes for anyone to be human."

"If that's true, will you still kill the Masks? What happened to your determination to wipe out their entire race in revenge for what they did to you?"

"I'll still wipe them all out, but not in revenge. I'll kill every last one of them. I have to. It's the only way to put them out of their misery."

Chapter 24

R hodes woke up from his conversion cycle.....and immediately remembered every detail of his contact with the Masks during the battle on Drion.

Going through a conversion cycle rested him and made him more relaxed. He didn't feel as shaky as he did when he came back from the planet.

The conversion cycle didn't take the memories away—or the feelings. The same oppressive anguish, yearning, and obsessive need to find something hounded him everywhere he went.

He would have spent the rest of his life searching for it except that he already had it. His rational awareness separated him from the Masks' misery.

That tiny sliver of objective distance was the only thing keeping Rhodes sane right now.

He woke up later than his subordinates. He must have needed a longer conversion cycle than they did, which meant his system really did need the extra time to regulate itself.

His subordinates sat around the table talking the way they usually did. He interfaced with them the minute he sat up. He had no more reason to hold them at a distance.

Not interfacing with them would have been rude. He'd already done that too much yesterday. He owed these people better than that.

He stared at his feet for a while and ran his fingers through his hair, but he didn't stay like that for long.

Staring at his feet only made him think about Stonebridge and the Masks and... everything.

He got up, crossed to the table, and sat down on the end of the bench next to Dietz.

"How you doing, Captain?" Lauer growled.

"I'm okay, I guess." Rhodes rubbed his face. "Does any of you still feel attached to the Masks—or Stonebridge or any other part of it?"

A few people shifted in their seats.

"I guess I do," Fuentes murmured. "I mean....I guess I do a lot—but we're here now. We aren't with the Masks and we won't ever be with the Masks again. I guess wanting to go back to them was really just wanting to feel the way I felt in Stonebridge. I don't really want to fight the Legion or help the Masks. I just want to feel that way again. I mean...." He glanced around the hold and winced. "When could I ever feel that way again *here?* All of that is gone for me here."

"Anybody else?" Rhodes scanned the faces at the table. "Does anyone feel any lingering sense that the Masks might be our people?" He turned to the SAMs. "Do any of you?"

"It would be nice to know that we had a people," Dash pointed out. "It would be nice if we had an entire race of SAMs out there acting autonomously with independent bodies instead of just being computer programs in someone else's head."

"Wait a minute," Rhinehart snapped. "*You* don't feel any lingering loyalty to the Masks, do you, Sir? You've been the staunchest of all of us through this whole campaign!"

"I wouldn't go that far," Rhodes replied. "Dietz held up better than I did."

"But.....you can't start questioning now!" Rhinehart exclaimed. "We're free from the Masks right now because of you."

"We're free because of all of us," Rhodes pointed out. "None of us could have gotten out alone."

Rhinehart gaped at him in slack-jawed horror. "Tell me you aren't questioning whether to kill the Masks. Please...just tell me you still want to kill them."

Rhodes had to look down at the table. "Yes, I do."

"What happened to you on Drion?" Coulter asked. "You changed. You were so certain before."

"I wish I could explain it to you," Rhodes murmured. "I really wish I could."

"What's stopping you?" Thackery asked.

Rhodes might have tried if anyone asked besides her. Her voice broke something in him. He couldn't tell her. He wasn't sure who at this table he could tell—so he would tell no one.

His silence stretched long enough that the others started talking about something else. He stayed seated at the table listening to them shoot the breeze.

An hour into their conversation, Rhinehart got the idea to raid the ship for a deck of cards and a stack of chips so they could play Slaughter Power. It was better than nothing.

He left the hold for a while, came back with the goods, and everyone started playing—or rather, Rhinehart, Oakes, Coulter, and Thackery played.

Lauer kept insisting that he was doing the world a favor by sitting out because he was too skilled to play against such amateurs. Fuentes watched without playing.

The players didn't seem too concerned about Rhodes sitting there watching and listening even though he didn't say anything to join their conversation.

An hour into the game, he got another summons to present himself to the inquiry panel. He had too much on his mind even to care what the hell they wanted.

He left the interface open this time. He got another surprise when he walked into the conference room and found everyone standing around the table instead of sitting there facing him.

The whole panel was there, including Colonel Kraft and everyone from the Battalion 1 governing body. Drs. Osborne and Trudeau were there, too.

Rhodes stiffened when they all looked up at him, but they still didn't confront him. They bent over a bunch of charts of the Treaty of Aemon Cluster displayed on computer terminals.

"Come on in, Captain," Admiral Stabler called again. "We've been anxious to hear your opinion on this."

Rhodes inched toward the table. Colonel Neff and Captain Lake both stepped aside to make room for Rhodes to join the group.

"We're planning a big push campaign and hopefully wipe out all the Masks," General Hyde explained and pointed to a solar system on one side of the chart.

"The Regos solar system is closer to Preinea and the inner planets than any of us feels comfortable with, but it's the best place where we can make a stand and hopefully finish off the Masks," Colonel Volk explained. "We can't afford to let them rampage through the Fringes the way they have been. We need to find a way to stop them."

"We'll move our remaining resources into the system over the next three weeks," Admiral Stabler went on. "We'll pull all our ships away from the parts of the Cluster where we only anticipated other alien invasions. This is more important."

"The Masks just started on the Horus system," Colonel Volk added. "Going off the time frame the Masks have been using to conquer every other system in their path, we estimate it should take them four weeks to leave the Horus system and make the jump to Regos. Our fleet will make a stand at the outer planets to stop the invasion ships from entering the solar system. Our force should be able to stop the Masks' invasion there—or on one of the planets if we absolutely have to."

A few people at the table glanced in Rhodes's direction. He didn't get involved in the conversation.

"We've also located what we think is the city machine you witnessed during your captivity, Captain," Captain Lake announced. "One of the Masks' ships has been traveling behind the others. It's bigger than all the others and it's comprised entirely of computer components. It doesn't seem to be made of anything else. This ship stays out of the battle zone and lets the other invasion ships take the gunfire."

He brought up a schematic of a ship in question on the controls. He rotated the display in front of the whole panel.

The Legion was already putting this plan into action, landing platoons on the Regos system's outer planets, and stationing ranks of Ravagers to block the Masks from entering the solar system at all.

Everyone looked up at Rhodes. "Do you have any recommendation for this campaign, Captain?" General Hyde asked.

"No, Ma'am," Rhodes replied.

"You know the Masks even better than the platoons that have gone into combat against them," Colonel Volk. "You've proven your loyalty to the Legion too many times for us to question you...."

"What the colonel is too polite to say," Captain Lake interrupted, "is that you keeping silent makes it look suspicious—like maybe you don't want to fight the Masks."

"That isn't what I was too polite to say," Colonel Volk countered. "We all know Rhodes is perfectly willing to fight the Masks. He's fought the Masks more times than everyone in this room put together."

"I know that," Captain Lake snapped. "I'm saying him keeping quiet doesn't look good when he might know something that could help us win this war."

"I don't know anything that could help win the war, Sir," Rhodes replied. "I would tell you if I did."

Everyone turned around to face him. "We would really appreciate your recommendation, Captain," General Hyde insisted. "That's why we asked you to come and see us. We'd like you to help us coordinate this campaign so it works out in our favor."

"I can't do that, Ma'am," Rhodes replied. "I really wish I could."

"You can't or you won't?" Lake countered. "Are you keeping silent because you know something that could actually work to wipe out the Masks? Is that why you're keeping it to yourself—because it would be too devastating to them? Are you worried about causing an entire race to go extinct?"

"I don't know anything that could do all that," Rhodes repeated. "I don't know how else to explain it to you."

"Then give us your opinion on our proposed strategy," Admiral Stabler urged. "Give us your opinion on any of it. If we can stop them here, we could save millions of lives on the inner planets."

Rhodes hesitated to say anything, but it didn't look like these people were going to let him leave the room without saying something.

"If you really want to hear my opinion, Sir, I don't think you'll be able to stop them," Rhodes replied. "With this strategy or any other."

Colonel Volk gasped. A few other people opened their mouths in shock. "Not at all?!" General Hyde asked. "What makes you say that? There must be a way."

"I don't think so, Ma'am. I've thought about it a lot and I honestly don't see a way."

"That's impossible!" Colonel Volk exclaimed. "There's always a way."

"I doubt that, Sir," Rhodes replied. "The Masks have millions of individuals in stasis—maybe billions of individuals. You saw all that in The Grid feed from my experience inside the city machine. The Masks can release these individuals on us whenever they want to. I don't see that we have a force anywhere in the whole Cluster—or even a combined force all over the Cluster—that can stand up to these numbers."

"Then there must be a way to assault the city machine...." Captain Lake began.

"I don't see how you can do that when you can't even get past the invasion ships," Rhodes pointed out. "We haven't been able to make a dent in the invasion ships. The Masks will be even more defensive about stopping us from going near the city machine."

"There must be a way to defeat them," Colonel Volk repeated. "You interfaced with the Masks on Drion. Did you see or hear anything that might help us?"

"No, Sir. Like I said, I would already have told you if I did. I didn't see or hear anything that I didn't already know—nothing strategic, at least. If you know I interfaced with them, you know the only thing I got from them was another view of the Stonebridge landscape."

Admiral Stabler frowned and rubbed his chin. "We saw that, but we didn't think it could be as hopeless as that."

"I wish I could tell you something else, Sir," Rhodes replied. "I'm as anxious to make them all go extinct as you are. I would do anything to make it happen."

"If you don't have anything more to add, Captain, we'll go ahead with this campaign as planned," General Hyde told him. "This is our best chance to stop the Masks. If it doesn't work, then you'll be proven right, but I sure hope you're wrong."

"So do I, Ma'am," Rhodes replied.

"I trust you'll inform us if you gain any other information."

"Yes, Ma'am. You'll be the first to know if I come up with anything."

Chapter 25

B attalion 1 rejoined the 765th on board the *Rapho*. The battalion had been in stasis for an undisclosed amount of time while the Aemon Legion fleet fought a losing air battle against the Masks' invasion force.

Rhodes didn't keep track of too many of the details. He only knew that he and the battalion were now about to deploy on the planet Sarus, the outermost planet in the Regos system.

Rhodes knew Sarus well. It wasn't on the Fringes like most of the planets where the Legion had spent so much of the last several years fighting the Emal.

The Masks covered all that territory in no time. They'd already devastated the Horus system—the last Fringe system.

Now they were starting to carve their way into the central band of Treaty of Aemon Cluster solar systems.

The Masks kept migrating closer to Preinea. Rhodes no longer doubted that the Masks wanted the home planet itself. It represented the very pinnacle of all things human. Of course the Masks wanted Preinea.

The Masks hadn't made landfall on Sarus yet. The Legion had spent the entirety of the air war landing supplies, weapons, and other infrastructure on the planet in preparation to defend the planet against the Masks.

The air battle slowed the Masks down and bought the Legion time to fortify the planet and evacuate some of the population, but not all.

The Legion was far better prepared to defend this planet than the Legion ever had been before, but Rhodes still didn't hold out much hope of this working.

Seventeen platoons of Legion soldiers were already stationed on the planet. The 765th would be one of the last platoons onto the ground.

The battalion gathered in the landing bay, but no one could move around. Hundreds of soldiers from a dozen platoons all waited for the *Ero* to land so the platoons could deploy.

"What's Sarus like, Sir?" Fuentes asked.

"It's really nice," Rhinehart told him. "It's green, temperate, and has a lot of really nice forests, oceans, and an oxygen atmosphere. It's one of the nicest planets in the Cluster."

"But not for much longer," Oakes remarked. "It also has a big population. It's a perfect target for the Masks."

"At least we'll be able to use boosters here," Lauer muttered. "We won't be stranded like we were on Drion."

"Why doesn't the Legion evacuate the population faster?" Thackery asked. "Why do they take so long to get the civilians out of harm's way?"

"Evacuating the population isn't as easy as it sounds," Rhodes replied. "First of all, most of the Ravagers are already tied up fighting the war. The Legion can only spare so many to carry civilians around."

"Then there's the problem of where to send the evacuees," Oakes added. "Not everyone in the Cluster is too happy about a few million evacuees landing on their doorsteps with nothing but the clothes on their backs."

"Sometimes the population even resists evacuation," Lauer finished. "Sometimes people say there really isn't any danger and they decide they want to stay home and wait it out. They blind themselves to the danger because they don't want to uproot their whole lives."

Thackery rubbed her forehead. "Wow. That's complicated."

"And then there are those on the inquiry panel or whoever is making decisions about how to fight this war," Rhodes added. "Maybe some of them actually believed they'd be able to stop the Masks from entering the solar system. Maybe certain people didn't want to believe they had to evacuate at all."

"Who thought that?" Dietz asked.

"I don't want to name any names," Rhodes replied. "In fact, I don't know of anyone who did think that. I'm just saying, if they did, it would slow the evacuation down even more by not diverting Ravagers to the evacuation. How the hell should I know what they're thinking?"

"If we can save at least part of Sarus, it will be worth it, though, right?" Coulter asked. "We don't want a planet as nice as that to go down in flames."

"Maybe this campaign will actually work," Thackery agreed. "This many platoons in one place are bound to make a difference, don't you think, Captain?"

Rhodes shrugged. "It's a nice idea, anyway."

Coulter gasped. "You don't think it will work?! You actually think the Masks will take Sarus?!"

"You didn't see the city machine the way I did. This many platoons don't stand a chance against the Masks."

"So....why are we going down to fight them?" Thackery asked. "Why are we fighting a battle we can't win?"

"Would you rather give up?" Rhodes asked. "I wouldn't."

A few soldiers standing nearby turned around. Rhodes didn't know them. He didn't even know which platoon they belonged to. "You don't think we can win this war?" a corporal asked. His nametag read, *Greer.* "You don't even think we can save Sarus?"

Rhodes tried to shrug it away again, but he wound up squirming. "I'm just saying what I saw. The Masks have a lot more people than we do—people they can send out to attack us. They don't have women and children and hospital patients and old people who can barely walk. Every single one of their people can fight. We don't have that."

A different lieutenant took a step toward Rhodes. His nametag read, *Mickelson.* "If you know that, why aren't you doing more to stop this campaign?"

"I don't have anything to do with this campaign, Lieutenant," Rhodes replied. "I go where I'm ordered to go the same as you fellas."

The soldiers stared at him for a minute and then turned away muttering to each other. Rhodes put them out of his mind. He had enough to worry about.

The *Ero* entered the Sarus atmosphere and he used The Grid to scan the landscape, but it didn't tell him anything. The Masks weren't even on the planet yet.

The Legion had set up bases, supply depots, airfields, hospitals, and administrative blocks on every continent. No one knew where the Masks would make landfall. The Legion wanted to cover every contingency.

"So what's the plan, Sir?" Dietz asked.

"Fight the Masks, bro," Rhinehart interrupted. "What's so complicated about that?"

"I mean are we pulling any flanking maneuvers or anything like that—anything like what we did all the other times."

"How can we know that when we don't know where the Masks are or what they're doing?" Lauer asked.

"So....we just have to wait and see?" Fuentes made a face. "It isn't a very good strategy, is it?"

"What do you suggest?" Oakes asked. "What would be your strategy if the brass put you in charge?"

Rhinehart burst out laughing and slammed Fuentes on the shoulder hard enough almost to buckle his knees. "I'm sure you could do a better job than these dopes."

"I'd go on the offensive," Fuentes replied. "Sitting around waiting for the Masks to wipe their asses with us is for the birds."

"That's what I'm talking about," Lauer added. "Now you're thinking like a general."

"What about it, Sir?" Dietz asked. "Would you tell the brass about Rudy's idea?"

Rhodes shuffled his feet. "I'll mention you said that, but I'm pretty sure they already thought of it."

"Then why aren't they doing it?" Thackery asked.

"They want to assault the city machine and the Legion can't even get near it. The Masks are too smart to bring it into the battle zone, so we can't assault it. That's why we're always on the defensive."

"I don't believe it," Fuentes muttered. "I bet we could find a way to take it on the offensive if we really tried."

"You spend all that time on the terminal," Rhodes told him. "You study the war and let me know when you come up with something."

Oakes started to say, "Just make sure you take into account the...."

A bunch of other soldiers interrupted the conversation by coming over to the battalion just then. Two of these soldiers were Corporal Greer and Lieutenant Mickelson from earlier.

Almost everyone else in the group belonged to Lieutenant Lohr's squad from the 765th platoon. Lohr himself came with them.

"Mickelson here says you said we can't win this campaign," Lohr told Rhodes. "Is that true?"

"I guess everyone is entitled to their own opinion," Rhodes replied. "I'm as much an armchair general as Corporal Fuentes here."

"But you know something," Lohr insisted. "You know more about the Masks than any of us. You would know if we absolutely can't win."

"I only know what I saw," Rhodes replied. "I said the Masks have numbers on their side—but that's nothing you fellas didn't already know."

"Can't you stop the campaign?" Mickelson asked. "What's the point of us fighting if we're just gonna get slaughtered like always?"

"How do you say I should stop the campaign?" Rhodes asked. "I already told the brass everything I know and everything I think. They're the ones who decided to go ahead with this campaign regardless. If you have a problem, you take it up with them."

"Come on, man!" Lohr exclaimed. "You can't let us go to our deaths."

"I'm not letting you go anywhere, Lieutenant," Rhodes countered. "I'm going into the same battle with you. If someone is going to their deaths, we are."

"We don't have to go into battle," Greer interjected. "We could just refuse to fight the war."

"And hand over Sarus on a silver platter for the Masks to destroy it?" Rhodes asked. "I'm going in no matter what. I really don't care what you and yours do. I won't leave humanity to perish—not while I have breath in my body to do something about it. That's exactly what will happen if the Masks win—and they will definitely win if no one fights them."

Mickelson frowned. "I don't like it. The brass just keeps throwing guys to slaughter. They don't give a shit about us."

"It's like I just told Fuentes here," Rhodes replied. "You come up with some better plan. Then we'll all be Johnny-on-the-spot to carry it out. Until then, you better go into battle and do your best to defeat the enemy. That's what I'm doing. That's what we're all doing. I don't see how you have a choice but to do the same thing."

Lohr and some of his subordinates exchanged glances. Then Lohr and Mickelson exchanged glances. Greer hardened his features in stern determination, but he didn't actually glare at Rhodes.

The group finally took themselves off to a different side of the landing bay. "Boneheads," Rhinehart muttered. "Who the hell do they think they are? They think they're too good to fight the damn war!"

"I should have kept my mouth shut," Rhodes murmured. "The walls have ears."

"It isn't the walls," Wild growled. "They were standing right next to you."

"Everyone has a right to their own opinion like you said," Fisher interjected. "No one would have paid any attention if some grunt soldier said what you said. They latched onto it because it came from you."

"All the more reason to keep my opinions to myself."

"Is this going to cause us problems—if part of the platoon doesn't want to fight the battle?" Dash asked.

"That's their business," Rhodes replied. "We already know what we have to do."

"How can they not fight the battle?" Murphy asked. "They're minutes away from deploying."

Almost at the moment when the words came out of his mouth, the order came through to deploy.

The landing bay disintegrated into everyone crowding and shoving to get into the right position with their own platoons and squads to get ready to deploy.

Rhodes and Battalion 1 got caught in the confusion. No one could hear themselves think.

The *Ero* touched down at one of the Legion's new bases on Sarus's Eulara continent.

Another jumble of confusion followed with all the platoons leaving the ship. The captains and lieutenants reported to the command dome to get their orders.

Then the platoons assembled at the airfield to meet Ravagers and Dusters that would take the soldiers to meet the enemy wherever and whenever the Masks decided to make landfall.

Rhodes got a bad feeling when Battalion 1 got assigned to a different Ravager. He'd developed a dread of getting separated from the *Ero* in case the battalion needed to go through conversion cycles.

He resigned himself to the inevitable. One of these times, he wouldn't be able to get back to the *Ero* at all. Then he would just have to deal with it.

The battalion showed up at the right spot and found the same platoons waiting for the same Ravager. Everyone stood around talking here the same way they'd been talking in the *Ero's* landing bay.

"We could be waiting for days for the enemy to show up," Edgecombe pointed out. "They might land on a completely different planet or the Legion could engage them in another air assault. We might not get to fight the Masks at all."

"Keep dreaming," Captain Blackwell told him. "We'll fight them one way or another, either here or on another planet."

Right then, the Ravager in question touched down across the airfield. A certain Captain Bowen came out of the landing bay and waved at everyone. "765th Platoon, 423rd, 647th, and Battalion 1, you're clear to board."

"It looks like we're going," Rhinehart remarked. "The Masks must be making landfall somewhere."

Everyone boarded. The platoons and the battalion got crammed into the landing bay again.

This time, an air of tense excitement infected everyone. The only people who spoke did it in a hushed undertone.

Rhodes didn't hear any other comments except more remarks like Rhinehart's. The Masks were on the planet. It was crunch time.

Chapter 26

B attalion 1 deployed on the ground along with the 765th, 423rd, and 647th platoons. He couldn't tell any of them apart except for the men he already knew from the 765th.

The Ravager delivered the Legion force to another open grassland miles from any sign of human habitation.

The area reminded Rhodes of the Battle of Keonus where the Masks took control of the battalion and made them shoot Legion soldiers.

The memory disturbed the rest of the battalion, too. Rhodes noticed his subordinates tightening their facial features and casting flinty glances at the soldiers nearest them.

No one mentioned the obvious similarity. The inquiry panel's half-hearted attempts to test the battalion in Grid training sessions didn't mean a thing compared to this.

Now everyone in the battalion was about to find out for real which side they were on—and everyone in the battalion was about to find out which side every other person was on.

Captain Bowen went through the assembled platoons directing each to a different part of the battlefield.

In some cosmic twist of irony, Battalion 1 got positioned with the 765th again—with the same men the battalion fought with on Drion.

If the Masks hacked the battalion, Rhodes and his people would wind up killing these men that the battalion worked so hard to save.

"The enemy is advancing from the north," Captain Bowen informed them. "They're on course to intercept Veulia. It's one of the biggest population centers on the planet. We gotta stop them from getting there."

"Are any Ravagers assigned to give us air support?" Lieutenant Lohr asked. "Are we stuck out here with our asses hanging in the breeze?"

"I better not see your ass hanging in the breeze," Captain Blackwell interrupted.

"The Masks aren't using invasion ships to transport their ground troops directly to the city," Captain Bowen replied. "The enemy landed their ground troops out here—about ten miles north of here. They're marching toward the city on foot—and no invasion ships are assaulting the city yet, either. This ground force is the only threat to the city so far."

Rhodes frowned. "That's unusual. I wonder why they changed their strategy."

"Who cares why they do anything?" Edgecombe asked. "They just do shit at random. They're machines. They don't think."

Rhodes didn't contradict, but this didn't sit well with him. The Masks had developed an unbeatable strategy. They bombarded every city into the ground and then landed ground troops to mop up the mess.

Why change it now? Why remove their greatest advantage by not using invasion ships?

No one around here would explain it to him. The platoons had to stand around in the open fields waiting for the Masks to show up. The tension in the ranks escalated as the minutes ticked by.

When the Masks did finally show up, they trooped one steady foot in front of the other heading south.

Whatever the Masks planned to do, they didn't send an overwhelming force to annihilate the Sarus population. The Masks barely sent enough ground troops to meet these three battalions.

Rhodes didn't have time to speculate on the Masks' new motives. They marched over the hills. All the platoons braced themselves to engage the enemy.

The forwardmost squads raised their Jackhammers. The Masks didn't raise their fusion rifles. They just kept clomping over the rolling grassy swells on a steady track southward.

The forward platoons opened fire and took down dozens of Masks. Only then did the Masks raise their rifles to return fire.

Gunfire blasted back and forth. The two sides appeared equally matched for the first few minutes.

Rhodes didn't expect the Masks to send such a small force. It didn't make sense, but it did give him an idea.

He swiveled The Grid in the interface, signaled his subordinates, and fired his boosters to fly to the western side of the battle.

The Masks didn't respond fast enough before Battalion 1 carved into the enemy ranks from the side.

Rhodes started mowing down as many Masks as he could to draw them away from the platoons and to get the Masks to divert away from the Veulia population center.

The Masks completely ignored the battalion at first. The Masks kept bombarding the soldiers with rifle fire and fighting their way south toward the city in the distance.

The platoons tightened their formation and dug deep to hold their ground. They actually succeeded in forcing the Masks to halt their advance, but only because the Masks didn't bring enough ground troops to completely overcome these platoons.

Rhodes was just wondering what the hell game the Masks were playing when Lohr's squad and a bunch of other soldiers on that side broke off their Jackhammer fire, tore away from the other platoons, and took off running across the fields.

They ran east—away from the battle, away from the enemy—away from everything.

Rhodes didn't see what those men could possibly be running to. There was nothing out here, especially not any way for them to escape the battle. The platoons were alone and stranded in the middle of nowhere.

Lohr's desertion stunned everyone in the battalion and all three platoons. All the soldiers and everyone in the battalion stopped fighting to stare at Lohr and his men disappearing behind some more swells.

The Masks didn't stop fighting. They doubled down with fresh barrages of rifle fire. The Masks surged forward to fill the gap Lohr's men left in the Legion ranks.

Lohr's squad had been fighting between Edgecombe's men and Blackwell's squad. The Masks overran both squads in seconds and both squads went down under the Masks' onslaught.

The sound of gunfire snapped the battalion back to its senses. Rhodes blasted forward targeting Masks at his top speed. He had to use The Grid to target them so he didn't hit any of the surrounding soldiers.

The Masks got all mixed up with the platoons for a minute. Soldiers toppled all over The Grid faster than Rhodes could take down the Masks shooting at those men.

The situation looked truly hopeless. The other platoons moved in to defend the 765th, but the soldiers couldn't target the Masks as well to avoid hitting their own people.

The other platoons fired more slowly and made less of a dent in the Mask numbers. Battalion 1 couldn't keep up with the Masks slaughtering the 765th en masse.

Without warning, the Masks wheeled to confront Battalion 1 and opened fire. The Masks surged back toward the west and engaged Battalion 1 face to face.

Rhodes switched to swiping his lasers back and forth to cut down the enemy, but the platoons' close quarters tipped the scales in the Masks' favor.

They locked with the battalion and fusion fire hammered Rhodes's implants. He stumbled, tried to keep shooting, and screams echoed through the interface as more gunshots hit his subordinates.

The platoons and a few surviving soldiers from the 765th opened fire on the Masks from the south trying to help Battalion 1.

The Masks ignored the soldiers this time and kept up their steady bombardment of Battalion 1.

So many fusion shots exploded in Rhodes's face that he couldn't see for a second. He did his best to keep targeting the Masks, but he lost sight of The Grid in the confusion.

The mayhem cleared just enough for him to see Dietz and Lauer on the ground with some of their implants blasted out.

Rhodes charged over to them and planted himself over them to protect them just as another explosion hit Thackery.

Oakes and Rhinehart had gotten separated from the rest of the battalion. The two men pivoted closer to the platoons and faced the Masks side by side from the south.

Rhodes didn't see the Masks alter their position at all. They continued to pretend that the platoons weren't there.

That left Rhodes, Fuentes, and Coulter alone on the west side. They couldn't stand against so many Masks. The enemy made one last surge and another fusion shot erupted in Rhodes's face. That one shot took him down and he fell on top of Dietz and Lauer.

Chapter 27

As usual, Rhodes woke up in a capsule the very next instant as if no time had passed at all. He must be back on the *Ero.*

He groaned when he remembered the battle. So much for defending the population.

"Good morning, Captain," Fisher greeted him. "All your systems are functioning normally. It appears the doctors repaired your implants and your injuries."

"I don't want to know how bad they were," Rhodes muttered. "Just tell me everyone else in the battalion is okay."

"They're all fine. Thackery is still in a conversion cycle and will probably stay there for a few more days. Oakes, Rhinehart, and Fuentes didn't get injured at all."

Rhodes sighed. "That's good."

"Lauer, Dietz, and Coulter got out of their conversion cycles yesterday. They're in the capsule hold."

"So....are we still on Sarus? What's the story with the invasion?"

"We're on Sarus on a different continent. The Masks are still isolated on the Eulara continent. You might be interested to know they still haven't sent invasion ships against any population center."

Rhodes frowned. "That's odd. I wonder what they're up to."

"You have an order waiting for you when you get out of the lab, Captain," Fisher told him. "You're ordered to report to the inquiry panel."

"I can't wait," he grumbled. "What is it this time?"

"The panel is meeting with a board of JAG advocates tasked with investigating the desertion of Lieutenant Lohr's squad and others from the 423rd and the 647th. The advocates probably want to question you about Lohr's desertion."

"Did anyone from the 765th survive the battle? I hope the advocates are charging Lohr's group with multiple counts of murder."

"They are," Fisher replied. "More than thirty men from the 765th died as a direct result of Lohr's desertion."

Rhodes let out another heavy sigh. "This is the last thing we need right now."

"The advocates have already taken reports from the rest of the battalion. You and Thackery are the last two."

"Then I should get up and go see them."

Rhodes opened his capsule and sat up to find the two doctors waiting there for him. "How are you feeling?" Dr. Osborne asked.

"About like I usually do when I wake up from one of these cycles. How bad was the damage?"

"Life-threatening. The deserters are being charged with attempted murder of everyone who got hurt after they left the battle."

Rhodes didn't know how to feel about that. Getting injured on the battlefield was no one's fault except the enemy's.

That battle would have gone very differently if Lohr and his men hadn't abandoned the 765th when and where they did. The deserters left the whole Legion force exposed in the worst possible way.

Rhodes would have gone straight to report to the inquiry panel, but he had to take his time getting back on his feet after his conversion cycle.

He would have liked to grill Fisher and the doctors about how the Sarus campaign was going, but Rhodes didn't do that. He wouldn't be able to do anything about it from here.

He finally dragged himself upstairs to the conference room.

The inquiry panel was back to sitting on the other side of the table to face him. His days of standing around that table as their equal were over—for now, at least.

Three JAG advocates sat with them. All three were colonels named Andrews, Dupree, and Hollander.

Hollander was a big, hulking, tall man of fifty with white hair clipped into the squarest flat-top Rhodes had ever seen.

Hollander narrowed his dangerous blue eyes at Rhodes the minute Hollander laid eyes on him.

Andrews was a much younger guy who barely came up to Hollander's shoulder. Andrews's brown crewcut and brown eyes made him look so much softer compared to Hollander.

Dupree was a black man somewhere between Hollander's size and Andrews's. Dupree also had a quiet, observant look. His eyes dipped to Rhodes's implants, but neither Dupree nor Andrews displayed any change in expression when they saw Rhodes.

"Thank you for coming in, Captain," Admiral Stabler began. "These gentlemen are investigating the desertion charges against Lieutenant Lohr and the men who left the battlefield with him."

"Yes, Sir," Rhodes replied. "I know why I'm here."

"Do you know why Lohr abandoned the battle, Captain?" Colonel Hollander asked in a deep chesty voice.

"Why he abandoned the battle?" Rhodes repeated. "No, Sir, I don't know why he abandoned the battle."

"He claims you incited his squad to rebel against the Legion," Hollander countered.

Rhodes gasped. "Incited! I never incited them to do anything except to fight the enemy!"

"Lohr claims you told him and his men in the *Ero's* landing bay that the battle was hopeless and the Legion couldn't win," Hollander went on. "Is that true?"

"I repeated exactly what I told the panel when these officers asked for my opinion on how to defeat the Masks. I said they had overwhelming numbers they could send to fight us. I said the same thing in the landing bay, but I wasn't talking to the platoons. I was talking to my subordinates. Some men I don't know overheard me and repeated what I said to Lohr."

"He claims you were the one who pushed his squad to rebel," Hollander repeated.

"No, no, no, Sir," Rhodes insisted. "That's all wrong. I told him and his men to fight the battle anyway." Rhodes turned to Colonel Kraft who, as usual, stood there in silence through the interview. "The Grid should have recorded the whole conversation. You should have all that evidence already."

"As a matter of fact, Captain," Colonel Hollander cut in again, "multiple soldiers from the 765th and the other platoons overheard your conversation with Lohr. These other soldiers have already reported that you urged Lohr's party to do their duty."

"Then why am I here if you already know what happened?"

"The advocates need your report on how it all went down," Colonel Volk replied. "We have reports from the rest of Battalion 1, but you are their commanding officer so we need your report, too."

"The platoons state that Lohr's desertion left a gap in the center of the 765th," Hollander went on. "They state that this gap gave the enemy a perfect line to penetrate the platoon. These soldiers state that this unique position was the one factor that allowed the Masks to inflict such heavy losses on the 765th. Do you agree with that assessment?"

Rhodes looked away and nodded. "Yes, Sir," he murmured. "The platoon was standing firm until Lohr split away."

"What did you do when his party did split away?" Hollander asked.

"I was too stunned to do anything at first. We all were. We just stood there staring at Lohr's people disappearing over the swells. I couldn't figure out at first what the hell they were trying to do—excuse my language, Sir. There was nothing over there—no way for them to escape. We were all so floored that we all stopped shooting for a second."

"Did that give the Masks the opportunity to make their move—the fact that everyone stopped shooting?" Hollander asked.

"I guess it must have, Sir."

"Then what did you do?"

"I snapped out of it and attacked from the west—which is where I was before. I decided to flank the enemy before, but by the time I got there, the enemy was already so mixed up with the 765th that it was hard to see anything. The enemy leveled half the 765th before anyone could do anything.....and then it got so chaotic that the other platoons could hardly hit any Masks at all. Everyone was too concerned about hitting the men from the 765th."

"Did the Masks turn on Battalion 1 in retaliation for you defending the platoon?" Hollander asked.

"No, I don't think so, Sir. We fought them while they were engaged with the 765th. That went on for a at least few minutes before the Masks turned on us."

"What caused them to turn on you, then? Why didn't they turn on you immediately?"

"I have no idea, Sir. A lot of things the Masks did during that battle didn't make sense. None of it was their usual fighting style."

"And you have no explanation for this?" Hollander demanded.

"No, Sir. I wish I could figure it out. It doesn't give me a good feeling at all. If I had to guess, I'd say they were planning something."

"Something like what?" Captain Lake interrupted. "How could they be planning something when they've removed the invasion ships to weaken themselves?"

"I'm not sure, Sir. The only thing I can figure is that they're responding to the Legion moving such a large force into the Regos system. I really wouldn't like to guess beyond that, Sir."

Hollander scowled even more dangerously. "That will be all for now, Captain. I would warn you, though, that certain elements in the Legion already question Battalion 1's loyalty."

"Yes, Sir. I know," Rhodes mumbled.

"These elements will be looking to Battalion 1 for any indication that you think it might be a good idea to betray the Legion. These elements will take even the slightest hint of doubt from you as a sign that *you* plan to betray the Legion to the Masks."

Rhodes cast his gaze down at the floor. "Yes, Sir. I already regret saying what I did in front of the platoons."

"That's all I have to say about it, then," Colonel Hollander replied. "This matter is closed, but you and your subordinates may be called up to testify at the deserters' court martials if Lohr and his men decide to fight the charges."

"Yes, Sir. I understand."

"That will be all, then, Captain."

Rhodes started to turn away, but Admiral Stabler called him back. "Wait a minute, Captain. We have a few more things to discuss with you—apart from this investigation."

Rhodes faced the table. "I already made it clear how I feel about this campaign, Sir. I don't see what else there is to say."

"We've been investigating the Masks to try to find some critical vulnerability we can exploit," General Hyde replied. "We've studied destroyed Masks from other battles, but we haven't been able to find anything."

"I wish I could help you, Ma'am. I don't know of any critical vulnerability, either."

"Do you think you could interface with one of them again?" Captain Lake asked. "You could get the information from them that way."

Rhodes cringed when he thought about interfacing with the Masks again. Going back into their version of Stonebridge sounded like his worst nightmare.

Colonel Kraft said the words that were already forming in Rhodes's mind. "If it helps us win the war and stop this slaughter, won't it be worth it? I know interfacing with them is painful for you, but what other choice do we have?"

"Yes, Sir," Rhodes husked. "I'll do it. I don't know that I'll be able to find anything, but if you show me one of them, I'll do it."

"We would have to capture one of them on the battlefield," Colonel Volk suggested.

"Don't you have destroyed body parts already?" Rhodes asked. "General Hyde just said you did."

"All of those Masks fell in old battles," she told him. "We want a new one with more up-to-date information about what the Masks are doing."

"We'll send the battalion back into combat for the express purpose of capturing one of the Masks so you can interface with it," Admiral Stabler explained. "Then you can report to us on what you find."

Chapter 28

Rhodes, his subordinates, and the 423rd and 647th platoons gathered into the *Ero's* landing bay—again.

Lieutenant Edgecombe stood not far away. Ten men from his squad in the 765th had survived the assault when Lieutenant Lohr deserted.

Edgecombe and his men had been incorporated into the 423rd along with a handful of men from Captain Blackwell's squad. There was no 765th anymore.

Captain Blackwell had been transferred somewhere else. Rhodes didn't know where. No one told him nor did the men of the former 765th volunteer anything if they even knew.

"We are NOT doing this," Zen growled through the interface.

"I'm afraid we are, darling," Van replied. "We have our orders—unless you want to desert like Lieutenant Lohr did."

"We aren't going anywhere," Dietz interrupted. "If catching one of these machines helps us win the war, we'll do it. We'll catch the whole damn force if we have to."

"Catching one of them will be easy," Rhinehart chimed in. "We'll be standing right in front of them."

"We'll be standing right in front of their rifles, genius," Lauer pointed out. "The hard part will be catching one of them without getting our asses shot off."

"And without destroying the target in the process," Rhodes added. "The point is for the Mask we catch to still be functional and interfaced with the city machine. That's the only way we can find out what they're planning—or some other vulnerability that will help us defeat them."

"I'm glad you're the one who has to interface with them," Oakes remarked. "You wouldn't catch me doing it."

"That's the other hard part of this operation," Thackery pointed out. "We have to catch the Mask and then somehow stop all the other Masks from interfering with the captain while he interfaces with it. That could get a little dicey with a raging battle going on."

"You don't have to remind me," Rhodes muttered.

"Haven't we already interfaced with the Masks enough?" Rhinehart asked. "What is there to find out that we don't already know?"

"I guess we might find something," Rhodes replied. "I don't see how this war can possibly go any worse for us. If interfacing with them tells us anything, it will be a step in the right direction."

Lieutenant Edgecombe glanced over just then. He heard their conversation, but he didn't get involved in it. There was nothing to say that everyone hadn't already said a million times.

Everyone in this landing bay right now had received the order. The platoons had to engage the Masks in battle for the specific purpose of capturing one of them so Rhodes could interface with it.

Interfacing with the Masks was the absolute last thing on God's green Earth he wanted to do. Doing it in front of not just his subordinates but two whole Legion platoons would be the ultimate nightmare.

Doing it in the middle of a battle would make it astronomically harder. It was a recipe for disaster on top of all the other factors working against him.

At this point, he'd resigned himself to a steady parade of insoluble disasters he couldn't do anything to prevent.

That was his life now. The sooner he accepted that, the better.

He finally had accepted it. That was the scariest part. He already expected the worst. What actually happened couldn't possibly be worse than what he anticipated.

He held out no hope that interfacing with the Masks would tell him anything he didn't learn the last time. It would give him another bird's-eye view into the Masks living in Stonebridge.

He already knew what that would be like. Every Mask he interfaced with would be some combination of the boy-father character or the girl-Ora character. All the Masks lived the same scenario.

In a way, the Stonebridge landscape was the perfect defense. Anyone who tried to hack the Masks would wind up in Stonebridge. The Grid landscape wouldn't tell the intruder anything useful they could use against the Masks.

None of this speculation meant anything. Rhodes just had to do the job in front of him. The outcome would be the same either way.

The *Ero* landed at the same base and then flew the platoons back to the Eulara continent. Rhodes watched through The Grid as the ship approached the city of Veulia—the city the Legion had originally been trying to protect.

The Masks still didn't bring in invasion ships. They didn't need to. Maybe that was their point. They could steamroll the whole Treaty of Aemon Cluster without using their ships at all.

The ground troops went street to street through town killing everyone who stumbled into their path—which was a lot of people.

The ground troops used their fusion rifles to blast out the buildings' lowest floors. The buildings collapsed with everyone still inside. Anyone who survived to escape the buildings fell to the Masks' rifles.

Every available Ravager sat or hovered at another Legion base on the other side of town. Thousands upon thousands of people stampeded there trying to evacuate, but the Ravagers couldn't carry everyone.

Rhodes winced when he saw the slaughter going on. The Masks worked systematically into the city from the north. They worked methodically from one building to another.

A black line of scorched land, shattered pavement, and ruins extended behind them as the ground troops swept into town.

The rest of the city in front of them looked as perfect as always—except for the remaining population all trampling each other in their desperation to get away in time.

Legion platoons fought street to street trying every trick in the book to stem the Masks' tide. Nothing worked.

The Masks brought down buildings on top of the soldiers and kept on going. Fleeing civilians got in the platoons' way and made it impossible for the soldiers to target the enemy.

The Masks had reinforced their numbers while the battalion had been dealing with this whole desertion catastrophe. The Masks only sent out a small force at first.

Now they fortified their numbers with a vast mob of thousands of Masks. Nothing could stop them.

Dietz mumbled the words the whole battalion was thinking. "Do you seriously mean to tell me we aren't supposed to try to defend them? Are we really going down there to do anything other than stop the Masks from advancing? And don't give me that shit about our orders."

"Why do all of us need to help capture a Mask?" Oakes asked. "Why can't you just fly over the Masks, snatch one of them, and fly off with it while the rest of us defend the population?"

Rhodes shrugged. He was thinking the same thing, but just then, the *Ero* wheeled over the city ten blocks behind the line.

The ship touched down and the platoons charged out of the landing bay. They followed their orders and headed west.

The platoons already in battle against the Masks made a stronger stand at the center of the Legion position.

That left the two side flanks exposed. The Masks advanced farther forward there—or they could have if they chose to.

They stayed level with their comrades even when the Legion resistance slackened. The Masks maintained their straight formation so they could all advance together.

"How do you want to do this?!" Edgecombe asked Rhodes.

"We'll try it Oakes's way first," Rhodes replied. "You and the battalion will engage the enemy. I'll come at them from the side and try to grab one of them."

"And if that doesn't work?"

Rhodes squinted over the advancing Masks, but he was really checking The Grid. "The platoons have shot down a bunch of Masks back there—behind the enemy line. I'll go back there and see if I can find one of them that's still intact enough to use."

Edgecombe made a face. "Good luck."

Rhodes grinned at him, but they didn't have time to discuss it any further. The Masks swept forward another few streets.

The platoons rushed the enemy and the two sides clashed in a hail of gunfire.

The battalion got mixed up with the 423rd and added their fire to the assault. Rhodes just hoped it was enough to distract the Masks away from him.

He fired his boosters, zoomed away through a few different streets, and cut behind buildings he hoped would hide him from the Masks.

He swerved and blasted back toward the Masks' line. They were trying to divert to compensate for the platoons' assault.

He flew faster, slammed into them, clamped his arms around one of the machines, and pinned its arms to its body so it couldn't raise its rifle.

He ignited his boosters and blasted straight up carrying the Mask with him. A few more Masks fired at him from below, but he climbed too high and too fast.

He put them behind him and raced back through the same tangle of streets to rejoin the platoon.

He landed five blocks away. Explosions boomed from out of sight as the battalion unloaded dozens of Vipers on the Masks.

Rhodes set his captive on the ground in an alley adjacent to the street where he and the platoons disembarked from the *Ero*.

He heard and saw on The Grid that the platoons were already starting to fall back. They inched closer to his position.

He turned his attention to the Mask in front of him. It was perfectly intact and started to raise its rifle to aim at him.

He slapped the weapon away and brought up his laser. He planned to cut off the Mask's arms and legs so it couldn't go anywhere.

The minute he aimed his weapon at it, the machine detonated in a massive explosion that hurled Rhodes off his feet. He sailed across the alley, slammed into the wall behind him, and hit the ground blinking stars out of his eyes.

Chapter 29

R hodes came to his senses with Thackery bending over him. "Captain!" she bellowed over the noise of continuous explosions. "Captain—get up! We have to fall back!"

He started to get up onto his hands and knees. He must have flown closer to the street than he realized.

The platoons surged back to get away from the Masks. Rhodes didn't see any of the soldiers shooting at the Masks anymore.

Thackery dragged Rhodes to his feet. He couldn't hold up his own weight. He sagged against her and she propped him on her shoulder.

He faced the street as best he could just as Rhinehart staggered past carrying Dietz on his shoulder. The rest of the battalion ran behind Rhinehart.

Continuous explosions went off up and down the battlefield. Rhodes didn't see what caused them until one of the Masks burst out of position.

That one machine rushed into the battalion between Oakes and Fuentes. The Mask got within a few feet of both men, but the machine didn't try to shoot either of them.

The Mask exploded right between them. The bursting fireball took down both men and the shockwave sent Rhinehart flying. He lost his grip on Dietz and they both crashed onto the pavement.

Thackery let go of Rhodes and charged into the open with no thought for her own safety. She grabbed Dietz and started hauling him toward the alley.

The sight electrified Rhodes and snapped him back to high alert. He ran out there, grabbed Rhinehart, and used all his strength to drag Rhinehart back into the alley, too.

Once Rhodes got out into the open street, he saw exactly what the Masks were doing. They didn't try to shoot. They scattered and individual Masks ran here, there, and anywhere.

They sprinted into the platoons and then Masks blew themselves up taking out dozens of soldiers with each blast. It was an even more destructive strategy than bringing in the invasion ships.

Rhodes left Rhinehart lying on the ground in the alley, raced back out into the mayhem, slung Fuentes over his shoulder, and grabbed Oakes by one wrist.

Thackery, Coulter, and Lauer made it just in time to avoid another Mask exploding a few feet away.

Thackery collapsed against the wall and wiped blood off her face. Rhodes bent over Dietz. At least he was conscious which was more than anyone could say for Rhinehart.

Everyone else in the platoon had sustained injuries and damage to their implants.

"Tell me you captured one of them," Oakes panted.

"I did—and then it blew itself up right in front of me."

Oakes's eyes sliced toward what was left of the battle. "The Masks are in front of us. We're behind them."

"Now's our chance to see if we can find one that's already damaged," Rhodes replied. "Stay here and stay hidden."

He stepped to the mouth of the alley. The Masks no longer kept their straight-line formation. They scattered, ran down any clusters of soldiers, and blew themselves up.

Rhodes shouldn't have been surprised by this. It was the perfect strategy considering how many individual fighters the Masks had. They were expendable. They were walking suicide bombs.

They all had their backs to him now as they advanced farther south. The self-exploding technique left no platoons to slow the Masks down.

They didn't seem too interested in blowing up buildings anymore. Maybe they planned to come back and finish the job later.

Rhodes took his opening and turned left heading back northward. He had to travel ten blocks before he got back to the place where the Masks and the platoons had actually been shooting at each other.

It didn't take him long to find the Mask he wanted. He only had to look for one with light still glowing behind its eye slit.

He found one with its arms and legs shot off. The rest of it was still intact.

The thing jerked in his hands as soon as he picked it up. It started speaking to him with B's voice. "Captain Rhodes—what a surprise. I didn't think we would meet again so soon."

"Shut up, you piece of shit," Rhodes snarled. "We aren't here to socialize."

"What are you going to do with me?" B asked.

"I'm not going to do anything with you, asshole. You're a computer program in the city machine's mainframe."

Rhodes walked away carrying the robot. Part of its severed left arm dangled mid-bicep with wires and tubes hanging out of it.

"You won't accomplish anything by this, Captain," B told him on the way.

"Did I ask for your assessment of my plans? I told you to shut up."

"If you want information about us, all you have to do is ask. We want you to understand us."

"I think I understand you well enough already, pal. Besides, I wouldn't trust a word that came out of your mouth."

"What are you going to do?" B asked again.

"Don't worry. It won't hurt."

Whatever Rhodes did wouldn't hurt B any more than the Stonebridge landscape already was hurting him, but Rhodes didn't say that.

Rhodes didn't plan to torture B. Rhodes didn't even know if he *could* torture B, but that didn't matter.

B was already being tortured worse than Rhodes ever could have hoped. He wouldn't have wished the Stonebridge landscape on his worst enemy.

The Masks were his worst enemy and he could only think about trying to help them get out of it. They couldn't get out of it. Their own desperation to be human kept them locked into it even though it didn't work.

Rhodes took the Mask back to the battalion. Rhinehart was just starting to stir, but he still had his eyes closed.

Rocky was back on the interface. "How bad are his injuries?" Rhodes asked.

"The damage to his neural core appears to be minimal, but we won't know until he regains consciousness."

Rhodes made a cursory check on the rest of his people. Dietz was still groggy.

Oakes had suffered the worst injuries. His right mechanical arm had gotten crushed. He couldn't use it, but other than that, he appeared to be fully functional.

"Are you sure you can interface with this thing, Captain?" Coulter asked when he saw the Mask.

"Interface!" B exclaimed. "You want to interface with me? How will you do that?"

"I told you to shut up," Rhodes snapped and turned back to Coulter. "I interfaced with one of them on Drion. I won't have any trouble doing the same thing now."

"What will that accomplish, Captain?" B asked. "I told you I would tell you anything you wanted to know. I already told you during our last meeting that we wanted you to understand us."

"I swear to God, B, if you don't be quiet, I'll take you offline and interface with you that way. Now keep still and try to cooperate. This won't hurt and it won't damage you any more than you already are."

"Do you know this thing, Captain?" Lauer asked.

"It's a computer program," Rhodes explained. "The Masks used it as a representative to talk to me when we were their prisoners. The city machine can send this program into any Mask. They don't have individual personalities."

"Are you sure?" Thackery asked. "What if you kill it?"

"I'm sure. Don't start sympathizing with them. We have enough of that already."

"Captain Rhodes is right, of course," B added. "We don't have individual personalities and I am a program that the city machine can send into any Mask. I acted as a doctor to you in our lab and...."

"B—shut up!" Rhodes snapped. "Now just keep still. I need to concentrate."

Rhodes laid the Mask on the ground, squatted over it, and clasped both hands on either side of its head.

The thing turned its head trying to see his hands. "What are you doing?"

"I'm going to send my grid lines into your head. Now keep still....."

Another explosion startled everyone in that second, and just then, a blast hit a nearby building across the street outside the alley.

Rhodes glanced over his shoulder just in time to see another tornado of exploding debris and disintegrating walls pinwheel across the street from a different building.

Lauer jumped up and rotated into the mouth of the alley. "Interface with it now, Captain! Hurry up and do it now before they come back!"

Coulter and Thackery scrambled to their feet to join Lauer in defending the alley.

Oakes got onto his hands and knees. He had to use one arm to try to pick up Dietz.

Rhodes crouched over the Mask and concentrated his whole attention on sending his grid lines into the thing's head.

He didn't have to power up its neural core. Everything about the Mask still functioned the way it should.

Rhodes drilled his grid lines into the Mask's neural processing system and found the Stonebridge landscape. This machine had been living the exact same program as Ora's husband and the father of the same two children. It never changed.

Rhodes kept searching until he found the memories of the city machine with all the other Masks in stasis in their conversion stations.

Rhodes tried to find his way out of those vast fields of stations. He had to find whatever part of the city machine made decisions for the entire Masks race.

More explosions behind him kept distracting him. His secondary awareness saw the battle sweeping back toward the battalion's hiding place.

The Masks circled the platoons and drove them back north. The platoons retreated away from the rest of their own people.

The Masks used all three of their new fighting strategies. They fought facing the platoons with guns blazing. The Masks kept blowing up buildings as they went and slaughtering any surviving civilians.

The Masks also sent individual robots running into the platoons to blow themselves up along with the soldiers. The Masks left bodies strewn in their wake no matter where they went.

Coulter charged over to Rhodes and grabbed him by the shoulders. "Come on, Captain! We gotta get out of here! COME ON!!"

He tried to pull Rhodes away from the Mask. Rhodes took too long to withdraw his grid lines. His awareness remained tied up with the Mask and the city machine.

Coulter tried one more time to yank Rhodes away, but right then, he saw the outer perimeter of the conversion fields.

Solid walls of computer components covered every inch of the city machine exactly the way the inquiry panel said. A few Masks walked through corridors leading between the components.

Those Masks worked on the machinery. They understood it. Rhodes just had to hack one of them to find out how the city machine worked.

He felt Coulter trying to drag him away. Explosions boomed outside the alley, and at that moment a different explosion went off.

This one didn't hit in the street outside. It didn't demolish any building.

This one came from inside Rhodes's own head. It knocked him out cold right there on the pavement.

Chapter 30

Rhodes blinked and found himself staring up at the sky. A few smoky clouds drifted past up there. He couldn't see anything else up there.

He tried to remember where he was and how he got here. He glanced around and the whole horrible memory came back in a flash.

The Mask he captured lay right next to him. No light glowed behind its eye slit anymore. The thing had completely powered down or maybe it really finally destroyed itself.

The rest of the battalion lay all around Rhodes. Each of them had fallen right on the spot where they'd been sitting or standing when that blast hit Rhodes.

Lauer, Thackery, and Fuentes lay unconscious in the mouth of the alley. Rhinehart hadn't moved and neither had Dietz.

Oakes lay sprawled on his face across Dietz's body. Oakes must still have been trying to pick up Dietz when whatever that was took out the whole battalion.

Coulter was just opening his eyes, rolling onto his side, and groaning when Rhodes sat up.

The world didn't look right. It didn't feel right, either. He couldn't put his finger on exactly what was wrong with it.

Then he realized. The Grid was down. He couldn't access his grid lines or read any of the surrounding terrain.

Fisher wasn't there anymore, either, and none of the other SAMs interfaced with Rhodes.

His limbs and joints didn't function correctly, either. His implants didn't give him any information about his surroundings....and then he realized that he could only see out of his left eye—his organic eye. His right eye implant didn't work at all.

"Captain...." Coulter groaned.

"I'm here, Corporal. We're okay. Can you get up?"

Coulter kept growling under his breath, but he eventually sat up and looked around at everyone. "What happened?"

"The Masks took us offline—our implants anyway. Everything is down."

Rhodes experienced a sudden surge of terror when he thought his weapons system might be offline, too. He couldn't use The Grid to check.

He raised his arm and tried to fire his thermal cannon into the brick wall next to him. Nothing. His laser didn't work, either.

He fought down the urge to panic. He and the battalion were stranded in a war zone without their implants, without The Grid, and without any weapons.

He scrambled to his feet and went from person to person. "Get up! Get up—all of you! We have to get out of here!"

He shook them, but it still took them way too long to sit up. They were all too dazed to think straight. Dietz and Rhinehart were still only semi-conscious from their original injuries.

Coulter got to his feet, but he kept blinking at Rhodes in numb shock. "What....what's wrong with The Grid? Murphy isn't here."

"The Grid is down!" Rhodes called over his shoulder. "All our SAMs are offline—and we don't have weapons, either. We gotta get out of here and fall back to the Legion before the....."

A distant boom of explosions startled him out of his wits. An explosion like that shouldn't have bothered him so much.

He had no way to defend himself. No one in the battalion did. They couldn't see where the enemy was or where they were going.

Rhodes finally got Thackery, Oakes, and Lauer on their feet. Fuentes stood up last, but the strain of losing both The Grid and their SAMs took a toll on everyone.

Fuentes wrung his hands, bit his lips, and whimpered in terror while his eyes darted back and forth without seeing anything. "Gone! They're all gone!"

"They aren't gone!" Rhodes snapped. He had to fight down hysteria. Losing his implants must be playing on his sanity, too. "The SAMs are just offline. We can get them back. Now come on."

He herded everyone toward the mouth of the alley. He couldn't even tell if it was safe for them to go out there.

It would never be safe. All these people were blind, deaf, and defenseless.

The problem got a thousand times worse when it came to taking Rhinehart with them. Lauer picked up Dietz and slung him over his shoulder. Dietz groaned, but he didn't protest.

No one in the battalion could carry Rhinehart. Rhodes went over to him, grabbed Rhinehart's arm, and tried to haul Rhinehart into a sitting position. He weighed a ton.

"You gotta help me, Lieutenant!" Rhodes gasped. "You have to stand up! I can't carry you! Come on, Lieutenant! Don't make me leave you behind!"

Rhinehart floundered out of his stupor just enough to realize what was going on. He tried to sit up, collapsed, and fell on his face before he pushed himself up on his hands and knees.

He wavered there with his head hanging down while Rhodes tried again and again to make him stand up.

"I'm trying, Captain," Rhinehart rasped. "I'm trying."

Rhodes cast a desperate glance toward the street. The sound of battle still echoed through the streets coming from somewhere.

The surrounding buildings reflected the noise. The walls made it impossible to tell which direction the gunfire was coming from.

Rhinehart crawled to the nearest wall and used it to push himself up. Rhodes got under his arm. Plenty of Rhinehart's weight fell on Rhodes.

Rhinehart staggered every few steps and nearly buckled Rhodes's legs, but he couldn't wait any longer. "Go! Go now!"

"Where are we going?" Coulter asked.

"I don't know! Head south! That's all I know!"

The party set off through the streets. Not having any weapons or being able to see anything in The Grid racked Rhodes's nerves.

His neural processors weren't working right. He wasn't coping as well as he should have.

He jumped at every noise. Even tripping over things made him startle. He couldn't keep an eye on every other part of the surroundings with Rhinehart next to him.

Rhodes heard sobbing, whimpering, and moaning behind him. He didn't dare to turn around to see his people going through the same turmoil.

They'd all become hopelessly dependent on their SAMs, The Grid, and their implants. The battalion might not be able to survive without them.

The battalion would have to survive without them. The noise of gunfire and explosions inched closer. It seemed to come from every possible direction.

He led the group four blocks south before they ran into another gunfight between the Masks and Legion platoons.

The Masks had their back to the battalion again. Battalion 1 would have to fight their way through the Masks to rejoin the Legion.

"What do we do?" Fuentes whimpered.

Rhodes glanced around, but the streets, buildings, and alleys nearby didn't tell him anything. He didn't even know if he *could* rejoin the Legion to the south—not to mention anyone who might be able to help him.

"Come on," he murmured. "We'll go this way."

He turned Rhinehart aside and headed to the right. Maybe, by some miracle, the battalion could circle the battle without getting shot at—by anyone.

"Captain...." Rhinehart wheezed. "Give me....a weapon..... please ....."

Rhodes opened his mouth to tell Rhinehart that Rhodes was just as unarmed as the rest of them. Then he had an idea.

He steered the battalion into a different street. Dead soldiers lay in gory pieces all over the ground.

"Pick up their Jackhammers!" Rhodes panted. "Arm yourselves...."

He barely got the words out before the gun battle he just witnessed poured into this street. Masks and soldiers nearly flattened the battalion with gunfire erupting all over the place.

Rhodes dove for the nearest fallen Jackhammer and wound up dropping Rhinehart in the process. Both men hit the ground and landed on top of piles of dead soldiers.

Rhodes's grateful fingers closed around a Jackhammer and he yanked it up. He rolled onto his side jerking the weapon in all directions.

He fired at any Masks he could see, but he couldn't see many of them. The Grid no longer targeted for him.

Smoke and debris got in the one eye he still had left. Shadowy figures flitted across the area in front of him. He couldn't be sure which side they belonged to.

Jackhammers went off in his ears. Was that the battalion shooting—or the platoons—or the Masks? Were they coming for him?

He couldn't see anything. He staggered to his feet and sidestepped back toward where he thought he got separated from Rhinehart.

"Rhinehart!!" Rhodes bellowed. "Lieutenant—where are you?"

Another roar answered him from Rhodes's left. That was Rhinehart's voice. Rhodes kept going and found Rhinehart on his feet.

He bared his teeth and thundered at the Masks while he unloaded his Jackhammer on them again and again.

Rhodes didn't see anyone Rhinehart might be shooting at, but at least none of the Masks came near him or Rhodes.

Rhodes tried to locate any of his people in the confusion. He didn't dare to fire his weapon in case he hit someone friendly in the smoke.

He held out his hand to draw Rhinehart back toward the south when another squad of soldiers inched backward out of the fog.

Edgecombe and his men kept up a steady barrage on a party of Masks advancing from the north. Edgecombe's men bombarded the enemy with all their firepower, but the Masks still drove the soldiers back.

Rhodes and Rhinehart sprang forward to join the squad, but these Jackhammers didn't do as much damage as the battalion's own weapons.

Rhodes caught Edgecombe giving him a strange look. This was the first time Rhodes had even held a Jackhammer since that day when the Duster crashed on top of him.

Rhodes didn't have time to explain anything. The squad retreated farther and overtook Coulter and Thackery shooting at three isolated Masks in an alley.

The battalion located Oakes and Dietz among the fallen. Oakes had taken another gunshot to the chest and collapsed along with Dietz.

Rhinehart picked up Oakes, threw him over his shoulder, and then hefted Dietz in his left arm. Rhinehart kept shooting with his right and roaring at the Masks in wordless, animalistic rage.

Rhodes glanced around, but he didn't see Fuentes or Lauer anywhere.

Rhodes didn't have time to look for the rest of his people. He and Edgecombe's squad retreated a few more blocks before Rhodes happened to glance into a different alley.

Fuentes sat at the far end huddled in a fetal ball. He whimpered in terror and kept his face turned toward the wall so he wouldn't see anything.

Lauer lay unconscious across the mouth of the alley with a gunshot wound to the organic part of his side under his ribs. Blood poured from the wound. He must have gotten hit defending Fuentes.

Rhodes looked around at his people and discovered Thackery making eye contact with him. Her eyes pinched at the corners and her mouth twisted in misery. Everyone in the battalion was suffering from the same problem. No one could fix it.

Rhodes picked up Lauer. He weighed only slightly less than Rhinehart and Lauer couldn't walk on his own or even help Rhodes.

Rhodes hauled Lauer onto his shoulder. Rhodes did his best to keep his weapon up, but Lauer's weight made it impossible to aim straight.

Thackery went over to Fuentes, squatted in front of him, and got in his face. "Come on, Rudy. We're going back to the *Ero*. Dr. Osborne will bring Van and the other SAMs back online. Come on. We're going to be okay."

He didn't respond at all. She eventually had to drag him to his feet and force him out of the alley.

She steered him with one hand while she kept her weapon pointed outward with the other.

Rhodes tried not to notice Edgecombe and his men staring at the battalion. This wasn't the Battalion 1 the platoons were used to.

The battalion had spent so much of the last several battles defending these very soldiers. Now no one in the battalion could take care of themselves. Battalion 1 wouldn't have survived this long without Edgecombe's squad saving their lives every few blocks.

Now the soldiers were the ones who moved in front of the battalion to block the Masks from coming near them.

Edgecombe never asked Rhodes for any explanation. Rhodes would never forget that as long as he lived.

The Masks rushed the squad again and again. Soldiers fell under enemy fire. Edgecombe and his men had to pick up their own wounded to carry everyone off the field.

Every injured man left the squad and the battalion more at risk. The Masks made one last charge and would have taken down the whole group.

Right then, another platoon swept in from the west. The newcomers attacked the Masks while Edgecombe's squad defended the battalion the rest of the way out of the city.

Chapter 31

R hodes collapsed under Lauer's weight. Rhodes barely lowered Lauer onto a bed in the Legion field hospital before Rhodes's knees gave out.

Rhinehart put Dietz on another bed and Oakes on another. The medical team surrounded Lauer....and then stopped.

The doctor in charge blinked down at Lauer. The doctor opened and closed his mouth a few times. "Um....what are we supposed to do with this?"

"You need to....contact....the *Ero*....Captain Ackerman....." Rhodes gasped. "You need.....to call....the ship......"

The nurses and medical team abandoned the battalion when Edgecombe and his men staggered in carrying their own wounded. The medical team knew how to deal with them.

Edgecombe laid three of his men on different tables. He got so busy giving reports to the doctors that he didn't notice the battalion until after the medical team took Edgecombe's wounded away.

Thackery guided Fuentes onto a different bed, but there was nothing wrong with him—not physically. She and Coulter seemed to be fine, too.

Rhinehart buckled onto the bed next to Coulter. Rhinehart's great strength drained away and his shoulders slumped. He hung his head and rested his elbows on his knees.

Coulter gripped his shoulder, but no one could do anything to help the battalion—not here.

Rhodes felt himself shaking. The feeling that he was about to fly apart into a million pieces—it didn't come from fear or even the exhaustion of carrying first Rhinehart and then Lauer.

It came from somewhere else. He would have thought his implants were malfunctioning, but his implants weren't online at all.

He allowed himself to topple over onto the bed. He couldn't keep himself upright anymore. Everything was shutting down. His neural core no longer regulated all his systems for him. Would he ever get them back? Was this the end?

His vision started to blur. Right before he lost focus completely, he noticed Lieutenant Edgecombe and his men standing there staring at the battalion.

The expressions on their faces made this so much worse if that was even possible. The Legion bet everything on Battalion 1 being able to find a way to defeat the Masks.

Now these soldiers—the soldiers whose lives Battalion 1 saved so many times—these soldiers were the ones seeing Battalion brought low, helpless and defeated.

If the battalion couldn't salvage this war, it couldn't be salvaged, but Rhodes already knew that. Now even that faint hope evaporated along with the last of his concentration.

He woke up on board the *Ero* again, but this time, he woke up in his capsule in the battalion's old familiar hold.

Rhodes saw Thackery walking around out there. He didn't see anyone else from the battalion. They better not be dead.

Rhodes waited, but Fisher didn't come back online. Everything felt and sounded eerie without the SAM constantly intruding on Rhodes's awareness. Did Thackery get Koenig back online?

Rhodes took a long time to decide whether he wanted to open his capsule cover. Part of him kept waiting for Fisher to wish him good morning and to ask how Rhodes was.

Rhodes couldn't make up his mind if he liked it better this way or not. What would life be like without Fisher always talking in his ear? Rhodes was about to find out.

The Grid still didn't work, either. The Grid should have fed him readings on all the other capsules in the hold and whether his subordinates' systems were functioning normally. Now he couldn't even see anything beyond this capsule cover.

Thackery passed his capsule and didn't come back. His mind started to play tricks on him again. Was he alone now? Would she ever come back?

He lost track of how long he lay there thinking, but eventually, the silence and isolation got to be too disturbing. He'd been living with fifteen other people in his head for weeks. He wasn't used to living alone.

He opened the capsule cover, sat up, and realized instantly that his implants were still offline. He could only see out of his one organic eye. None of his limbs worked the way they should.

He actually had to exert some effort to move his arms or legs. His joints didn't bend automatically the way they did before.

Thackery watched him from the table across the hold. She didn't smile or try to talk to him.

He saw right away from the haunted, suspicious strain in her features that none of her implants were working, either. He didn't have the heart to ask about the rest of it.

He stumbled through the hold checking the other capsules. Fuentes was the only one functioning normally. The controls said he'd been in a conversion cycle for a week.

He must have been so out of his mind that the doctors left him in a conversion cycle until they could fix whatever was wrong with the battalion.

Either that or Fuentes locked himself in a conversion cycle so he wouldn't have to deal with any of this. Rhodes didn't blame him.

Lauer's injuries had been repaired. He was due to stay in stasis for another week before he got up for the first time.

The others had been in and out of longer and shorter conversion cycles. Oakes had been awake for three days when the battalion first came back from Sarus.

He'd been in a continuous conversion cycle ever since. This must be everyone's way of coping.

Dietz and Rhinehart had both been treated for head injuries. They'd been in conversion cycles all this time, but they were due to wake up anytime now.

Rhodes couldn't stand hanging around the hold like this. The sight of his subordinates made his skin crawl.

The feeling that he was about to go insane became more acute the longer he stayed awake. No wonder they all locked themselves in their capsules.

He didn't ask how Thackery managed to function. Rhodes left the hold without exchanging one word with her.

He didn't have to explain why he wasn't interfacing with her. He couldn't interface with anyone.

He kept expecting Fisher to show up and start talking to him. Fisher's absence really started to get to Rhodes.

He went down to Dr. Osborne's lab and found Trudeau there.

"We're trying everything we can to bring everything we can back online," Trudeau told him. "Trust me, if we knew how, we would have done it already."

"What's the holdup?" Rhodes tried not to snap, but his nerves threatened to crumble any second now. "Why can't you just reactivate our implants?"

"There's nothing wrong with your implants. All the battalion's implants are functioning normally."

"Like hell they are," Rhodes countered.

"We don't understand it, okay? That Mask did something to your neural core. The connection between your implants and your neural core are all fried. We might have to go through each of you and refuse or replace every connection one at a time."

Rhodes's blood ran cold. "Don't say that."

"That's what's taking so long, okay? We're trying to come up with some alternative solution so it doesn't come to that. Try to be patient. I know it isn't easy. Believe me, I've had to explain this to each of your subordinates when they came in here. That's why they're all in stasis. They can't stand being awake."

Rhodes looked away. He didn't want Trudeau to see the toll this was taking, but Trudeau must already know.

"If you need to go back into stasis, then do it," Trudeau went on without asking. "You don't have to suffer. Just go back to sleep and we'll wake you up once we figure this thing out."

"Where's Dr. Osborne?" Rhodes grumbled.

"He's been running interference with the inquiry panel. They're all hot under the collar to find out if you learned anything while you were....."

"I didn't. I already told them it wouldn't work. You can tell them that the next time they ask."

Trudeau bit back a smile. "Okay. I'll tell them—or I'll tell Osborne to tell them."

Rhodes shuffled his feet. He didn't want to leave the lab.

He'd gotten used to coming here to get anything fixed that might go wrong with him. He didn't want to walk away empty-handed.

Trudeau waited. He didn't suggest again that Rhodes go back to his capsule and stay there—maybe forever.

What if the doctors never fixed what was wrong with him? What if he got stuck like this for the rest of his life? What would he be then?

He would be human—exactly the way he wanted to be.

The thought horrified him so much he left the lab without saying anything else to Trudeau.

Rhodes had been so anxious all this time to find even the slightest trace of evidence that he was still human. Now he found out firsthand what that meant.

He had no boosters, no implants, no Grid, no weapons, and no SAM.

He had to use his own energy to make himself walk down the corridor back to the hold. He had to use his one remaining eye to see where he was going.

This was how human beings lived all the time—in this silence inside their own heads. He remembered that from before his time in the battalion.

He couldn't count the times he'd wished he could just go back to that. Now he couldn't make up his mind whether this was a good thing or a bad thing.

The battalion would never get sent back into battle without their implants. The brass would take the battalion off duty and send everyone back to Coleridge Station if the panel didn't order them all taken offline for good.

He returned to the hold. Thackery sat at the computer terminal. She didn't look at him or talk to him when he came back in.

He sat down at the table trying for the life of him to decide what to do with himself. He didn't feel like drawing. He didn't feel like doing anything. He didn't even feel like living.

This was human life. He remembered enough of his old life to remember that, too.

Being alive was a constant battle to keep pushing back against the force of gravity. Sitting in one place for long threatened to tow him down into the floor until he never got up.

What was the point of anything? What in the known universe was worth the effort of actually standing up and doing it?

He couldn't think of even one thing worth his time or energy. Not even winning the war against the Masks motivated him enough to fight this lethargy and numb emptiness inside him.

The war would keep going without the battalion. If he was right about the Masks' numbers making victory impossible, the battalion's absence wouldn't make a lick of difference.

Did it really matter in the end if he and his subordinates died in battle or if the doctors just shut everyone off while they were in their conversion cycles?

Maybe that's where all of this was going. Rhodes and Thackery would crack under the strain, go back into stasis, and the doctors would take the battalion offline while they slept. None of them ever had to wake up.

That outcome sounded pretty damn good about now.

The other members of the battalion must have been going through this turmoil and hopelessness, too, during the times they were awake.

Oakes and Fuentes must have gone into their capsules resigned that they might never wake up again.

Rhodes glanced over at Thackery. She looked up at him for a split second before she looked away.

He couldn't read anything in her expression. The Grid and the interface no longer told him what she was thinking. She was a total stranger to him now. They all were.

How could anyone live like this? How could any normal human being stand the silence and isolation?

Chapter 32

Rhodes strolled through the *Ero's* many corridors. He watched the crew carrying out their duties, but he remained outside it all. He wasn't really here. He was just some ghost passing through.

Nothing bound him to these people or any business they might be engaged in. Whatever war they happened to be fighting no longer concerned him.

In the week since he came back to the *Ero,* he'd gotten used to the quiet and isolation of being.....normal.

He wasn't normal. He would never be normal again, but he was a lot closer to it now than he was before.

Doing things for himself without his implants actually started to make a kind of primitive sense. He started to remember what it was like to get up every morning and go through a normal routine.

None of that brought back the urge to fight the war. There was no war for him anymore. He didn't even try to find out where the *Ero* was, where it might be going, or what the brass had in mind for the battalion after this.

He'd spent the last week putting the whole subject out of his mind. He accepted now that he wouldn't get Fisher back or any of the bonus abilities his implants gave him.

He resigned himself to this new life with numb indifference. Nothing mattered anymore.

Watching these people go about their lives gave him a kind of vicarious pleasure. They carried out all their little dramas in front of him as if he wasn't here.

They talked about their relationships, complained about their superiors, criticized the government, and some of them even made out in front of him. He was invisible to them.

The fact that they didn't treat him as human didn't bother him. It actually made him feel better. No one in the Legion was pinning their hopes on the battalion anymore.

Everyone knew by now that the battalion was just a bunch of normal, mortal, vulnerable people. The Masks could defeat the battalion whenever the Masks chose to.

That somehow put Rhodes on the same level with all these people. They didn't think he was special or even noteworthy. This was all he'd ever wanted in life. Now he had it.

He returned to the capsule hold to find Lauer sitting up. He didn't look any happier than usual. "So everything is still down," he muttered. "I might as well go back to sleep."

"You might as well," Rhodes told him. "The doctors don't know when they'll be able to fix anything."

Lauer glanced at the other capsules. "Is everyone else okay?"

"They're as okay as they can be under the circumstances. There's no reason for any of us to be awake for this—unless you want to be."

Lauer looked around and his features spasmed. "I really wish Wild was here. I was starting to like having him around."

"I know," Rhodes replied. "It's spooky without the SAMs here."

Lauer kept silent for a minute while he made up his mind.

Rhodes started to turn away to go about his business—which he didn't have any to go about.

Just then, the two doctors walked in. "We're ready to reactivate your SAMs," Dr. Osborne announced. "We found a way to bring them back online, at least."

"Yes!" Lauer pumped his fist. "Perfect."

"Do you have to bring them back?" Thackery asked.

Osborne raised his eyebrows at her. "Of course. Why wouldn't we bring them back?'

"What if I don't want my SAM back?"

He stared at her in horror. "Why not?"

She shut her mouth and looked away. "I just don't. I would rather stay like this."

"We have to reactivate your implants," Osborne insisted. "Your systems can't regulate themselves without them."

"I know, but can't you bring my implants back online without my SAM? We all came out of stasis before you activated our SAMs."

"I don't think it's a good idea not to reactivate your SAM," he told her. "Your systems are designed to integrate with a SAM, especially when you go into The Grid. You'll need both the next time you go into combat."

Her head shot up. "Combat! Are they sending us back?"

"Of course—but not before we work out all the bugs in your systems. We wouldn't send you back until you're all fully functional—which means we'll need to run tests."

She groaned, collapsed back on the bench at the table, and turned away.

Rhodes stayed out of the conversation, even when Dr. Osborne frowned at him for some explanation of Thackery's reaction.

Rhodes related to both her and Lauer. One of part of Rhodes couldn't wait to see Fisher again and talk to him about everything.

The other part would have been perfectly happy—more happy, in fact—never to see Fisher's bird face ever again.

The doctors went through the hold one capsule at a time and woke everyone up from stasis.

The doctors tinkered with Rhinehart's, Oakes's, Fuentes's, Dietz's, and Coulter's cranial implants before they fully regained consciousness.

The five of them were still groaning, stretching, and rubbing their eyes when Dr. Osborne went over to Lauer. "I just need to adjust something on your cranial implant. Then you should be able to communicate with your SAM again—and you'll all be able to interface with each other, too."

"Thanks, Doc," Lauer exclaimed.

Dr. Trudeau came over to Rhodes. He had to sit down on the bench so Trudeau could reach his implant.

Trudeau fiddled with it for a minute before The Grid blipped back on. The lines twisted, adjusted themselves, and then started to tangle into a messy blob in front of Rhodes's eyes.

Osborne activated Thackery's implant next. As soon as he finished, she stormed out of the hold and vanished. She didn't interface with anyone the whole time she was gone.

Rhodes could just imagine what she said to Koenig once he came back online. It couldn't have been anything good if she didn't want him back at all.

The lines in front of Rhodes formed an outline and then the squares between them developed color, texture, and shape.

Fisher looked all around him. "Ah, I'm back! Good morning, Captain."

"Good morning, Fisher," Rhodes replied, but he didn't get a surge of delight and relief at seeing his SAM again.

Fisher studied everything, including Rhodes. "Your implants are offline," Fisher remarked.

"I know that. The doctors only just restored The Grid this minute. We've been like this for a week."

Fisher cocked his head. "Did the doctors say when they would reactivate your implants?"

"They didn't say."

Fisher inclined his head the other way. This was by far the most wooden conversation Rhodes ever had with his SAM.

The thing brought up so many confused ideas and emotions. The face looked unfamiliar even though Rhodes had been looking at nothing else every day for so long.

Who the hell was this person talking to him right now? Rhodes knew nothing about this thing—because Fisher didn't have a past. He didn't have a story like a normal person.

He never went through any of the dramas, conflicts, or tensions of normal human beings. He wasn't human and never would be.

Rhodes had been watching human beings every hour of every day since he woke up. They were all so different from Fisher.

He would never understand them—which meant he would never understand Rhodes. Fisher only understood the Rhodes he'd seen since Fisher first came online.

Fisher didn't know jack shit about who Rhodes had been before this. Fisher didn't know Rhodes's story and never would.

This person looking back at Rhodes right now was a machine exactly like B, Ora, and the other Masks. The SAMs weren't the same kind as Rhodes or his subordinates or the rest of the Legion.

Rhodes had gone out of his way to find out as little as possible about all his subordinates' histories. He knew the most about Thackery and Henshaw.

Rhodes didn't need to know their individual stories just like they didn't need to know his.

Knowing their stories wasn't part of the job, but at least they had stories. He knew they did. He wouldn't have been able to stay in the same room with them if they didn't.

How was he supposed to relate to this person in front of him—this thing with no substance? This thing would never understand him.

The interface kicked back on one SAM at a time. Wild and Koenig appeared on The Grid first. Then Zen and Rocky reactivated as Dietz and Rhinehart sat up.

"Oh, it's good to be back!" Koenig exclaimed. "That was awful!"

"You didn't even feel anything," Wild growled. "It could have been a lot worse."

"That's what was so bad about it," Koenig went on. "It was the closest thing to death I can imagine."

"You were offline before the doctors ever activated you," Zen chimed in. "Don't tell me that was awful."

"I didn't know any better then."

"Did we miss anything?" Van asked when Fuentes sat up.

"You missed a bunch of battles against the Masks," Wild told her. "We've been locked up in this hold ever since the Masks shut us down."

"What's happening with the war?" Rocky asked.

"I don't know," Rhodes replied. "I haven't been keeping track of it."

"Are we at least still in the Regos system?" Koenig asked.

"Did you just hear the man?" Wild snapped. "He said he hasn't been keeping track of it."

"I just asked a simple question," Koenig insisted. "I thought anyone who stayed awake would at least want to know how the Legion is doing."

"I didn't think there was much point," Rhodes replied. "I figured we'd be out of the war for good unless the doctors could bring us back online."

"We're back online now," Van pointed out. "I guess they'll send us back into combat."

"Our implants aren't back online," Zen pointed out. "We won't go anywhere unless we get our weapons systems back."

"That's what I figured," Rhodes agreed. "Trudeau said he and Osborne might have to refuse all our neural connections one at a time one person at a time—which could take ages. Even then, our implants might never come back online—which means we're out."

"That would be a disaster," Rocky exclaimed.

"It would be great!" Wild countered. "We wouldn't have to fight this pointless war."

"What's pointless about defending the Treaty of Aemon Cluster?" Van asked. "It's our duty. We couldn't leave all those people undefended."

"What rock have you been living under, honey?" Wild growled. "We would be leaving them undefended even if we were standing right in front of them with our weapons pointed at the Masks. It's time to pull your head out of the clouds and catch up with current events."

She sniffed at him. "You don't have to get nasty about it. You're always so bad-tempered, Wild."

"I'm a realist. You'll be facing reality one way or the other. You might as well hear it here first."

Rhodes found himself smiling at their dynamic, but his smile drained away when he spotted Fisher watching him again.

Rhodes turned away, but of course Fisher followed him everywhere.

Rhodes would have liked to resume his walks around the *Ero* and see the crewmen whose lives he'd become so familiar with.

He couldn't do any of that with Fisher watching his every move. Rhodes didn't want Fisher to see the crewmen, either.

Rhodes would have felt like he was betraying them if he let Fisher peek in on their private lives. Those crewmen obviously didn't mind Rhodes watching them grope each other in secluded corners.

He wouldn't invite some stranger to watch them, too. That was private. It was none of Fisher's business.

Rhodes felt the old resentment creeping back in. He wanted to get rid of Fisher and go back to just being Rhodes by himself.

This time played out differently, though. Rhodes already knew Fisher. Fisher had proven his worth too many times. Rhodes would never be able to really hate Fisher again—not the way he did before.

This resentment—this burning impulse to carve Fisher out of his awareness—this was the same disorientation process Rhodes went through the first time.

He told himself that, but it didn't make the feeling go away. The simmering rage to stab himself in the head to put a stop to all this—it kept building with every passing second.

He crossed the hold to his capsule. He didn't want to be around if any of his subordinates snapped, got violent, or tried to kill themselves or their SAMs.

He shut himself in without a word of explanation to anyone, but of course Fisher was still there.

"Are you angry with me, Captain?" Fisher murmured.

"Of course not," Rhodes muttered. "You haven't done anything to make me angry."

"You're angry about me being here."

Rhodes drew in a shaky breath. "I'm going through a reorientation period about getting you back."

"Would you like me to make myself invisible and silent?"

"No, that won't help. I need to get used to you again."

"Did something happen while I was offline?" Fisher asked. "Did something make you wish you wouldn't get me back?"

"No, nothing happened, pal. You don't have to worry about that. Like I said, I just have to reorient. I oriented to not having you around. Now I have to reorient to having you around. That's all."

"Orienting last time nearly killed you. It caused you extreme distress."

"It won't cause me extreme distress this time because I already know you. We've been through a lot together."

"But you aren't happy to get me back."

Rhodes would have liked to roll his eyes and groan in exasperation. "I'm sorry I can't be happy to get you back, pal. I *am* happy to get you back. I'm happy I'm getting you back and not some other SAM."

"I'm happy about that, too, Captain. I'm glad I have you and not one of the others. It's an honor to be your SAM."

Rhodes's eyes snapped open and he stared at Fisher. For the first time ever, Rhodes experienced a pang of affection for his SAM. This frustration and aggravation really was just an adjustment phase Rhodes was going through.

For the first time, Rhodes considered ending the formality of Fisher always addressing Rhodes by his rank title.

Rhodes would have preferred to be on a first-name basis with Fisher. It no longer felt appropriate for Fisher to address Rhodes so formally.

What would Rhodes have Fisher call him? Calling him Rhodes didn't sound right. Rhodes didn't want Fisher calling him Corban, either.

Fisher might not even feel comfortable calling Rhodes either of those names. Hearing Fisher call him, *Captain,* felt natural and easy now. It was the most obvious thing for Fisher to call him.

Chapter 33

R hodes returned to the conference room to meet with the inquiry panel. After another week of testing with the doctors, they'd finally brought the battalion's implants back online, including the battalion's weapons systems.

The battalion had gone through three different training sessions to make sure everything was working right.

This was the first time the panel had called Rhodes to discuss his disastrous attempt to interface with the Masks.

He didn't see the point of this meeting. They already knew what happened, but the whole battalion knew now that they would go back into combat again.

Thackery had come back from her walk that first day and reestablished the interface with the rest of the battalion. She continued to behave normally—except that she didn't talk to Koenig anymore.

She talked to everyone else in the battalion, including the other SAMs. He talked to everyone else in the battalion, too, including the other SAMs.

They both studiously pretended the other wasn't there. Koenig spent training sessions informing her about battlefield conditions and letting her know about threats, dangers, and any changes to the environment.

She responded to these without talking nor did she ask him anything about the environment or each scenario.

She didn't acknowledge that he was speaking to her beyond simply reacting to the information in the most appropriate possible way.

She never spoke to, acknowledged, or even looked at him at any other time.

Their situation reversed itself with the relationship between Van and Fuentes. They were back on speaking terms in and out of training sessions. He even laughed at her jokes and talked to her apart from the rest of the battalion.

Rhodes reserved judgment about all of this. Everyone in the battalion went through a range of emotions about getting their SAMs back. Lauer couldn't be more tickled to get Wild back.

Coulter and Murphy had a few raging fights over Murphy's constant remarks about whatever Coulter happened to be doing at the time.

Coulter cut the interface and went for a walk around the ship. He must have had a serious talk with his SAM. When they came back, Murphy kept his opinions to himself more often than not after that.

Rocky came back online with his horse face and higher, softer voice. Rhinehart didn't go through the same problem of wanting to kill Rocky.

Dietz and Zen sailed through the whole process without a hiccup. Both of them clicked back into perfect synch with each other.

The relationship between them seemed almost to work better now than it did before. Dietz never gave the faintest hint that he ever mistrusted Zen in the Stonebridge landscape.

Rhodes didn't mention it. He was beginning to come to the conclusion that he wasn't qualified to tell any of these people how to do anything—especially not when it came to dealing with their SAMs.

Rhodes was no saint. He'd wanted to kill Fisher more than once. Rhodes even went through a few bouts of that in the last week.

He didn't tell Fisher that, though. Rhodes didn't tell anyone that.

He reentered the conference room where the panel greeted him as usual. "Welcome back, Captain," General Hyde exclaimed. "I'm glad to see from your test results that you and the rest of the battalion are returning to full functioning."

"Thank you, Ma'am. I apologize for not being able to come back with any useful information about the Masks."

"We're grateful that you tried, especially considering how much the attempt cost the battalion," Admiral Stabler replied. "I hope you understand that we can't let you do that again."

"No, Sir, of course not. The Masks would only shut us down again."

"In which case, we have no choice but to fall back on our last-ditch plan to defeat them." General Hyde changed the display on the charts in front of her. "We're planning to assault the city machine and hopefully weaken or defeat the Masks that way."

"The city machine isn't here," Rhodes pointed out. "You said before that no one could get near it because the Masks kept it too far in the rear."

"They did, but that was before. They've landed the city machine on Sarus."

Rhodes's jaw dropped. "Are you serious? What for?"

"We have no idea, but it can't be for anything good. The Masks have razed three cities while the battalion has been down." General Hyde readjusted the chart in front of her. "The Masks are on course to attack the Lilithea Cluster—here. It's a conglomerate metropolis of fourteen cities with a population of more than twenty million civilians. Three more large population centers are standing in the Masks' path—Estra, Triowa, and Chaivis. Their combined populations total over fifty million."

Rhodes stared at the chart with a heavy weight sinking into his stomach.

"The Legion isn't trying to evacuate the city," Admiral Volk went on. "There are too many people and we don't have enough Ravagers that aren't already involved in the war. The population would panic if we announced that we were evacuating. They would stampede and kill each other the way they did at Veulia."

"Which means we have to stop the Masks before they get there," General Hyde finished. "Fighting the Masks on the ground or in the air won't stop them. The city machine is our only chance to shut down all the Masks at the same time. It's the only way to stop the Masks from sending out more and more troops."

Rhodes couldn't tear his eyes off the chart. All those people.....

Nothing would stop the Masks from killing every last one of them. If the Legion couldn't stop the Masks from razing the Lilithea Cluster, then the Legion wouldn't be able to stop the Masks from doing anything else.

The Legion wouldn't be able to stop the Masks from razing Preinea itself.

General Hyde broke in on his thoughts "Captain? Do you have any suggestions about how we can assault the city machine? You're the only person in the whole Legion who has seen it."

"No, Ma'am," Rhodes mumbled. "I don't have any suggestions on how to assault the city machine. I don't know if it has any vulnerabilities. I don't think it has any. I only know the Masks will do absolutely anything to defend it—and heaven knows they have the numbers and the firepower to do it."

"It being on the ground may work in our favor," Admiral Stabler suggested.

"Then again, it may not," Captain Lake countered. "The Masks haven't brought in invasion ships since they entered the Regos system. We wouldn't be able to attack the city machine with anything other than Ravagers. That will bring the invasion ships running if anything does. Once they get involved, we're finished."

"Can't you offer any more positive contribution than that, Otis?" General Hyde asked. "What's the point in even discussing it or mounting this campaign at all if there's no hope?"

"I'm just telling it like I see it," Lake returned. "Do you see any other way to attack the city machine besides using Ravagers? Forget about using platoons or any smaller aircraft."

"I wasn't going to suggest either of those," General Hyde replied.

"What about laying mines along its path....or shooting Vipers underneath it?" Colonel Neff suggested.

"We would only be able to shoot Vipers underneath it from Ravagers that were within Viper range," Captain Lake pointed out. "We don't have time to lay mines in its path. Even if we did, we would have to get platoons close enough to plant the mines—which would be too dangerous for the platoons."

"We'll just have to risk bringing in Ravagers and hope we make a dent in the city machine before the invasion ships catch up with us," Colonel Volk finished. "If we can destroy or disable the city machine, that could neutralize the invasion ships."

"Or it could make them twice as aggressive," Lake pointed out. "They could go after the Lilithea Cluster in retaliation."

"Well, we have to do something!" General Hyde turned back to Rhodes. "What do you think, Captain?"

"I don't know, Ma'am," he replied. "I'd prefer to stay out of any decision-making process."

"You can't," Volk snapped. "You're already involved in it whether you want to be or not."

"I beg to differ, Sir," Rhodes replied. "I'm just a soldier. That's all I've ever been. I've already given my opinion on the Masks. I'd prefer to just carry out whatever orders you give me. That's all I'm qualified to do."

Volk compressed his lips. "Then you're dismissed to return to the capsule hold, Captain. We'll inform you when we're ready for the battalion to deploy."

Rhodes made his exit. Why in the name of all that's holy did these officers insist on trying to drag him into their decisions? He already said everything he had to say on the subject.

They were on drugs if they thought they could get within a hundred miles of the city machine. He didn't know why the Masks landed the city machine here of all places.

The population density of the Lilithea Cluster may have attracted them—not that it mattered. No way in hell could the Legion destroy or disable the city machine.

The Masks would never let the Legion destroy or disable it. These officers were living in a fantasy world if they thought the Legion stood a snowball's chance in hell of that.

He didn't tell anyone that. He basically already told them. They didn't listen to him then. Why should he get involved in their discussion—so he could tell them again and they could contradict and ridicule him out of the room?

He headed back to the capsule hold, but on the way, he decided to take another walk around the ship.

He was still interfaced with the rest of the battalion, but he decided not to watch his old interests too closely.

He wouldn't do anything to make anyone in the battalion think any of the crew meant anything to him.

He wandered around, spotted some of his favorite people going about their lives, and moved on before he saw anything incriminating.

He finally gave it up. He couldn't keep putting off the moment when he went back to the hold.

Maybe it was better for the battalion to go back into combat. Sitting around with nothing to do was no way to live.

He turned off into one of the corridors leading to the hold. He stiffened when he saw five armed soldiers standing outside the entrance.

They stood face to face with Captain Blackwell, Lieutenant Edgecombe, and three of their men from the 765th.

All three men had fought with Battalion 1 on Drion. The same three men had also helped drag the battalion to safety during the Battle of Veulia.

Rhodes slowed when he heard the soldiers arguing back and forth. Their voices started rising and they shoved into each other's faces before any of them noticed Rhodes coming closer.

He glanced back and forth between the men he knew on one side and the armed soldiers he didn't know on the other. "Is something going on, fellas?"

"Thank goodness you're here!" Edgecombe exclaimed. "We were trying to talk to you, but these assholes wouldn't let us near your hold."

"Take it easy, Lieutenant," one of the soldiers interjected. "We're under orders not to let anyone near the hold."

"Since when?" Rhodes countered. "I never heard about this. My people and I have been walking around the ship at liberty since we first came on board."

"The whole crew is under orders not to talk to you, Sir," the same soldier replied. "We've been keeping your hold under guard...."

"You have? I've never seen you."

The soldier squirmed. He was only a corporal. "Captain Ackerman ordered us to keep it on the down-low so you wouldn't feel like you were prisoners on board or anything like that—but he was very clear about our orders. None of the crew is supposed to go near you or fraternize with you or talk to you at all."

"We aren't on the crew, dumbass!" Edgecombe spat.

Blackwell raised his hand and pressed his knuckles against Edgecombe's chest to make him back off. "We just want to talk to you," Blackwell told Rhodes. "If you aren't too busy."

"I'm not busy," Rhodes replied.

"Excuse me, Sir, but we have very specific orders about this," the corporal cut in. "We could all get in a lot of trouble if we allowed this."

"Then you can go tell Captain Ackerman right now," Rhodes replied. "Tell him this is a one-time thing and I'm making an exception for these men on account of how we've fought together as brothers-in-arms on multiple occasions. If Ackerman has a problem with this, he can take it up with me and Captain Blackwell. The three of us are equally ranked, so I'm sure we can work out some agreement. You can tell him that these gentlemen aren't members of the *Ero* crew and we won't make a habit of fraternizing or contradicting his orders where the crew is concerned."

The corporal and his men looked back and forth between Rhodes and the others. Then the corporal mumbled, "Yes, Sir," and left with his men.

Rhodes turned to Blackwell and the others. "What do you want to talk to me about?"

"Everyone is saying you aren't involved in making decisions about how we're going to fight the Masks," Edgecombe blurted out.

"That's right," Rhodes replied. "I communicate with the inquiry panel that has command authority over Battalion 1. I don't know how much they're in contact with the rest of the brass."

"But they've asked you," Blackwell chimed in. "They've asked you to get involved in making decisions about the war."

"Sure, they've asked me, but I already told you and them what I think. I'm just a grunt like you. I'm not in charge of this."

"Please reconsider," Edgecombe insisted. "Come on, man. We all know you. You know more about the Masks than anyone."

"That doesn't mean I'm qualified to run the war," Rhodes pointed out. "It only means I know better all the ways the Masks will defeat us."

"They can't!" Edgecombe exclaimed and Blackwell stopped him again.

"Listen, Rhodes," Blackwell murmured under his breath. "The reason the five of us came to find you is because we all have families either in the Lilithea Cluster or in line for the Masks' advance. If we don't find a way to stop them, all our families will die—and so will all those other people. Please reconsider. You're our last hope."

"I can't offer you any hope, man." Rhodes looked back and forth between Blackwell and Edgecombe. "I would tell you if I thought there was any possible way we could win."

"Please get involved," one of the other soldiers pleaded. "What can it hurt? If the situation really is that hopeless, then you getting involved will only help. Right? You sitting out can't improve things."

Rhodes didn't answer. He didn't want to get involved.

"Please just consider it," Blackwell went on. "If you're right about Legion brass farther up the chain of command making these decisions, then that just means they're that much further removed from the reality on the ground. We need you to be the voice of reason. You're the one person who has faced the Masks. If you say it's hopeless, then we believe you, but at least get involved. Don't just give up on us—on all of us."

"We don't stand a chance if you don't," Edgecombe chimed in.

Rhodes let out a shaky sigh. "Listen to me. The battalion is already going back into combat, so I'm sure we'll all wind up down there together again. The brass plans to assault the city machine and hopefully stop it before the Masks get near any population center. I can't think of any other strategy that might work, so I guess we're doing this. If I think of anything, I'll be sure to let the panel know. I'm sure they would take my recommendation if there was any other possible way."

"Thank you!" Edgecombe grabbed Rhodes's hand and nearly pumped it off his shoulder. "Thank you so much!"

"Don't worry about it, man," Rhodes murmured. "The battalion and I are already doing everything there is to do."

"Thank you," Blackwell replied. "That's all we ask."

Chapter 34

R hodes got another hopeless pain in his gut when he surveyed The Grid from the *Ero's* landing bay. The ship descended toward another open field miles north of Estra, another of Sarus's massive population centers.

Estra lay south of Veulia. The Masks had already leveled Veulia to the ground and killed everyone who didn't get lucky enough to evacuate during the assault.

The Masks kept advancing farther and farther south. They stayed on a straight-line course for the Eulara continent's most densely populated cities.

The majority of the Legion force assembled on that field. Ravagers, Dusters, and Predator fighter craft fought the invasion ships in the skies.

Dozens of Legion platoons locked together with Masks ground troops. The Legion tried every maneuver ever invented to try to break the Masks' line.

Rhodes widened his Grid. The Masks' city machine sat far behind the main front, but it always kept advancing south, too.

It wasn't a city or a machine. It was really just a gigantic ship miles wide. It rolled along the ground on hundreds of mechanized treads.

These treads hugged the ground. No one would be able to shoot a Viper underneath the ship.

Heavy metal cladding covered the outer hull. The plates armored the ship against assault—not that anyone could get near enough to hit the ship.

Ravagers bombarded the city machine from orbit where no one could hit them back, but the shots had no effect on the city machine.

Some kind of invisible electric charge burst from the city machine's armored hull whenever a Ravager's fusion loads struck the giant ship.

The Ravagers' shots exploded on the charge, but the impact always went off inches away from the hull. None of the fusion shots ever touched the ship.

Rhodes didn't comment on how hopeless the situation looked from inside the *Ero's* landing bay. He'd already gotten into trouble doing that once before.

Whatever this battle held in store, it would happen right now—one way or another.

He didn't see how Battalion 1 would be able to make any difference in this battle, but what the hell did anyone from Battalion 1 have to lose anyway?

The *Ero* set down as before in the fields behind the main front. The platoons streamed out of the ship and charged the front line to relieve the platoons that had already been fighting the Masks for hours and even days.

Rhodes and his people fired their boosters, zoomed out of the landing bay, and vaulted high in the air over the battle. It looked even more hopeless from up here—but what was more hopeless than hopeless?

Rhodes put that out of his mind. He put everything connected to the outcome out of his mind.

He dove headfirst toward the ground gaining speed, altered his grid lines, and the whole battalion changed into those long snake whips.

They punched into the ground full force and set off at high speed for the city machine.

The Masks kept marching straight over the battalion's heads. The Masks never knew the battalion was there.

It took a long time for the battalion to work its way all the way to the rear. Then Rhodes and his people had to travel over a dozen miles of open fields to get to the city machine.

The Grid gave the battalion their only view of the surroundings down here in the dark. Miles of grid lines kept pivoting past Rhodes's eyes.

"I'm not reading any charge around the city machine's underside," Fisher pointed out.

"Do you read any charge around the city machine at all when it isn't defending itself from Ravager fire?" Rhodes asked.

"Well....no......"

"Then that explains why the underside isn't charged. No one is hitting it."

"Do you have to be so sensible?"

"What about the treads?" Rhodes asked. "Can you locate the mechanism that makes them turn? If we can disable them and bring the city machine to a halt, the ground troops might stop their advance."

"It's worth a shot. The axels are all reinforced with the same cladding as the ship's outer hull."

"That isn't what I want to hear, Fisher," Rhodes countered.

"I'm sorry, Captain. The power source for the treads is coming from inside the city machine, too. The drive shafts are the only thing turning the tread wheels and they're all reinforced, too."

"We'll just have to try it." Rhodes signaled the battalion. "Here we go! Stay alert. These charges could damage us. Shoot into the treads from out of range."

The eight snakes burrowed through the soil closing on the city machine. The ship crawled southward without stopping once. It advanced at the same rate the Masks ground troops drove the Legion back.

Rhodes dove under the city machine and fired his Vipers upward into the ship's underside. The explosions hit the reinforced armor and the tread wheels' drive shafts, but the Vipers didn't damage the structure.

The rest of the battalion joined the bombardment. The city machine didn't let off any electric charges underneath it.

"Wheel back around for another pass," Rhodes ordered. "Lasers and thermal cannons this time. We know thermals work on Masks armor."

The battalion dove back out into the field, circled, and came back to dig under the city machine again. The tread wheels and all their mechanized parts kept churning right over Rhodes's head.

He flipped onto his back and kept snaking through the topsoil while he fired a laser from his right hand and a thermal cannon from his left.

Rhinehart and Oakes flanked him on both sides. All three men combined their fire, but again, neither weapon did any good.

"The cladding is too thick even for thermal cannons to melt it," Fisher reported.

"What other options do we have? Is there a way we can disable the electric charge—short-circuit it, maybe?"

Fisher started to say, "I don't see how....."

"Hold on!" Rhinehart yelled. "I have an idea!"

"Wait a minute, Lieutenant...." Rhodes began, but Rhinehart was already racing away.

He plunged back out into the battlefield, erupted out of the soil between the city machine and the Masks' rear flank, changed into another all-terrain vehicle, and bounced over the hills closing on the Masks from behind.

A big mob of them broke away from the main assault. Those Masks couldn't get near enough to the Legion to do any fighting anyway. Too many Masks crowded the field.

This group turned around to meet Rhinehart's charge. The Masks' main force kept pushing south. This group halted there to wait.

They played right into his hands with the city machine closing from the north. The Masks raised their rifles to aim at Rhinehart as he plowed toward them. Dirt clods spat from his wheels.

He hit one last swell, caught air, and changed again in mid-flight. He resumed his original form, landed on his feet in the grass, and the Masks pounced.

"What the hell is he doing?" Dash growled.

"Winning the war for us!" Thackery called. "Come on! We gotta help him!"

"Hey!" Rhodes yelled. "Where are you going?!"

He got his answer a second later when the Masks surrounded Rhinehart. They never got a shot off.

He dove into their midst, snatched one Mask after another off the ground, and sent them flying through the air.

They cartwheeled head over heel not knowing what hit them and fell inevitably straight into the city machine's electric charge.

The first Masks exploded and then one or two shorted out. Thackery caught up with Rhinehart and started doing the same thing.

Masks soared over Rhodes's head and struck the charge, but they didn't weaken it.

The trick worked to divert more Masks away from the battle, but even that didn't lessen the sheer tide of Masks crowding the platoons southward, always southward.

"This isn't working, Rhinehart!" Rhodes yelled through the interface. "We need another plan!"

"What do you suggest—that I fly into the charge myself and try to short it out?"

"That might not work, but maybe crashing a Ravager into it would do the trick," Dietz suggested.

"That would kill everyone on board, you psycho!" Lauer fired back.

"I'm just saying...."

Almost as if his words made it happen, four invasion ships ganged up on one Ravager right over the Legion front line. The invasion ships pounded that Ravager from all directions and its engines exploded.

It started to bank toward the ground and then its fusion reactor caught fire. A catastrophic plume of flame exploded from the hull. The ship listed farther to the west and dove into a death plunge.

"Let's go!" Rhodes ordered and he shot out of the ground flying at his top speed.

He didn't think once that he would be killing the whole Ravager crew. They would die on impact if they weren't dead already from the fusion core overloading.

Rhodes, Coulter, Dietz, and Fuentes launched into the atmosphere, caught up with the ship, and wheeled behind it to attack from the southwest.

Rhodes opened fire with his Vipers and all four men bombarded the ship with shuddering explosions. The ship pivoted farther north.

"Come on!" Rhodes yelled to the rest of his people. "Help us out before it's too late!"

Oakes raced up into the cloud to join the bombardment. Rhinehart and Thackery took longer, but they launched their Vipers and forced the ship to turn even more.

The city machine kept motoring over the swells, completely oblivious to the battalion's master plan.

The Ravager groaned farther onto its side. Continuous explosions went off inside the ship. Rhodes didn't want to think about what might be going on in there.

The ship plunged, but it wasn't falling far enough north to hit the city machine. Rhodes adjusted his Viper fire and hammered the Ravager in the nose along its underside.

The ship tilted up just a few inches while the rest of the battalion kept up their assault from the back. The ship altered its angle of descent and smashed full force into the city machine.

The electric charge let off a massive pulse when the Ravager detonated against the ship's hull. The city machine shuddered and ground to a halt.

"The hull isn't charged anymore!" Fisher called. "Now's our chance! Assault the city machine with everything you have! I'm interfacing with the Ravagers to bombard it now."

Rhodes didn't wait to be told twice. He banked toward the ground, fired his boosters to full power, and plummeted. He unloaded every Viper in his arsenal on the city machine's outer hull.

The battalion surrounded him all unloading on the ship. The Ravagers combined their firepower to drive the ship into the ground.

The city machine didn't move. It just sat there taking the bombardment on its hull. It didn't return fire.

The Masks ground troops didn't break off their assault on the Legion platoons, either. Apart from the city machine coming to a halt, the Masks force didn't change its behavior at all.

Rhodes pounded the ship with Vipers, and when that didn't work, he tried his thermal cannons again.

The Ravagers' bombardment made it impossible to touch the hull from above. He had to change his position to hit the ship's sides.

The battalion copied Rhodes, but their thermals didn't produce any more effect on the ship's sides than they did on its underside.

The Ravagers broke off. The mayhem cleared enough for everyone to see the city machine's top caved in.

The ship sat there motionless and unresponsive. The Masks ground troops never even turned around to see if their precious city machine was still intact.

Rhodes stayed where he was and stared at the ship. Nothing happened. The Ravagers didn't open fire again. It couldn't be over. It couldn't be that easy.

It wasn't because the Masks still fought the battle as ferociously as ever. Damaging the city machine didn't stop the Masks one bit.

Then, after a few minutes of motionless silence, the city machine shuddered and its treads started turning again. It motored forward at exactly the same speed as before.

Chapter 35

R hodes staggered back toward the front line to get away from the city machine. It kept crawling forward on its inevitable advance toward the population centers in the south.

An explosion startled Rhodes into spinning around. He didn't want to turn his back on the city machine, but when he did, he wound up with a whole new problem.

The Masks broke the Legion line, penetrated inside the platoons, and from there, the Masks had no problem cutting the platoons to pieces. It was the worst possible déjà vu of the Battle of Veulia when Lieutenant Lohr's squad deserted.

Rhodes couldn't stop the slaughter—not that way. "Follow me!" he called to his subordinates and took off into the air.

"Tell me you aren't running away!" Rhinehart yelled after him.

"I have an idea. It might not work, but anything is better than this."

Rhodes soared away from the Legion ranks heading back west. "Interface with the Ravagers!" he told Fisher. "Get them to come in from the south and assault the city machine from there."

"What difference will that make?" Fisher asked. "We already know Ravager fire won't damage it—not like that."

"We can draw out the Masks' numbers. They'll come out to defend the city machine. Then the Ravagers can cut them down while the battalion attacks the ship from the west."

"How will we attack it?" Oakes asked. "We don't have a weapon strong enough."

"We haven't used all our weapons. Signal the Ravagers, Fisher."

Fisher rotated The Grid so Rhodes could see the Ravagers in the atmosphere. They stayed up there out of the invasion ships' range. The Ravagers could hit the city machine, but they couldn't damage it."

"I sure hope you know what you're doing," Fisher murmured.

"I don't," Rhodes replied. "I'm shooting in the dark."

"The Ravagers are coming in. Stand by."

"What are we doing?" Coulter asked.

"As soon as the Ravagers open fire, use your grid lines to get inside the electric charge. Make contact with the damaged part of the ship's hull. We should be able to either bore through it or burn through it with our thermals."

"It's a long shot," Lauer muttered.

"Everything is a long shot. Nothing else is gonna work. Here we go!"

Twenty Ravagers dropped out of orbit. The invasion ships had been busy dealing with the Dusters and Predators.

The invasion ships were the only thing stopping the Dusters and Predators from bombarding the Masks ground troops.

As soon as the invasion ships broke away to attack the Ravagers, all those Legion vessels turned their guns on the Masks ground troops.

The Legion force inflicted heavy losses on the ground troops. The Dusters and Predators actually succeeded in bringing the ground troops to a stop.

Then the Ravagers opened fire.

They unloaded on the city machine with devastating firepower. The invasion ships got caught between trying to fight the Ravagers and trying to protect the ground troops. They couldn't do both.

Rhodes didn't wait around to see how it all went down. He launched himself at the city machine and transformed himself into a fighter craft completely encased in metal.

He whizzed across the battlefield and collided with the electric charge. It crackled all around him. It should have shorted his systems, but his grid lines insulated his outer skin. The charge didn't touch him.

He landed on the ship's hull, extended a boring drill from his underside, and started drilling into the most crumpled part of the hull.

The rest of the battalion punched through the electric charge. Oakes fired his thermal cannon into a torn hull section. It started to melt.

The battalion went to work on the section of the hull that the crashed Ravager already damaged. Oakes's breach started to widen.

"Keep going!" Fisher called. "We're breaking through!"

"What do we do once we get inside?" Thackery asked.

"Find whatever is powering this thing," Rhodes replied. "Fly through the whole ship if you have to. Just find it!"

He doubled down his efforts. Red-hot metal shards flew from his drill and bounced off his face.

The hole under his drill widened. It spread almost to the size of a person. It almost got big enough for him to get inside.

"I'm through!" Oakes called. "I'm going in!"

Oakes reared off the hull. His grid lines morphed. He started to change himself into a Striker so he could fly inside the city machine.

At that moment, a brutal thump hit the whole battalion. It didn't come from the electric charge. Rhodes didn't know what it was.

The impact ripped him off the hull, threw him into the air, and he crashed down on the grass with the whole battalion around him, but the fall didn't hurt him. They bounced and lay still.

He pried his head out of the dirt planning to make another assault on the ship. He froze when he saw thousands upon thousands of Masks pouring out of the enormous ship.

The ship opened a port in its side and a black cloud of Masks marched out. They blackened the landscape and formed a massive flock flowing across the hillsides.

Their rifles carpeted the ground with shots, leveled all the Legion troops, and then all those guns turned on the Legion aircraft hovering above the battlefield.

Explosions detonated as fusion shots hammered Dusters and Predators. The ships blew one after another and left the invasion ships all the time in the world to turn on the Ravagers.

Rhodes couldn't tear his eyes away from all those Masks. The Ravagers' assault drew out the Masks numbers, all right. More and more of them emptied from the city machine's port.

The city machine kept trundling along the ground, rolled over hundreds of dead Legion soldiers, and continued its deadly journey toward the population centers in the distance.

End of Book 4.

Keep Reading

Battalion 1 Series: Book 5: Blood and Hope

With the lives of billions of people in jeopardy, Captain Corban Rhodes and his team of super soldiers are facing down unstoppable odds with no way to turn the tide. As battle after battle turns against him, Rhodes must find one tiny scrap of hope in a landscape of death and destruction. Could humanity's darkest hour be the moment when Rhodes finally discovers what it really means to be human—and to win back a little of what the Battalion 1 project took from him—including his own humanity?

With those he most cares about under fire and with no way to save them, Rhodes must grasp at any lifeline to find the key to unlock the mystery of the Masks and try one last, hopeless time to shut them down for good. It just might cost him everything in the process, including his own life.

You can find it at your favorite book retailer.

Sign Up Once--Get all Theo Mann's free books including brand new releases

S ign Up Once--Get all Theo Mann's free books including brand new releases

Commander Layton Raines was just doing his job when he got shot down on the battle defending his platoon's retreat. His whole life changes when he wakes up in the hospital implanted with cybernetic limbs, but Raines is nothing like anyone else who has ever gone through the Battalion 1 project.

With the fate of the galaxy hanging in the balance, the future will depend on the one man who has never been good with authority, following orders, or staying within the lines. With the mission in jeopardy and Battalion 1 pinned down by overwhelming odds, it will take a miracle to save their lives. It just might take a mutiny to throw out the rule book and forge a path no one has ever taken before.

Sign up at www.theomann.com to read it for free

About Theo Mann

I write 70 books per year—and yes, before you ask, all these books are my original creative work. Nothing written under my name is AI-generated or ghostwritten because I write better than AI and any ghostwriter out there.

People don't read fiction for entertainment or to escape from reality. People read fiction to see their humanity reflected in another person's character and story.

This is my promise to you. When you read my books, you'll see your own humanity reflected in the characters and stories. I take this commitment to my readers very seriously. My books are an intimate form of communication between us. I would never disrespect my readers by turning that over to a machine or another writer. This is my bond between me and you as my reader.

I write 20,000 words per day as my daily work output. If anyone with a public platform would like to challenge me to prove this in a controlled environment, feel free to contact me on this website's contact page.

I worked as a professional ghostwriter for fifteen years. Now I'm on a mission to set a Guinness World Record by writing 700 books over the next ten years and 1400 books over the next twenty years, all originally written by me. See my website for the full book list.

I'm also the author of *Proof for the Existence of God* and the *Crimes Against Fiction* blog. You can find all my nonfiction work at www.crimes-against-fiction.com.

If you have a story idea, or if you would like me to explore a series in more depth, or if you'd like me to explore a character by writing a spinoff series about that character or world, leave me a message on my website's contact page. I answer all reader emails, so ask me anything, tell me what you liked and didn't like, and let me know where you'd like your favorite series to go. I would love to hear your ideas and find out what you'd like to read next.

Find out more at www.theomann.com.

Also by Theo Mann (so far)